A TOUCH OF FIRE

A SISTERS IN SIRENS NOVEL

KATHRYN K. MURPHY

Caraway Press

For my Family

CHAPTER 1

H ank Chapman turned off the TV after the applause had ended and threw the handle on his La-Z-Boy recliner he got for Father's Day twenty years ago. He braced his hands on the arms and pushed himself up, fighting the arthritis from many years of working too hard for too long. He put on his house shoes, the kind the doctor prescribed, pocketed his flip phone in his overalls, and grabbed the empty bowl.

"Come on, Levi, let's clean up, get a cup of tea, and head to bed."

Levi, the golden retriever with a now-gray face, followed with a slight limp after lying in his oversized dog bed through the news, *Jeopardy,* and *Wheel.*

Hank ambled toward the old-fashioned kitchen he had always known. The yellow countertops and wood cabinets were the same color his mom had picked out back when his dad had redesigned the ranch house before he was born. The appliances were white and of medium quality, replaced as the old ones went with time, but all of the dishes and linens were still the ones Barbara had bought in town when they had moved in forty years ago.

Hank put his bowl in the sink next to the small saucepan he had used to heat up the can of Campbell's chicken noodle, then filled the tea kettle, leaving the water running to fill the sink. The click click click of the gas on the white range poofed into a little blue flame which he turned up before he set the kettle to boil. While the water heated, he grabbed the Dawn and an old sponge and set to work, with Levi watching him.

With two dishes done, he left them to dry in the rack next to one glass and a coffee cup from this morning, drained the sink, and passed the sponge around it to wipe away the water stains. He and Barbara had always been so careful about keeping the place clean, believing things lasted if you took care of them, which Hank had almost always found to be true.

Speaking of antiques, he pulled out the coffee mug with the Purina red and white checkerboard label which had been a gift from the man who sold feed in the eighties. Both the man and Hank had retired years ago from all things cattle, a fact that bothered him. Hank's mind was fine, but his body couldn't do the work of a young man anymore. He knew what needed to be done and had always hated laziness and waste, which was a hell of a feeling to be had with age.

Before, he could work from sunup to sundown, but now he could only manage one or two things a day before having to rest. The ranch had outrun him a long time ago, and time was widening the gap between what needed to be done and what Hank could do. Hank was still able to do most things, just with more time for the job and the recovery from it. Still, pride and finances meant he was the man for the job.

When Hank had gone to his doctor, frustrated with the situation, his doctor had listened with a patient smile, as if he had heard this a hundred times, and urged him to just tackle one thing a day and do what he could. Hank complied, but he hated it. The ranch wasn't just his home, it was the house his father had built, where he was raised. It was the house he and Barbara took over and added on to while raising two boys. Seeing the disrepair around the house and ranch was a constant reminder of how far things had come.

Now it was just him and Levi. Hank righted the cup next to the ticking tea kettle, pulled down a box of tea from the cabinet above, and unwrapped a bag of Lipton's decaf to plop inside. He pulled open the Sears refrigerator to grab the low-fat half-and-half when the tea kettle whistled.

"Alright, alright," he said as grabbed the kettle with a pot holder and poured the boiling water into the mug.

A sloshing noise had him setting down the kettle and grabbing another towel from the drawer on instinct.

Next to the fridge, Levi lapped up water and was managing to get about half of what he wanted in his mouth.

"I gotcha, buddy," Hank said, grunting as he bent over to wipe up the floor with the faded floral tea towel, taking care to lift the edge of the bowl and pass the rag under. Water on a floor was never good.

"There you go," he said as he patted his old friend on the head. "No worries here."

Levi looked up and panted his typical loving retriever smile, while Hank tossed the used rag into the washer, which was just to the left of the kitchen.

Returning to his tea, he added a dollop of low-fat half-and-half small enough to appease his doctor and replaced the carton in the fridge.

"Time for bed," he said, picking up his cup. "Two magazines came today. *AARP* and *Guns and Ammo*. What should we read tonight, buddy?"

Hank hit the kitchen light switch on his way out like he

had countless times before and walked upstairs to the bedroom following Levi, never looking back into the dark kitchen where he would've seen the pot holder next to high blue flame.

CHAPTER 2

Megan White hopped down from the six-man-cab fire engine into the orange glow of the inferno that resembled a two-story farmhouse. Angry orange flames licked out of a small window on the side while smoke billowed into the night sky, blending with the clouds.

Megan pulled her helmet on while the radio squawked out the orders in her ear, not that she or the new rookie, Nick, needed any. Buzz had them all so well trained as a team, each assisting the engineer with parts of the hose to push back the blaze in support of the fire attack, when Buzz made the call.

At least one occupant still inside, transitional fire attack. Save lives, not the building. The seven hundred and fifty gallons of water might not save the structure, so it would have to cover the team as they went into rescue mode. That was Megan's specialty.

Buzz supported the engineer with the hose and ordered Megan and Nick to take the lead.

There was no hesitation from either.

Megan took point and entered through the unburned

side, which happened to be the front door. A few chops of the irons and it came away freely, revealing a scalding hell on six sides of the kitchen, the roar of the fire mixing with the shrill screams of the fire alarm. Four walls, floor, and ceiling all moved in waves of red energy licking every surface for fuel.

"Nick, follow me when Buzz takes over door control."

"Got it," he said, already inside crouching down, ready to help regulate air and steam flow but also to help her find her way back. "Go get them."

Megan was already heading straight into the blaze, scanning for signs of life. It was almost nine o'clock, so she headed for the staircase, testing it with her boot before taking them two at a time.

"Behind you," Nick said in her radio. As she turned on the landing, she saw him at the bottom and a figure that was her captain at the door.

She finished the staircase, crouching and looking for occupants through the thick black smoke.

"My name is Megan White. I'm with Station Three here to help. Tell me where you are," she said, yelling above the sound. There was a moan followed by coughing to the right of the stairs.

An older gentleman in pajamas lay on the floor of a smoke-filled bedroom next to his flip phone, holding a pillow to his mouth. His hand stretched out to her, and his eyes were wide in his red face.

"I got you. Sir, we're going to get you out. My name is Megan and this is Nick. He's going to help you out."

He sputtered and coughed again. "Wait, please, my dog is here. I don't know where he went, but Levi ran off after the smoke alarms started."

"I'll find him. Nick, take him and go."

Resigned and filled with worry, the man started to shake.

Nick crouched low. "Sir, can you walk? I'm going to help carry you out."

Megan hoisted up the man and draped his arm over Nick's back before scanning the remainder of the room. No dog.

"Megan, we're having luck with the temperature down here. Workin' to save the ceiling, but move fast. We can see Nick coming now."

She hit the radio button, taking care to avoid the emergency button which would send in the cavalry. "Got it. I'm looking for a dog. We need EMS to check the occupant out."

"Will do, but when I say get out of there, you better move your ass."

"10-4." Megan scanned the room, closets, and looked under the bed before moving to what appeared to be an older boy's room. Even through the smoke, she could see it had not been used in some time.

There was one more room down the hall. Megan pushed in through the smoke and peered into the closet again, noting it was full but, judging by the conditions, hadn't been used in some time. A whimper turned her attention under the bed, where she crouched down to see an old golden retriever easing back against the wall, shaking.

"Easy boy, easy."

A gruff woof followed by a growl and whimper had him retreating farther.

"Come on, Megan. Tank's almost out of water; we've got to go. Moving to exterior attack."

"One minute," she said, knowing she was on borrowed time.

Checking to make sure she was alone, Megan did the unthinkable. She pulled off her helmet and removed the oxygen mask.

"Come on, boy. It's okay. I got you."

The dog perked up but shrank back from her glove.

"Okay, fine," she said, pulling off her glove and extending her hand to the animal.

Sure enough, one inch, then another, followed by a careful exploratory lick, and then the dog came forward enough for her to grab his collar and drag him out into her lap where the big guy curled and continued to shake while licking her face.

"We're not out of the woods yet."

A loud crash told her something had fallen down below.

"Time to go, buddy."

The smoke was darker now in the back hall as the flames traveled up one of the exterior walls, probably through the kitchen window up the outside. There wouldn't be much to save at this point.

The heat smothered the oxygen in the house, gobbling it up in a frenzy of greed, pulling it out of her lungs. Sparks flew like fireflies in the black clouds that mixed with the steam from the hose. The temperature was rising with all three elements, and while she had every faith that Buzz and the crew had a handle on things, there was only so much they could control if they couldn't take out one of the three ingredients of the fire—oxygen, heat, and fuel.

A large crack echoed through the smoke ahead of her.

"Megan, the staircase is starting to go; get down here now."

"On it," she said before coming down the hall and heading for the stairs, blinded by the smoke in her eyes. A few sparks landed on her arm, but as usual they just felt warm. No pain. No marks. No burns.

Part of the door to the bathroom at the front of the hall broke away with the flames and landed on the carpet, blocking the path. She tried to nudge it out of the way with her boot, but it wouldn't go, not because of weight since it looked hollow, but how it was awkwardly wedged in between the walls.

Muttering a curse under her breath, not that anyone could hear, she put the dog down right next to her.

"Don't you move an inch," she said, looking Levi in the eye.

Still shaking, the dog's soulful eyes met her gaze and seemed to communicate obedience.

Megan turned back to the piece of the door and grabbed it through the flames with her bare hands, feeling only a little warmth. She couldn't get burned, never had been able to, which was the whole reason she was here in the first place. Megan gave it a few good tugs. Nothing.

"Come on!" She threw her body against it, which was enough to cantilever it out of position, clearing the way.

"MEGAN. We're almost out of water," Buzz said in her ear.

"Path was blocked; cleared it and coming down now."

She went to put her glove back on, but Levi squirmed away and barked. He had stayed put crouched and backed up against the wall, shaking.

"It's okay. No one else can see, still me," she said before putting on her oxygen mask, which was a welcome relief from the smoky air. She might not be able to get burned, but she could still asphyxiate from lack of oxygen, so she needed to be careful when she took off her mask, making sure not to leave it off for too long.

Megan fixed her helmet and glove too while she could, taking care that no one would see the breach in protocol. After she was all settled, she picked up the shaking dog and cradled him against her.

The sound of the hose streamed against the fire in the kitchen as Megan descended down below, taking care on the blackened steps now that she was approximately seventy-five pounds heavier.

The flames had died back away from the door, which was the standard fire attack strategy with two in two out. Keep the exit open to get the people out, which was exactly what Megan was doing now.

Nick and Buzz waved her down toward the door through the smoke and the steam, cranking down the water of the hose to let her pass through the door with the dog to step into the night, illuminated by the orange glow of the house behind them.

CHAPTER 3

With everyone out of the building, Megan and her crew from Station Three moved into an exterior attack to keep the fire from spreading and save as much of the building as possible.

Laura and Jordan hadn't been far behind with the ambulance and had been treating Levi and his owner with extra oxygen and an examination to rule out any other injuries from the smoke or flames. Judging by the way the man had been lying when she found him, Megan would bet he had scored himself a trip to the hospital, but then every patient could refuse treatment.

No doubt he was in excellent care. Especially with Laura and her special ability of being able to heal people or at least kickstart the healing process.

They had bonded over that, when Megan had seen Laura's hands glow with a golden light as she healed an overdose call they had responded to about eight months ago. Before she had a chance to explain, Laura had panicked and tried to run to another town, fearing Megan would out her secret, which was hilarious considering Megan had a secret of her own. The two had sorted it all out at the teahouse downtown, when Megan had revealed her own ability. After that, they had gone from friends to secret sisters.

Laura had explained she had always acted when the patient was unconscious so they wouldn't see, and she could be sure they needed the help. If they were conscious, that brought in a lot of sticky questions like consent and explaining that they weren't hallucinating and she was actually helping.

For now, Megan could see Laura out of the corner of her eye, evaluating the man on the edge of the ambulance with a foil blanket around him and an oxygen mask on his face. It was a good sign that he was sitting up and conscious.

Levi was leaning against his leg with his golden fluffy tail wrapped around his shuddering body.

"Go ahead and check on them," Buzz said, clapping a big, gloved hand on her shoulder. "Tank is empty. We're going to stand by, but that's all we can do."

"Got it," Megan said, but felt the sadness sink into her chest. There were no water pipes out here in the country, no water source to save the building. They had no choice but to let it burn, but it sucked to see the flames engulf a house slowly while you stood by and watched.

"Good job again. I don't know how you do it, but I'm glad we have you," Buzz said, turning to go.

"Thanks. I wish I could do more."

"We all do, but all we can do is our best with the resources we have."

Megan nodded but didn't agree. It didn't feel right to sit by and watch a home turn to charred wood. She was an optimist and a problem solver by nature and hated to give up and settle. As it was, her feet were already walking toward Levi to check on him.

He shrank away as she approached until she remembered to take off her helmet and gloves.

"Hey boy, hey now." She crouched down a few feet away, and the trembling tail began to weakly thump against the cold dark ground.

Unlike his owner who was still wrapped in a foil blanket, Levi wasn't still wearing an oxygen mask, but she still pulled out a pair of gloves to begin an examination. Laura was talking with the man, and Megan waited until they were finished to introduce herself.

"My name is Megan White. I'm a firefighter, EMT, and a vet tech. Can I check on your dog?"

The man blinked a few times and nodded, watching her as she crouched down again.

"Hi Levi, remember me?" He glanced up at his owner, who nodded his head once, and walked forward into her outstretched arms.

"It's a good thing the SPCA provided the oxygen masks; he was a little weak when he came over," Laura said in her ear.

"You look like you've perked up now, boy, huh? It's going to be all right. Can I check your paws?" She took a pen light Jordan offered her and shined it on each pad, checking for burns or cuts. Finding none, she went on to check his eyes, ears, and mouth, which all looked great, thankfully.

"So far so good. You're such a good boy," she said, while continuing to pet him. "Such a brave, beautiful boy. Let's take a listen to your lungs."

On cue, Jordan handed her a stethoscope, and Megan took a listen to his heart, going strong, and his lungs which were clear.

"All right, that's done, and you passed with straight As. Have you had anything to drink tonight?" she asked, eyeing the clean kidney dish filled with water next to the truck.

His brown eyes looked back with a soulful connection only dogs could have, which was part of the reason she had always felt more at ease with animals than people.

"Not thirsty, huh? That's okay, maybe later. Let's get you a blanket while we sort everything out."

She petted him again and pulled over the blanket that had slid off him earlier, tucking him in and rubbing his boxy, soft head before walking him back to the leg of his owner, where he rested his head on the man's pajama-clad knee, the soulful eyes looking up.

It struck her how the man wasn't sitting inside the warmth of the ambulance. April in Montana and tonight was in the forties. He sat slumped in a crumpled foil blanket with the oxygen mask obscuring his mouth, the orange glow of the flames reflected in his exhausted eyes that remained fixed on the house in front of him.

She wanted to say something or wrap him in a warm hug and promise everything would be okay, but couldn't find the words or make that promise. She exchanged a glance with Laura, who had been watching him for any signs of distress, off to the side with her arms crossed.

"Is there someone we can call for you?" Laura asked with a gentle voice.

The man sighed and looked away from the house to answer her.

"Just my son."

"Is he local?"

The man shook his head and resumed watching the fire, looking so alone.

"I recommend we take you to the hospital to get checked out further. They have people who can help arrange for a place for you to stay."

The man didn't acknowledge Laura but kept rubbing

Levi's head, with movements so slow, Megan almost didn't notice.

"Would it be a help if I looked after Levi? You could come and pick him up the second you're released."

The man turned and studied her before letting out a sigh, crumpling further into exhaustion or maybe it was resignation, but he nodded.

"I wouldn't have said yes, but you talked to him like I do. And besides, I don't see another option."

Megan gave him a warm smile. "I'm off tomorrow and can meet you when you're ready. I'll make sure he has everything he needs."

"Thank you for your kindness, and for saving him. I…" He paused, almost succumbing to the emotion. He caught his breath, swallowed, and looked at the ground blinking. "I'm so grateful you could save him. Everything else is gone."

Megan's heart broke, and she stretched out her hand to lay it gently on his shoulder.

"I know you have done all you can, but I just don't know what I'm going to do."

Laura stepped over and crouched down in front of him, waiting until he looked her in the eyes.

"The only thing you need to do, Mr. Chapman, is focus on your health tonight. We will sort out everything else one step at a time."

He nodded and seemed to sigh, slumping further under the weight of his grief. "Thank you all for your kindness."

CHAPTER 4

Levi had a great time at Megan's house. Her cats, less so. Having a big happy dog lying in the middle of the apartment's tiny kitchen had soured the mood for the two spoiled cats.

Megan had talked with Laura when she had gotten back to the house. Laura had even swung by with some dog food, which had been great since Levi had eaten, drunk, and fallen asleep hard on the old pillows she had put down for him. No doubt he was still recovering from last night.

Her hands twitched, itching to pick up the phone and call Mr. Chapman to see if he was okay, but she didn't want to disturb him or interrupt if the doctor was in treating him for whatever had happened. Laura hadn't known any details, but his heart was erratic and they feared a heart attack, especially after viewing the ECG on the ambulance.

Just thinking about it, Megan had to stand up again and pace the apartment, even though she had just sat down. Feeling the need to settle herself, she began the process of making a cup of tea on autopilot, while her thoughts ran their course. He had looked weak and with poor color, but the lighting and the stress from the fire would've been reason enough. Still, if he'd had a heart attack, it was amazing he had sat up that long, insisting on watching the house as long as he could. There had been a sheen of sweat reflecting the fire, but again that too could be explained. It had been easy to miss, which proved the value in being taken in as a precaution. In her heart, Megan had a feeling he wouldn't have gone without Levi being taken care of, even if it was by a stranger. As a matter of fact, that was evidence alone to his condition.

She reached past Lincoln into the cabinet to grab a tea towel from the stack under the sink and knocked the flashlight over by accident. There was a hiss, and four sharp claws sliced into her hand with searing pain. She jerked back and cradled her hand with a hiss of her own before peeking at the wound.

"You really got me deep, you know that? You should be ashamed," she hissed while applying pressure to her wounded hand.

Lincoln, her orange tabby tomcat, lifted his leg and proceeded to lick himself without any concern for the blood streaming past the ruined dish towel and down the drain of her sink. Thank God she had already done the dishes last night, or she would've had a much bigger mess to clean up.

An affectionate nudge followed by a graceful smooth pass of fur along her leg had her looking down. Of course it wasn't Lincoln ready to apologize. Popsicle, her smaller, chocolate-colored cat clearly felt her pain. She always was a more affectionate and understanding creature.

Megan looked down. "Thank you. And you better not give me the same reaction when I have to give you medicine."

The big green eyes stared up at her with nothing but curiosity and obedience. Popsicle sat down next to her foot and flicked her tail right around, waiting and eyeing the cabinet over the coffee pot.

"For you? Yes. Because *you* listen." Ever the sucker, Megan tied the towel around the nasty four scratches on the inside of her hand and retrieved the box of kitty crunchies.

A deep meow signaled the approach from Lincoln, who turned his big yellow eyes on her in a complete farce of innocence.

She eyed Lincoln, almost tempted to give in despite her throbbing hand.

"None for you, Mr. Attack Cat," she said, heading to the bathroom in search of a first aid kit, taking care to tiptoe past Levi, who was snoring.

The trip wasn't a long one as her whole apartment was smaller than a thousand square feet. The layout was a little odd as she lived in an old downtown bank building, which was close to everything—a luxury that she paid a lot for.

True to form, the kitchen had an exposed brick wall that faced the island and the living space where two windows with arched tops looked onto the street below. Her bedroom and bathroom were blocked off by walls installed much later than the original construction, but the plumbing was a creative journey.

"Hi guys," she said, using her good arm to pull an old towel off the cage in front of one of the windows next to an old, secondhand, pull-out couch.

Salt and Pepper squawked hello as she passed the two parakeets. Both of them hopped to the side wall when she walked by, hoping to be let out for a quick zoom around the place. Megan had let them out before when they had careful supervision in case Lincoln and Popsicle decided to get hungry for something other than kitty crunchies. Neither one had even taken an interest in the birds, preferring to sleep upside down on their cat beds scattered around the floor.

Her bathroom was a war zone of laundry, hair care products, and Leo's tank. Leo was short for leopard because of the pattern on his shell or for Leonardo from the *Teenage Mutant Ninja Turtles*—the previous owner wasn't exactly sure. Either way, Leo was her box turtle she had inherited from a local science teacher a few months earlier. He had outgrown the tank in the school and was about to outgrow this one. It was another thing she'd have to worry about later.

"Come on, you stupid thing." Megan wrestled with the first aid kit's overprotective latch until the lid flew open with a flurry of Band-Aids everywhere.

Megan let out a stream of words her grandma would not have approved of at all, even though she had heard her say more than a few when her grandma had thought she was alone.

Trying to clean, treat, and wrap four deep scratches with her nondominant hand left her sweaty and ten minutes behind schedule.

A small tube popped out and flew onto the floor behind the desk. Not a total pig, Megan finished up, gathered the Band-Aids, and retrieved it only to laugh when she saw what it was.

"Burn cream. That's hilarious. Won't be needing this. Guess I should clean this out more, shouldn't I, huh, Leo?" She tossed the expired ointment into the trash can next to her desk, stopping to right the pictures she kept there.

If anything, her desk was more of her keepsake area, since all of her banking and email happened on her phone. Since she wasn't in school right now, her computer normally sat in the drawer, but it was out as she had been completing her applications for vet school, hoping to get contacted for an interview in a few weeks. Assuming they liked her portfolio, the interview would be the last step, and she could realize her dream of being a vet. Just thinking about it made her anxious. She had wanted this for so long, and with every step closer it all became so nerve-racking.

Animals had always been her companions, and Laura and Ash had learned not to go to the park with her, unless they wanted to greet every animal that walked by.

Megan had wanted to be a vet for as long as she could remember and had been on track until life had other plans. Some things were more important than school. Megan's eyes slid over to the other things.

Her most prized possessions were artfully arranged on the cleanest spot in the apartment. There were two pictures, one of her grandma holding her as a baby, surrounded by her parents and siblings, and another of just her and her grandma at her high school graduation. They sat next to an array of her grandma's antique perfume bottles, jewelry, and her most cherished item—a music box that used to be white, but that still played the sweetest music. She knew the melody, but not the name of the tune.

Her phone beeped, right as she shut the box. She spun around and tripped over a work boot, catching herself before she fell on her face inches from her bed. The phone was still going off somewhere in the mountains of her pillows and covers strewn haphazardly all over the bed.

"Hello?" she answered, out of breath.

"Megan, it's Laura."

"Hey, what's up? Have you heard anything?"

"Yeah, it's not great, but not as bad as it could've been. Heart attack, but minimal damage."

Megan stopped and sank down onto the edge of the bed. "Oh no."

"I know. They're calling his son now and getting him to come home. He'll be able to live on his own soon, but—"

"His house."

"Yeah, so you may want to give him a call or pass a

message to the nurse to let him know about his dog. Give him some peace of mind."

"Of course; I can do that today. Do they know how long he'll be there?"

"Not sure, but given he doesn't have a place to go back to right now, it'll be a while."

"I feel so bad for him."

"I know. I talked to Carter about helping him, and he's going to reach out and make some calls to see if there is anything he could do. I'll keep you posted if I hear anything."

"Okay, sounds good. Tell Holden Mimi loves him."

"Will do."

Megan ended the call and came out of the room.

Levi flopped over and let out a yawn. As if he could read the worry in her face, he stood and walked over to sit next to her and looked up with those brown eyes. She rubbed his soft ears when he let out a low whimper.

"It'll be okay, buddy. I don't know how, but it'll be okay." She drew in a breath and added, "It'll have to be."

CHAPTER 5

"You have got to be kidding me." Troy had been fighting a headache since getting to work, and today hadn't done anything to fix it.

"No sir, I wish I was. The commander wants the seating chart done again."

Troy's phone buzzed again on the desk, but he hit ignore for the third time today and rubbed his head.

"It's a military ball, not a wedding. We had an easier time ordering ammo during the shortage. Alright well, what time is it?" He glanced at his watch and swore again. "You head out, and I'll take another stab at it tonight."

Not needing to be told twice, Sergeant Nelson thanked him with a smile and headed out. Not that Troy could blame him—as it was they were supposed to be done at five, but the army always had a way of holding on to people. It was well past seven when Sergeant Nelson left, and the clock was closing in on eight thirty by the time Troy powered down his computer and slipped his CAC card out of the reader and headed home.

It wasn't a long drive off post to his home at Fort Campbell. He had an apartment, which was pretty decent. He liked the modern design, security, and the kitchen, but mostly it was nice to get away from work for a little bit. Sometimes, when he had time, he would drive over to Nashville, which was one of the cleanest towns he'd ever seen. The good food and the music scene always fit the bill.

Troy pulled his truck into his spot, killed the engine, and climbed the stairs before letting himself in to the second-floor apartment, welcomed only by the shrill beeping of the alarm system. He punched in his code to cut it off, before resetting the alarm for staying in, then headed for the bathroom, cranking the shower to hot. The bathroom, like the rest of the apartment, was all modern and clean lines. He didn't care about the finishes as much as that it was new and spotless. His deployments had taught him the value of two things—good food and clean bathrooms.

Troy stripped out of his uniform and stepped under the spray, grabbing the soap and going to town, still reworking the seating chart in his head. By the time he accounted for everyone's rank, everyone's spouses, and everyone's precious little feelings, he was getting a headache all over again. As it was, he had to finalize the menu and the list of speeches with the sergeant major in the morning.

He stepped out, tied one of the towels around his waist, and headed out into the kitchen, stopping to put the TV on a YouTube documentary about the Apollo Space Program on the way for some background noise.

In the kitchen, Troy grabbed his usual Perrier and a can of soup, which hardly constituted a great meal, but he decided to class it up with a day old chunk of bread from the bakery and the good butter he kept on the counter so it would stay soft. While the soup warmed, he changed in the bedroom into an old T-shirt from Fort Bragg and some boxers, with a quick glance to make sure the blinds were still closed, since it was well past sundown.

Once everything was heated up and his soup in a bowl, he set his dinner on the coffee table and plunked down on the couch to listen to the narrator tell him what he already knew about Alan Shepard and Buzz Aldrin while he ate. He had always loved history as a kid, but he had taken more of an interest as an adult. Being in the military and seeing things firsthand that would end up in media like this documentary brought a special appreciation for those that came before him. He had read somewhere online that men his age either got really into smoking meat or World War II, and he was decidedly in the second camp.

He ate and finished the program, browsing YouTube's recommendations for whatever he should watch next, which as usual was on point and freakishly accurate. At first he hadn't been used to the online streaming world, but the History Channel was mostly about aliens and weird BS these days, and his buddy had recommended a few online channels which he enjoyed.

The countdown to the next video told him this would be on the use of gunpowder in ancient China, which was all fine and good but wasn't his primary focus, so he opened up his phone and began swiping through tonight's lineup of women on the newest dating app. Troy had expected the apps to be a waste of money, but sometimes he met some pretty cool people who weren't looking for anything serious, which worked for him. He had seen enough heartbreak, divorce, and affairs to give Cupid himself strong doubts about love these days. He had no problem with romance, companionship, and a good time, but was not interested in pressure or drama.

Tonight's lineup was a mix.

The first woman was pretty and had a picture of her son.

He was a cute kid, but children needed stability and long-term relationships. Troy respected her for putting it out there and not trying to hide the fact that she was a parent, but he still swiped left with his thumb to move on to the next one.

The second woman had a neck tattoo, which was kinda hot but intimidating at the same time. She liked concerts, bars, and the BDSM club downtown. Not his vibe. Swipe left.

Woman number three posed with a hand on her hip and her head cocked to one side, like most women did these days and always made Troy think of back problems. Pretty face, but her profile mentioned wine with the girlfriends, beach trips, and how family was the most important thing to her. He checked out a few more pictures to discover they all were of her in various wedding parties. Red alert, swipe left.

The fourth lady was a little older and had a nice smile. In every picture was one of what looked like three dogs. He was just about to scroll down to read more of her profile when an incoming call flashed across his screen.

Shit, he never called those other numbers back today either. Might as well add it to the to-do list.

Since it was Goldvein's area code, he picked up, expecting to be reminded about his car's nonexistent extended warranty. Since the telemarketers had started to mimic people's area codes, it made it so much harder to screen calls.

"Hello, is this Troy Chapman?"

Here we go. "This is he."

"My name is Matthew, and I'm a case manager here at St. Olaf General Hospital. We've been trying to reach you."

Oh no. On instinct, Troy got up and started pacing. He'd had this call before.

"What happened to my dad? Is he okay?"

The calm, matter-of-fact way the case manager spoke did nothing to ease his fears.

"Mr. Chapman, I'm sorry to tell you there was a fire, and your dad was brought in by the paramedics."

"A fire? This doesn't make sense. When? What burned?"

"It was a house fire late last night."

Troy stopped dead. The house. The ranch. His dad. Memories of his mom, Adam, and Dad all started running through his head at a mile a minute. Childhood memories, sounds, smells, Mom's kitchen, Dad's chair, Adam's room left just like it was. His dad. Oh God, that house was his life. What would happen now?

The case manager was still speaking, but Troy couldn't follow.

"I'm sorry, could you please repeat that? What about the house?"

"Of course. We're waiting on the building inspector to come and assess the damage of the house, but until then we need to talk about a care plan for your father."

"Is he okay? What happened? Where is he now?"

"He is in stable condition right now. He was found on the floor of the bedroom, and the firefighters were able to get him out where the paramedics treated him for smoke inhalation. When he got here, he was very weak with an erratic pulse, and the ECG showed he suffered from an apparent heart attack."

Troy slowly sank down into the chair.

"But he's stable. That's good, right?" His voice didn't sound like his own. Instead, it was monotone and flat, like a person who was going through the motions of his own life while he watched from a distance.

"He is stable, but very weak. We are making arrangements for his care plan after he leaves the hospital and wanted to reach out as you are next of kin. Are you able to make yourself available to assist him once he leaves the hospital?"

"Assist him?"

"Yes. While he is stable, he is weak and will need care with daily tasks such as managing medication, feeding himself, and hygiene care. Are you able to make yourself available at this time?"

Troy blinked a few times, trying to digest the news. "No. I'm in Kentucky at this time. It's hard for me to get away."

"Are there any other members of your family that could be available?"

"No. It's…uh, just us."

"Are you able to take leave or FMLA?"

Leave? FMLA? What in the hell was happening?

"No, I'm in the military, but I do have leave. I'm going to need some time to organize this all. Do you have a number or a way I can get in contact with you?"

"Yes, let me know when you're ready and I'll give it to you."

Troy grabbed a notepad from the junk drawer in the kitchen and scratched down the number as Matthew rattled it off.

"Additionally, we will need to discuss living arrangements."

"Right. You said the house needs to be inspected before he moves back in. How bad is the house?"

"I haven't seen it myself, but I'm told the inspector still needs to see the extent of the damage. It did start in the kitchen."

Troy sat in stunned silence. His mom's kitchen was his favorite place to talk with her. Most of his memories were of her in that room, and when he dreamed, he was always in that room with her at the stove. The memories and his dreams overlapped so much he was no longer sure which memories had actually happened and which had not.

She was humming over the sink doing the dishes, wearing a yellow apron with pink flowers and those big yellow rubber gloves. She turned around and smiled at him, pretending to accidentally put soap on her nose before making funny faces and failing repeatedly to wipe it off. She was like that though. Always smiling. Always laughing.

"Mr. Chapman?"

Troy gave himself a shake, blinking to clear his eyes and focus on the paper pad in front of him.

"Yes? I'm sorry. Could you, um…repeat that again?"

"Of course. Is there another property or location I could put down for his discharge paperwork?"

"We have another house on the ranch. It's been vacant for about a year, or maybe two years ago now. I can't remember, but it's loosely furnished. Winterized, I think, so the water and heat will need to be turned on, but um, I don't think that will take very long."

Troy rattled off the address as best he could remember until the case manager was satisfied.

"Alright, I think that is all I need at this time, but I'll reach out and be in touch if we need any further details from you."

"Wait—how's Dad? Can I talk to him?"

"I believe he's resting now, given the time, but I'll leave a note in the chart for the nurse to see when he's awake."

"Thank you, I appreciate that."

"Thank you, and please let me know when we can expect you to arrive."

Troy ended the call, clicked the mail app on his phone, and typed out a quick email to his therapist.

CHAPTER 6

Three days later Megan sat outside the hospital with her fingers drumming on the wheel of her Subaru. She had fiddled with the radio, first scanning through all of the pop stations, tried a podcast, then watched funny cat videos online but was still so restless she had settled on a calm story she normally used to fall asleep. The narrator's soothing voice and subtle sound effects of an imaginary train chugging on a track calmed her just enough to stop her from biting her already raw nails. She loved helping people but dreaded talking to them afterward. The gratitude felt awkward, and she never knew what to say.

As if he understood, Levi whined behind her, and she reached around to scratch the soft boxy head. The golden retriever was curled up on some blankets, and though the breed was happy by nature, he kept glancing out the window toward the glass doors, waiting.

Megan had scribbled her number down for Mr. Chapman as he had been secured in the back of the ambulance. She had gotten a call this morning saying he was released, and he asked if she would mind meeting him at the hospital so he could get Levi. Not knowing who he would call, and since she felt sorry for the older man, she offered to give him a ride, which to her surprise he accepted.

She didn't know how he was doing, but he had said ten o'clock, and her clock said five till. Thanks to her grandmother's insistence, Megan always liked to be early. It was just the anticipation on any social interaction that was the killer.

Levi's tail started to thump against the blanket she had put down for him when she saw the glass doors open and a man in scrubs rolling Mr. Chapman toward her. Levi barked a few times and started pacing in the back.

She opened the door and walked around the car to stand by the back door where Levi was waiting. "Hello, Mr. Chapman. Levi's missed you!" she said, getting out of the car just like she had rehearsed in her mind, while Levi went from excited to ecstatic in the back seat.

Mr. Chapman gave her a smile and a wave before murmuring a thank you to the nurse, who helped him stand up. Megan opened the door to the onslaught of love. Levi went berserk jumping, barking, and licking while his tail went a mile a minute. Mr. Chapman laughed and rubbed both ears, flopping them all over so much his hospital bracelet shook on his wrist. He then pressed his head to Levi's and closed his eyes, in the way only pet lovers did, silently sending his love and thanks to his counterpart. Levi's brown soulful eyes blinked slowly in understanding and singular love.

He was carrying a bag with his pajamas, which still smelled of smoke. She didn't know if he had a wallet, but he was going to need to make some purchases soon since everything in his bedroom was in the same boat. As far as she knew, Buzz and the inspectors hadn't cleared the house yet.

"Thank you again for watching him."

"He was no trouble at all," she said, rubbing Levi's head. "I have two cats, and they got along pretty great."

"He's a good boy. I can't thank you enough. I—" He swallowed and shook his head once, coming up empty for words.

"I was happy to do it."

"Thank you for the ride. I'll pay you for your gas and trouble."

Megan, who had been having anxiety about not knowing what to talk with him about, found herself nodding before she could overthink it more. They got in the car, and he eased into the seat with some evidence of stiffness and other pains, but was moving on his own which was a good sign. His pills rattled in the a little white bag he carried.

She found it a little odd that he had accepted her offer of a ride, when she knew he had two bedrooms for children at home. Neither had been occupied, but surely his sons would come home to see about him.

"Would it be too much trouble to stop for breakfast? Drive-thru is fine."

"Not at all. Where would you like to go?"

"Do you have anything against McDonalds? It's my favorite, and I could use a pick-me-up."

Megan smiled. "That sounds perfect."

It was a short drive from the hospital, and they ordered through the mic and ate in the parking lot. Mr. Chapman ordered a senior coffee and pancakes with sausage and eggs, and Megan ordered an orange juice and sausage biscuit. Not at all shy, Levi had stuck his head in between both of them, giving the eye, which earned him two sausage patties.

Megan took notice of him while eating. He had showered and washed off the soot and gotten some clean clothes. The sun came through the window and glinted off his worn, gold wedding band.

"This is the best meal I've had in days," he said with a hint of a smile that cracked through the sadness.

"I'm sure after three days anything gets old."

He shook his head and kept eating. "Bunch of worriers obsessed with health. "

"Were the people at the hospital able to help you make a plan?"

He took a sip of his coffee, which was black. "The Red Cross came and got me in touch with insurance and helped me get new credit cards and paperwork. Assuming none of that can be recovered."

Megan didn't meet his eyes. "I'm not sure it's safe to go back into the building until an engineer and inspector have checked it."

His only sign of further grief was a slight pause in eating. "Then paperwork it is."

"What about living arrangements?" she asked before taking a sip of orange juice and wiping her mouth with the paper napkin.

"There is another house on the property. It needs some work, and they're getting me some donations for furniture and housewares, since it's empty now. I should be able to manage well enough; my son should be coming in tomorrow."

Four days after his dad had lost everything? Megan was not impressed.

"Well, let me know what you need until your son can get here."

He shook his head. "He's in the army, and I didn't want to distract him with this, but the case manager insisted." He took another sip of coffee.

"Does he live nearby?"

"Kentucky."

"It'll be good to have him home to help out."

Mr. Chapman nodded. "It will be nice to see him. I haven't seen my son in over a year, and he's the only family I have left."

CHAPTER 7

The drive back to Montana had taken an agonizing thirty hours, which with two overnights meant he arrived on the third day, one day after his Dad had been released.

He could've flown, but given how he had handled the drive, it had been the right decision not to. For one, he needed his truck since he would be there for six weeks. Dad would never part with his old one, and Troy needed to have that freedom.

Worries about his dad's health, loss of the house, and how they would pay for everything weighed down on top of everything else he was dealing with too. At one point in the middle of the first day, a truck had swerved and almost hit him head-on. The blinding lights had kept him awake in the motel, where he tossed and turned from one nightmare to the next. Since he hadn't slept well, the second day was worse. Normally his safe space, the truck's cabin started to feel overwhelmingly small. He couldn't stretch his legs or arms or back, his breath coming in short panicky bursts, while a wave of sweat washed over him. He barely made it to a rest stop where he was able to park and duck out into the grassy common area. It had taken him a full thirty minutes to get his bearings and calm down enough to continue. Troy was determined to make it. He had no choice.

Dad didn't have his cellphone with him, but Troy had spoken with his dad while he had still been in the hospital.

The conversation had haunted him. It had been a relief to hear his old man on the other end of the line. That rugged voice that had always been a stern, salt of the earth rancher, was weakened with age and exhaustion.

"Troy?" his dad had answered, through what sounded like labored breathing.

"Yeah, Dad. It's me. How are you doing? I'm on my way."

"Man, I hate to bother you with this. I tried to tell them here at the hospital I wasn't that bad off."

"Dad, they told me about the fire." He hadn't known what to say at that point. He didn't know if he should be apologizing for not being there, telling him how much he loved him, or begging him not to go like his mom and Adam had. There were too many emotions to say.

His dad's voice had cracked, which was a sound Troy had only heard on two other occasions. "The house—I don't know. It looked bad. It was my fault."

"No Dad, that's not important."

"It was. I know it. Once I heard the smoke alarm, I knew. It's all my fault. All of the pictures, memories."

Troy had to pull over and clench his eyes against the welling of tears. Everything remaining of Mom and of Adam was in that house. Not to mention the generations that had come before.

He took a minute to breathe and steady himself before he steadied his dad. "Those are just things, Dad. The important thing is we have each other. That you're okay."

"I'm okay," he said through labored breathing and blowing his nose.

"They said you had a heart attack."

The pause on the line let him know more than words ever could. "I didn't want them to tell you. I didn't feel anything, so it must've been minor."

"I'm in Iowa now, will be there in a couple of days. We'll sort it out, one thing at a time. Don't do anything dumb until I get there."

His dad let out a whisper of a laugh, which led to more heavy breathing. "It's hard for me to get into trouble with all of these nurses around."

"Good. I'll be there as soon as I can. I love ya, Dad."

"I love you too."

"Get some rest."

"Drive safe."

He hadn't spoken to his dad since because the next time he had called, the nurse had let him know he was discharged. He had called the cellphone, which went straight to voicemail, meaning it was probably left in the house and destroyed. A thought he chose not to dwell on right now.

Troy wasn't sure how his dad had gotten home, but he was a survivor, had lived his whole life in that town, and was not afraid to ask for help. That was a good thing since he was so far away.

The moment he had hung up the phone with the case manager at the hospital, he had texted his CO explaining the situation and putting in for six weeks of leave. He wasn't sure if that was enough to assess the situation, but it was a start. Leave was granted with well wishes and off he went. He was lucky this didn't happen when he was in Kuwait or Iraq. Once he was deployed, it would have been much more difficult to get home.

He arrived at two in the afternoon, riding through the

familiar scenes of town buffered by rolling farmland that in a few months would be filled with crops. He turned onto the main drag through the old downtown area and passed his high school hangout, Joe's Diner, which looked just like it had twelve years ago. It was like he was driving through a memory instead of going home.

He tried not to think of his mom and Adam, but with each red-brick facade of the tea shop here and the grocery there, the memories echoed louder and louder in his mind. They only increased as he headed out of town toward the ranch.

God, what if he couldn't bear looking at the rubble? Everything his dad had worked so hard to build. Hell, the house his grandfather had built. All of his mom's memories and Adam's belongings in the closet—

No. He had to get a grip. They were things. Not people. Things could be rebuilt and replaced.

Not exactly, his annoyingly accurate subconscious pointed out.

For someone in the army who had moved around, seen different countries, met different people, he hated change. It wasn't that he was inflexible, but this was the one thing that was never supposed to change. He relied on Goldvein to be the exact same as he left it. He counted on his dad to always be there, doing the same things in the same house.

The sight of the black fence brought him back to center, while his pulse kicked up another notch.

This was it. Their property. The ranch.

There were no animals, and the fence needed a good coat of paint, which made him frown. He knew Dad had semire-tired, but it was unlike him to let things like this slip.

Troy popped the blinker on and turned into Mountain View Ranch. He was home.

The gravel driveway sounded the same with the crunch

of his tires. Even though this car had never been here before, the ranch whispered its familiar greeting as he drove deeper into the nearly three-thousand-acre ranch. There were a few gates in the four square mile area, but this one was the closest to the main house, one of the smaller ranch houses, and the old original wooden barn his grandfather had built.

There were two more houses on other parts of the ranch for employees to stay in while they monitored their area, but those houses hadn't been occupied in years. It made sense to guess that his dad would stay closest to home.

His dad had picked out the property from his grandfather's tract of land, which had been sold off to support the estate. This was the last original piece, and though he hadn't always appreciated it, his sense of tradition meant he had to keep the legacy going when the time came.

The rolling hills swept up into mountains that mingled with clouds at the horizon. He could track the ridgeline from memory, including the notch that seemed to be cut out about half a mile in. The mountains weren't on their property anymore but were a landmark dividing them from others. Right now everything was still bleak and gray, but in the summer, the blue sky would stretch on for miles over a golden prairie speckled with wildflowers. He had grown up here, and back then couldn't wait to leave.

He crested the hill and… "Oh, thank God."

He loosened his death grip on the wheel and let out a gush of air in relief when he saw the outline of the main house standing strong. Not a total loss. He could work with that. He could deal. Whatever it would take, they could salvage and rebuild. Then get a damn dry hydrant because, as God is his witness, this was never going to happen again.

Rather than dwell on what was lost, he turned past the barn, which had more peeling paint, and headed for the closest house.

He parked and hopped down from the truck, hitting the hard ground with a thud. The frost-covered ground was no good to dig in for a needed hydrant, but if he could, he would at least get the site approval for once things thawed. He needed it now, but Montana's weather didn't change because you wanted it to.

A slice of wind cut right through his army field jacket and nearly knocked him flat. He shoved his hands in his pockets and turned against the spring wind that still had a bite in it to go into the house, reaching out to open the knob when the door swung open without him.

His brain scrambled trying to reconcile what was in front of him with why he was seeing it.

Standing in his path was the most beautiful woman he had ever seen in his life.

CHAPTER 8

"Uh…excuse me," she said, edging to one side to pass him, as if he'd let her go without an explanation.

Levi barked from somewhere in the house before trotting up to Troy and giving the sniff test. Apparently, he passed because the tail started going nuts.

"Troy, is that you?" called his dad from somewhere in the back of the house. It was a relief to hear his dad's voice before his anxiety could assume something had gone wrong. She must have been some sort of nurse.

"Yeah, Dad. Where are you?"

"Come on back. Megan was just helping me unpack some stuff."

He heard his dad but eyed Megan, trying to telepathically tell her to stay until he could figure out more about her. Torn between following his dad's voice and staying rooted to the spot, he broke away in a huff and walked back through the small double-wide, manufactured home to the main bedroom.

His dad sat on the edge of the bed in a white T-shirt, and a warm smile tore across his face.

"My boy," he said in a voice cracked with emotion as he held his arms outstretched and tried to stand.

Troy went to him and held on tight, soaking in the familiar smells. Coffee and Irish Spring soap filled his nose with memories of home. His dad's arms were thinner, and he could feel him giving more of his weight, which he was glad to bear.

They stood like that for a long time, each holding on to the other, when his dad let out a sigh and leaned back to look at him.

"How was the trip?"

Leave it to Dad to get right to the point. He was a practical man with practical emotions. A rancher through and through, he was a tough old cowboy, but his hair was fully white, unlike the last time Troy had visited, and his face was gaunt with worry and exhaustion.

Troy propped his hands on his hips. "Long, uneventful. I'm more interested in you. You have a nurse helping you, and why are you out of bed?"

Troy's dad waved a hand but eased himself back down onto the bed despite his show of force. "Megan's just being nice, and I'm fine."

He wanted to ask his dad more about the beautiful redhead in his house, but knew there was time enough for that later.

"Fine is not what I heard on the phone the other day."

His dad clapped his hands in front of him and let them fall on his lap.

"I'm going to the cardiologist in a few days for a follow-up. Been taking some pills. Feel okay."

Troy eyed the McCafé cup, knowing full well how much his dad loved the golden arches.

"I'm no expert, but French fries won't be his favorite thing."

"Well, I will deal with that when I talk to the doc. There are other things to deal with. The inspector said the house is uninhabitable as it stands right now. Might be a loss, depending on if we can get the money to fix. Insurance is only covering fifty percent of the possessions and none of the appliances." His dad glanced up at him with brown eyes just like his own. "Have you seen it yet?"

Troy let out a breath in response. "Just the outside. I came right here."

His dad nodded, the lines in his face carving farther in while a slight sheen of sweat formed on his brow. There weren't any curtains hanging in front of the open window. Broken blinds hung at odd angles, with sun scattering through reminding Troy of shattered glass. A few plastic bags from Wal-Mart lay on the ground with some fresh clothes inside waiting to be unpacked.

He hadn't even thought about the clothes and the housewares. All of that would have to be replaced. He had been so focused on the past that he had neglected to focus on the implications on the present. It could be fixed, but the toll it would take was just starting to set in.

Levi whined next to the bed until Hank reached out and rubbed his head.

"Why don't you take a rest, and I'll unpack a little. We can...assess the situation and sort things out tomorrow."

"Okay, yeah. I think that might be good."

Troy helped Hank into bed and covered him up, reminded of how many times his dad must have done the same for him, and Levi hopped up to curl at the foot of the bed. He folded the pants his dad had been wearing and placed them on the small dresser which stayed with the house. They were new along with everything else he could see through the cracks of the open drawers. Nothing from the house was here other than Dad and Levi.

With his dad settled, Troy came back down the small hall, careful not to make any noise despite still wearing his field jacket which was anything but quiet. He peeked out the door, frowning when he only saw his car. Clearly, Megan hadn't gotten his mental message to stay put.

He came out into the kitchen and living room space, noting the old, worn furniture. The carpet needed to be replaced but had been freshly vacuumed, and more Wal-Mart bags were in the kitchen.

He pulled open the fridge and found more evidence from McDonald's, along with a fresh half gallon of skim milk, some bread and cold cuts, and a few apples. A quick inspection of the cabinets revealed Cheerios, oatmeal, and a handful of dishes.

The house was furnished, but very basic with nothing fancy. If this was going to turn into a long-term situation, there would need to be a few other upgrades including a TV, which he hadn't seen in the bedroom or in the living room in front of the kitchen.

Troy brought in his luggage and set them in the other bedroom, which had a pack of new sheets on the naked mattress. He could hear snoring through the wall so decided against unpacking.

Coming back out, he decided to make a list of everything that would need to be purchased. His dad had covered the basics, but Troy could only go so far without a coffee maker, and McCafé wasn't his cup of tea…er, coffee at all. His dad might be happy enough eating a literal heart attack in a bag, but Troy had always loved to cook, a skill he had learned from his mother.

Grabbing his keys and his list, Troy headed out to the car to drive over and inspect the house for himself. Later he would go into town to pick up a few more things, and during dinner he fully intended to question his father more about the mysterious Megan.

CHAPTER 9

"So the son finally showed up, huh?" Megan's friend Laura said before taking a bite of her roast chicken.

"Yeah, I know." Megan rocked back on the red vinyl booth that was the hallmark of Joe's Diner. The fifties-style restaurant was known for meatloaf and milkshakes while Elvis played on repeat. She grabbed a French fry and shrugged. "Hank said he had driven from Kentucky."

Ash, who completed their trio, had stopped by from the police department to join them for lunch. She hadn't responded to the fire since a police presence wasn't needed, but the others had filled her in on what had happened. She took a bite of her salad and frowned in thought. "He must not have the money if he didn't fly."

Laura shook her head. "I don't know. But Hank has lived here all his life, and people want to help since he's mostly alone."

"How was the son? This must have been a shock."

Megan took a drink from her iced tea and took a moment to think that over. Ash was an excellent read of people, and Laura had known her long enough to anticipate her thoughts. What she didn't want to say was he was the most handsome man she had ever seen. She also didn't want to say that he looked like he had been through hell and wasn't interested in chitchat.

"He was wearing an army jacket, but Hank had said he was in the army, so that wasn't a shock," she finally said. "I didn't hang around long enough to find out more." Partly because his demeanor had been so intense, but mainly because she wanted to give him and his dad their privacy after over a year apart.

Laura nodded. "He may have had to get leave or was coming from somewhere. I guess if he didn't know how long he'd be staying, he'd want a car."

Megan nodded in agreement.

Ash chewed on her sandwich and what Megan had just said. She could almost see her friend's violet eyes turning it over in her mind as she stared at the table with a slight line between her brows. "Maybe."

"Well, either way, he's finally where he should be."

"About damn time," Ash said.

"Mhmmm," Laura agreed. "It was really nice of you to help him out."

Megan could feel her cheeks go pink with the praise, which was always hard to take. She loved to help people but always felt so awkward about it. "I really enjoyed it. It was nice to hear his stories about his life and the family's land."

It had been more than nice. Having someone to care for and help shop for got her out of her routine. She enjoyed unpacking groceries for him while he told her about the history of the town. It had only been one day, but it was nice to run errands and have someone to visit with. She got the sense he needed it just as much as she did.

"Did you get the little house all set up?" Laura asked.

"For the most part. It'll do. He has some basic clothes and

groceries. Toiletries, linens, and a few lamps were what I was working on when his son showed up. I pretty much left right after that, but most of it was done. Honestly, I'm just checking in on him. He likes to go to McDonald's."

Laura grinned. "We should introduce him to Holden. He loves the Happy Meal."

"Sounds like Carter's doing."

"Oh yeah. Big time."

CHAPTER 10

Troy stomped across the cold, hard-packed ground, braced against the wind that sliced through his jacket. He hadn't preheated his truck, but being out of the wind felt as good as balmy, even if he could still see his breath. He cranked the engine over against its will and headed out toward town.

It was early, and the sun's golden light was just starting to peek across the horizon. Dad wasn't up yet, which was telling. The man had spent so much time as a rancher that it was his innate nature to be up at four thirty every day without fail, sometimes even earlier. His body was trained that way, so when Troy woke up to snoring yesterday and today, he knew how much his dad had slowed down.

It wasn't a surprise. They had talked all day after his arrival, and he had insisted on seeing the medical paperwork for himself. From a healthcare standpoint, Dad was lucky. No major damage. Rest, exercise, reduce stress, take meds, improve diet, and all of that. He was lucky. The house, on the other hand, wasn't.

When he had walked through, the initial shock had been

overwhelming. Just as he had expected, seeing the smoke-scarred kitchen was a punch in the gut. The house was a shell of what it had been, with a gaping hole in the roof. The building inspector had come out and condemned the property, and while insurance was working on getting them an estimate and check, he and his dad were making do in the small house, talking about the future.

Country people like his dad mourned deeply, but in such a way that required action. It wasn't long before they were talking about plans for the future and what that would look like. There was no way his dad wanted to sell, meaning Troy was next in line once he got out of the army.

They talked about hiring a salvage company to reclaim as much as they could from the original structure to carry those traditions and materials forward, but with updating the layout. A new, larger kitchen would make way for newer appliances which always seemed to be getting bigger, and would be an easier fit with electric and plumbing instead of shimmying a new oven into an old space.

They also had talked about finances, which was another sore subject Troy intended to get to the bottom of this morning.

From what he gathered when talking with his dad, everything was a shitshow. All of it had burned in the fire, so there were no paper records to verify until he got to the bank. His old man hadn't believed in—or was too cheap for—hiring an accountant.

In the recent mail, which had been delivered since the fire, Troy found statements from nine different credit cards with rolling balances that thankfully had zero interest rates for the first year. Most of it didn't make any sense. Three hundred dollars here, a couple of thousand there. All of it was low enough that it should've been able to be paid off easily. To make matters worse, his dad had taken out seven loans at various points.

It wasn't uncommon or unheard of for a farmer to take out loans to get the crops in and the livestock fed before the sale of the product. The money would be earned back and the debts paid. All it did was add a little more cash to get the farm going, but it was a dangerous game to play. The banks always took their cut, leaving little to squirrel away for the next season, repeating the same dangerous cycle of dependency.

Troy's appointment this morning was to consolidate everything, and if his math was right, it should add up to the tune of one hundred and twelve thousand dollars. If the land wasn't paid off and owned outright, his dad would have no choice but to sell or go bankrupt. Knowing his dad, both options were out of the question.

As it was, Troy had one thing on his mind now. Tax season. If he couldn't pay the taxes, the whole lot would go up for a tax sale, and the land his family had poured blood, sweat, and tears into for generations would go to the highest bidder at a strong discount.

Troy shuddered at the thought. If they lost the property, he couldn't imagine what that would do to his father.

To keep his mind off that unpleasant possibility, he took a minute to think of Megan. Dad had told him a little about her, but not nearly enough to satisfy him. All he knew was she had offered to care for Levi and had been helping out, though Dad did look a little disappointed to hear that she had left after Troy had arrived.

Thinking of her light-blue eyes and pale skin and that small pink smile calmed him. Would she get freckles? He didn't know, but he liked the idea of it. He didn't even know her, but wanted her to be carefree and in a sunny spot on a porch, with bare feet tracing the grain of the wood as she rocked back and forth. The thought made him feel lighter, as if he didn't have any troubles.

It was a welcome break because he had plenty of troubles. At least one wasn't time management. The bank didn't open until ten, so he had time to grab a coffee and maybe browse the bookstore downtown. It wasn't open yet, but the coffeeshop next to it was. He turned the truck into a spot and crouched against the wind to get inside, welcomed by the tinkling of a little bell above the door.

The smell of cinnamon and coffee rushed around him in a warm hug as he walked inside. Honey oak floors creaked under his feet while an acoustic guitar played in the background, but both sounds were overtaken by the steaming milk from behind the counter. The overall vibe was a little artsy for him, but he liked good food and cold brew was where it was at. Why go through life with shitty coffee and stale, dry pastry?

There wasn't a line, so the girl behind the counter with a gauge in her ear waved him over with a bubbly smile and took his order for the daily special and a ham and cheese croissant because it had been a fucking week and he deserved it. He ran the card through the sleek iPad right as she put a cup of tea at the pickup station.

The color of the hair was a dead giveaway and had somehow seared into his mind as the only color red hair should actually be. He hadn't consciously digested what was happening before he heard himself call out her name.

She flinched as if she didn't want to run into him but turned around. At first her shoulders were caved slightly in, but before he could take it personally, she straightened and looked him in the eye, taking his breath away again.

A spring goddess stood before him.

"Hi." She looked at him, then back at her cup as if she

didn't know what to say. He wasn't sure if she even knew his name.

"I'm glad I ran into you. I wanted to thank you for taking care of my dad." He stuck out his hand, hoping she'd take it and forcing some connection with her. "My name's Troy."

She only had the slightest delay before reaching forward, and despite her slender hand, her grip was strong. Actually it was strong enough to surprise him.

"It's nice to meet you. I'm Megan. How's your dad doing?"

"He's doing okay. Going back to the doctor in a few days for some follow-ups. He really has talked a lot about you."

A pink tinge hit her cheekbones as she smiled and looked down. "I'm just glad I could help."

"I think he misses you. Levi too. Dad would love for you to come back to the house for dinner sometime."

"Oh, I would hate to intrude. I know it's been a while since you've seen each other. After everything he's gone through, he needs to be with family."

"Not much of us left," Troy said without thinking. He wished he could take the statement back along with the chill that entered his voice. "Seriously. I think it'd be good for Dad. He has mentioned it several times and wanted to thank you, and I owe you too. I mean, I got here as fast as I could, and I'm thankful he had someone looking out for him."

She looked at him with an odd look, almost as if she wanted to say something but decided against it. If he had been cheekier he would've offered her a penny for her thoughts.

"I'm working tonight, so maybe later."

"Here," he said as he scribbled his number on the back of his receipt. "I know you have Dad's number, but here's mine. I'd love to talk more about when we can meet up."

She took it and thanked him before leaving with her cup of tea, which sadly was to go.

Troy flashed his brightest smile as she walked out, knowing full well that he wanted her to come visit as much as his father did. He watched her go, imagining the curves that were hidden under her green sweater dress and wishing it hugged her figure more. He tried not to stare at the two or so inches of skin that were exposed between the dress and her boots, and he prayed that she would text him soon.

CHAPTER 11

Megan ended up driving back out to the little house to meet Troy three days later, mainly because Mr. Chapman had called and invited her. She only texted Troy because Mr. Chapman still hadn't gotten the hang of texting, and even that was just to let him know she was on her way, to which he responded with a "sounds good" and a happy face. She didn't answer him.

She bounced along on the gravel driveway of the ranch with a bottle of wine and some bread from The Perfect Cup, which was her go-to spot where she had run into Troy. Of all of the people she had seen in there, the cocky, too-good-looking-for-his-own-good man was the last person she expected to run into while in her happy place.

When she first had seen him there, she had attempted to hide in the ladies' room, only to be stymied when he shoved his hands in his pockets and sauntered right into the path to her escape. Not only did this mean she had no choice but to interact—thank God she had ordered her tea to go since she hated small talk—but annoyingly it meant she couldn't see his ass squeezed into some Wranglers, which looked better than any of the buns in the glass case.

Megan hated herself for ogling. It wasn't as if she didn't admire the view of a fine specimen, but of all of the people to find attractive, she hated that it was this selfish, arrogant bro. If she was honest with herself, she didn't know him like that and was making a lot of assumptions. Still, she didn't have any living family and he did, yet it took him far too long to come home to his dad, even if he was in the military. People who didn't appreciate what was in front of them drove her crazy.

Then, to add insult to injury, the way he had looked at her with a lopsided, sexy grin and casually mentioned dinner to give her his number like it was a gift was just an eyeroll. Sure, he was hot. That he knew he was hot was annoying.

She liked Mr. Chapman a lot, though, and was genuinely looking forward to visiting with him. When they had been together, he had reminded her of the grandfather she had never known. He would've been a little blue-collar for her very proper grandmother, but Megan liked to think that they would have gotten along well. Grandma always appreciated hardworking gentlemen who knew how to fix things and took pride in their work.

Megan drove past the burned original house which now was wearing a big blue tarp like a bandage. The little house wasn't too much farther, and in no time, she was parked next to Mr. Chapman's old, reliable pickup and Troy's newer one.

Both matched the personality of their owners. Mr. Chapman's was plain white with a few dings and scrapes, but overall in good condition. She couldn't see inside the cab, but she had a feeling it sounded like old-school country, smelled like McDonald's.

Meanwhile, Troy's was newer and bulkier, but at least it

didn't have the lift kit or any annoying bumper stickers. There was hope yet.

She braced for the cold, windy night and went to the little covered front porch. Even though spring was right around the corner, here the wind still had a bite to it. She raised her hand to knock on the door, but it swung in courtesy of Troy who gave her another lopsided smile.

"Right on time."

Levi pushed past him, with his tail going a mile a minute as she knelt down to give him scratches.

"Hi buddy! I'm so glad to see you again! I missed you."

Troy let out a laugh to her left. "I see why you agreed to come."

Megan stood back up and gave him a smile. "I wasn't sure what to bring, so I picked these up." After he shut the door behind her, Megan handed over the rolls and the bottle of wine, which she hoped was good. She didn't drink and didn't know wine. All she knew was red wine was good for the heart, she liked the label, and it was at eye level, which maybe meant it was good?

Troy eyed the wine and looked impressed. "Thank you. This will actually go great."

Before she could say anything else, Mr. Chapman ambled around the corner.

"Megan. There you are! Was wondering where you got off to, you turkey."

She stepped into his outstretched arms for a quick hug, noticing he was wearing the new overalls she had picked out when she had run into town for him.

"Well, I've been working and wanted to give you two some time together."

"Come in and sit. Troy has made a feast."

"Thank you."

The small table was set for three, and Troy had already

poured ice water and was uncorking the wine, which he placed next to her. Megan fought to keep her nose from wrinkling at the thought but wanted to be polite, since Mr. Chapman was clearly happy and feeling well.

He asked her about her pets, and she talked about Levi who was resting and smiling happily, his big golden head in between the two of them watching them talk.

Troy stepped forward and picked up the plates. "Salad, mashed potatoes, and steak good for you?"

"That sounds great. Thanks."

He gave her a quick nod. "I went for medium, but can let it go longer if that's a problem for you."

The arrogance of him assuming how to cook her steak was annoying, but what made it worse was that he was right.

He slid a plate in front of her, which she had to admit looked delicious, then slid an identical one to his father and sat down to a face of disapproval.

"Where's the ranch?"

"Terrible condiment and you're lucky you're getting steak. Doctor's orders." Troy glanced at Megan and smiled. "Tonight's a special occasion. Let's eat."

Megan hadn't had steak like this in, well, as long as she could remember. She didn't take meat often, but when she did, it never tasted like this. Tender and cooked perfectly, it almost melted on her tongue. She swirled her fork in the potatoes, which were light and buttery and mixed perfectly. Everything down to the light dressing on the mixed greens was restaurant quality.

Before arriving, she had her usual social anxiety panic in the car, but now that the food was so good, she relaxed and ate, realizing just how hungry she was. Stopping to sip her wine, which wasn't that bad and went nicely with the steak, she caught Troy watching her.

"This is really delicious," she said as she paused to wipe her mouth.

"Thank you."

"I'm on a diet. Troy hasn't let me go to McDonald's," Mr. Chapman piped in.

"No sausage biscuit?"

"No grape jelly either."

"The hospital nutritionist sent over a list of foods, and we're working to follow it."

"I don't think I had a heart attack. It's fine now, other than a little arrhythmia. Been like that for years. Too much coffee."

"Better safe than sorry," Megan offered as she dug in again. If he was eating like this, then he was taking a step up from the golden arches.

"Megan let me go to McDonald's, and she knows about this stuff."

She looked at him to catch his smile, which deepened the lines in the older man's face, making his brown eyes crinkle at the corners.

"Don't bring me into this. I was just helping you run errands until Troy came home."

"You did a great job." Troy's voice seemed lower from across the table, and maybe it was the steak, but he looked a lot nicer over there than before. "I really appreciate you being there for him after the fire. That was so kind of you to do after you met at the hospital."

Megan froze with her fork in midair, then resumed the bite and chewed slowly, eyeing Mr. Chapman who was polishing off his potatoes, not seeming to notice what was just said.

She chewed and swallowed, picking her words carefully. "I was happy to do it, but we didn't meet at the hospital." Surely, Mr. Chapman would've mentioned it to his son.

Troy frowned and looked confused. "I thought the hospital sent over a nurse. Dad, that's what your doctor said."

Mr. Chapman waved a hand and took a sip of his wine. "Nah, I sent them away. Didn't need all of those exercises. I feel fine."

Mr. Chapman turned then and smiled at her, the same look of hope and gratitude that endeared him to her from the night he was sitting on the edge of the ambulance.

"Megan saved my life, and then went back into the fire to carry out Levi. I owe her everything."

Megan felt the blood rush to her cheeks, and she smiled into her lap. As if on cue, Levi put his boxy head in her lap and looked at her with his big brown soulful eyes echoing his master's emotion. She played with his ears in between her fingers, feeling the soft fur.

"Hold up." She glanced up to see Troy's face frozen in shock. "You mean to tell me you're the firefighter?!"

CHAPTER 12

Megan's spine straightened on instinct. Familiar with the shock, disbelief, and the inevitable oncoming questions, she looked him in the eye.

"Yes," she said. "I am."

Troy had the good sense to shut his trap, but through his eyes she could see the gears turning and the math not adding up. He looked her over and then glanced at his dad.

"Shit, if I'd have known, I would've taken you out in town. Dad, you didn't think to mention this?"

Mr. Chapman hadn't moved a muscle and gave his son a plain look before he shrugged. "I figured you knew. I'm sorry I didn't mention it."

"It wasn't just me," Megan added quickly before this turned into hero worship and got even weirder. "The team was there too. Nick helped your dad out. I just got there first, but we always go in together while the engineer watches the fire engine with the highest ranking person, which that night was my Lieutenant Buzz."

"She reached me first, then went back for Levi who took off."

At the sound of his name, Levi looked up and grinned while panting in the way only goldens could.

"It's a team effort all of the time."

"We need to do something for all of you," Troy said almost more to himself than to either of them.

"Oh, that's not necessary. The whole team works there because we want to help people. It's really a family."

"So do you often dog sit and take care of errands for people you save as well?" Troy asked, his brown eyes peering at her as if he was seeing her for the first time. Gone was the playboy attitude that seeped Netflix and chill. Now he was all business and interested in her as a person.

Only took him realizing she worked in a male-dominated field. Typical.

Megan shrugged. "I try to step in when anyone doesn't have family nearby."

She didn't enjoy conflict, but had enough practice and coaching from Ash to know where to place a sting when she needed to.

Troy considered her for a second and pulled his lips in tight before looking back down at his plate.

"I just really appreciate it. That's all."

Megan gave him a smile and let it go at that. No reason to continue. He was here now and that was that. It wasn't right for her to judge how fast he could get home. She knew nothing about him, and he clearly cared for his dad, enough to withhold ranch dressing and sausage biscuits. Maybe this was the best he could do.

Either way, after dessert and coffee, which she was considering bailing on depending on which way this turned, Troy Chapman wasn't her problem anymore.

It was a bit of a pity considering how handsome he was, but hey, she had already run into him around town once.

"So what made you get into firefighting?" Mr. Chapman

asked, distracting her from Troy's face, which was perfect timing.

"I just wanted to help people," she said, hating herself for the lie. She felt like an impostor, a total fake. If she was normal she would've already died, and if somehow she had made it out alive, she never would've signed up for this.

For once she just wanted to tell people the real reason.

"That's very admirable," Troy said with deep meaning.

Ugh. Megan wanted to vomit.

"Thanks."

"How often do you work at the station?" Mr. Chapman asked. Very reasonable question.

"Three days a week typically. They are twelve-hour shifts, and we all rotate as a team. My best friend used to work with us, but she doesn't run calls too much anymore."

"Firefighter?" Mr. Chapman asked.

"Paramedic, but she's going to school now to be a doctor. It's what she's always wanted."

"How nice for her."

Yeah, lucky her.

"Yeah, we're a little family. My other best friend is a cop. She used to hang out a lot more, but has been working on some bigger assignments, so it's just me and the boys now."

"Boys? So you're the only woman?" Troy asked, with a strained look on his face.

Here we go again.

"Yep, just me. They're like a bunch of brothers," she said like always to get ahead of the next obvious assumption.

Troy nodded—was he smiling? Mr. Chapman still had the same expression, a polite smile and genuine interest, but she could see his eyes were starting to droop. Time to pull out the old get out of jail card.

"Well, thank you for dinner; this was really delicious. I

need to leave soon to get back, but can I help clean up before I go?"

"Not so fast, Megan," said Mr. Chapman.

Rats. Foiled again.

"Yes?"

"I want to talk to you both, which is why I invited you."

She glanced across the table at Troy who gave a small shrug and looked as surprised as she was.

Mr. Chapman leaned back and crossed his hands on his stomach and started to speak, pausing every now and then to give weight to his words. She watched as his eyes glassed over, seeing something other than the three of them sitting there at the small table. Levi rested his head on his master's lap, his ears twitching to the baritone filled with gravel.

"I'm an old man. I don't have a fancy education, and I've lived my life in this town. I've had one wife and lost her. Two sons, and lost one. One house, and now that's gone too. I almost lost my life if it hadn't been for you and the other firefighters."

Megan and Troy exchanged a glance. There was pain in Troy's features at the mention of his brother and mother.

"I see a lot in you both. Potential. Youth. A life ahead of you. So I hope you'll listen to the wisdom I've learned because it came at a very high price. The highest."

He smiled in a distant way as he took a mental turn and visited with some unseen memory.

"Out of everything I've done and everything I've seen, the most important thing is family. At the end that's all there is. Even though half of mine is gone, I have memories. A lifetime of memories."

He smiled again and closed his eyes for a few moments. Megan thought maybe he had fallen asleep until his lids fluttered open again.

"You young people are just like I was. Too busy to see

what's in front of you and focus on what you have. Don't waste this life on work. It's important, don't get me wrong. Hard work provides for family, but if you don't have one, what's the point? Legacy?"

He let out a laugh and coughed.

"The most important thing in this world is love."

Troy shifted uncomfortably and looked down onto his empty plate.

Megan was watching Mr. Chapman as he looked from Troy to her and back again.

Oh no.

No, no, no, no, no, no.

"I want you to get to know each other."

Megan cleared her throat. Absolutely not. This is why she shouldn't help people outside of her job. In fact, tonight pretty much ruined her for helping anyone ever again.

"That's very kind, but I don't think—"

"Dad, I'm not sure she'd want to—"

He held up his hands and silenced them both. "Fine, fine. Maybe that was a bit pushy."

A *bit?*

"I love you, son."

"Thanks, Dad. I love you too, but I don't—"

"Megan," he said with his head on a swivel. "You're a nice girl..."

"Thank you."

"...with a good heart. I'd like to see you settled too. If not with Troy, then with someone else."

"I really appreciate that, but I'm happy. Really."

He let out a sigh and smiled in a sad sort of way. "We spent a few days together, which I'm very grateful for, so I know you crave connection."

Well, shit.

"Listen, think it over. I don't know where young people

go to meet other young people, but I think you both should give it a try. What's the worst that could happen?"

The visit came to an end as soon as Megan could manage it without being rude and thankfully only involved one broken dish in her attempt to help clean before fleeing into the night.

She thanked Troy and Mr. Chapman and gave a quick round of scratches to Levi before grabbing her jacket and diving out into the dark, cold night.

God, the frigid air in her lungs was a literal breath of fresh air. It cleansed her soul from the weird awkwardness of that setup. Troy looked mortified, but Mr. Chapman looked satisfied with how the evening had gone, seeing as his plan had blindsided them both.

Megan got in her car and collapsed against the headrest with her eyes closed for a solid ten seconds while the engine heated up. It felt so good to be back in her own space with her little air freshener. The familiar scent and hum of the engine smoothed over her like a balm to heal the awkwardness from the night.

Two raps on the window had her jumping out of her skin.

Troy smiled through the window and did a little finger wave.

She rolled down the window, wondering what he could possibly want.

"Hey, um, look, I'm really sorry about that. Dad's been weird ever since, you know, everything that happened. Going on about life and living for the present and all of that. I guess a near-death experience does that, huh?"

"I guess so."

Where was this going?

Troy blew out a breath, looking more tired than he had inside. He pulled a hand over his face and let it drop.

"Look, I wanted this dinner to be nice to thank you for everything you did before I could get here. I didn't know he'd do this. I know it's got to be awkward hearing this, but I'd like to take you to dinner *without* Dad."

Megan looked at him and tried to digest his statement. He was asking her out *minutes* after his dad had just tried to set them up. What was he thinking?

At her blank stare, he continued.

"I owe you a lot more, and I admire the shit out of what you do. Please, just think it over. One dinner and then if you never want to see me again, I promise I will personally throw myself off the face of the earth."

Despite herself, Megan smiled and started to laugh.

"How about I check my schedule and get back to you?"

And that was how they ended up setting up a date one week later.

CHAPTER 13

Megan slid into a parking spot outside Osaka, the Japanese steak house in town. Laura had come here with Carter and had raved about the hibachi, but Megan had never been before. Of course, when she had called earlier to ask Laura what to wear, that got her friend's attention.

"So you're going?" Laura had asked when they had spoken on the phone two hours ago.

"Yep. So you think the black dress?"

"You're a knockout in it, but it depends on how much you like him. If you really like him, wear that green dress with the low back."

Megan had pulled a face and opted to stick with the black. It didn't show a lot of skin, but had a fun skirt that flared out and fit her figure nicely. It was comfy, and she thought she looked nice in it. Better to play it safe.

"Okay, dressed. Hair up or down?"

"You always have it up at work. It's so pretty down."

Taking her advice through speakerphone from where the phone lay on the bathroom counter, Megan pinned part of it back just behind the ear and fought her way through getting a slight curl at the bottom. Her bright red hair almost came down to her hips, and the curl gave it a nice sense of body so it didn't just hang like a curtain.

"I don't want to feel like I'm going to a funeral."

"Well, you could've worn the green, but you said you're not that into him. When are you going to wear the green dress? You've had it in your closet for a long time."

The silky green dress draped over the hanger still had the tags. It had been on clearance, and Laura had insisted that she not only try it on, but also make the purchase since it was "made for her."

"I'll get to it eventually when I have somewhere to wear it."

"God, you look great in it. Maybe this is good practice to get back out there. See how it feels and if you like it, then fire up the dating sites. Carter's groomsmen were nice. A few of them have asked about you."

Megan had let out a sigh. She had tried to get to know a few people for Laura's wedding and had even had high hopes that one of Carter's friends would sweep her off her feet, but it was just the usual uninspired conversations.

"I feel like I try, but nothing clicks. Everyone is too predictable. I have a feeling this will be the same way. I don't know why I even agreed to it."

Laura let out a sigh. "Because you're a good person. Try to have fun. It might be nice."

"He got *that* look when he found out about my job."

"Yeah, I know, but give him another chance. If nothing else, the food is great."

Megan had thanked her friend, thrown on a peacock pin her grandma had loved, and arrived at the restaurant a few minutes early. Troy had offered to pick her up, but seeing as she didn't know him all that well, Megan felt much more comfortable in her own car. It always felt safer that way. Like a home away from home.

She fought to keep her hands from twisting in knots in her lap. She never knew what to do in these situations. Should she wait until she saw him to get out? She knew his truck. Would it be better to wait inside? Then she would just be awkwardly standing by the hostess stand.

What if he didn't show?

"Thanks, social anxiety," she said alone in her car, proof she was losing it. "As if I didn't have enough to worry about."

As if summoned, Troy's truck rolled into the lot and pulled into the spot next to her, and moments later he was angling his head to see if she was still sitting inside.

Megan took in a deep breath and opened the door with a friendly, but not too friendly, smile.

"Hey." He looked great. Better than great.

Even in the dim reddish light, he looked different from before. Gone was the army T-shirt and Wranglers. Standing in front of her now was a very handsome man in a fitted suit. She couldn't tell if it was black or dark gray, but he had on a crisp white shirt that was open at the collar. His shoes glinted in the light from Osaka's sign, and as he walked forward, she smelled the most subtle, delicious cologne.

"Sorry, I'm late. I wanted to get here first." He gave her a smile that dazzled, then pulled out a trio of yellow roses. "Didn't want to show up empty-handed."

Megan accepted the gift, trying to get her brain to rewire and work again. Words. She was supposed to be speaking words.

"Thank you. I didn't expect this. They're l-lovely." Damn stutter always showed up at the worst of times. They were beautiful. She couldn't remember the last time she'd gotten flowers outside of a wedding party.

Now what did she do? Should she leave them in the car? Was that rude?

"You're welcome. You look beautiful tonight."

"Thank you," she said with a smile. "You do too."

"I clean up okay when I want to. I called ahead and we have a reservation. Ready to head in?"

He held out his arm, and she nodded and took it, carrying the flowers right in with her.

He reached to open the door, when one of the hosts rushed out to get it for both of them.

Tones of dark wood and deep red mixed in an artful take on a sleek styling. They followed the impeccably dressed hostess past a rough-cut stone waterfall surrounded by an array of tropical plants. The tables were spaced out around the hibachi flat top with lights placed intentionally to make diners think they were the only ones there. On the far side, there was an ornate bar, with backlit shelves to the ceiling with colorful bottles that looked like gems in the light.

They kept meandering through the restaurant to a table in the back, framed by two lush red silk drapes. Megan slid into the booth opposite Troy who sat down after her, taking care to unbutton his jacket and thank the host who delivered two menus with prices higher than Megan had seen in a while.

Troy smiled and asked as he looked at her above his menu, "What looks good tonight?"

Megan eyed the menu and decided to play it safe as usual. "Not sure yet. What are you thinking?"

Turns out Troy was thinking a lot.

"Probably the mango lobster roll to start, maybe the New York Strip and some tempura udon."

"Wow. Okay, let me catch up. I don't know where to start."

"Do you like sushi?"

"I've never really tried it."

"Well, if you like seafood you can try some of the mango lobster roll. It's going to be a big size, and then if you like it, we can always get more."

Was he being generous or just trying to show off? Too soon to tell. In fact, the last date she went on—was it really over a year now? Wow. That time was just lunch and he got change from a twenty. Already it was looking like that might not even cover the tip here.

"Oh, we don't have to do that. I'll just try yours and get something else." She eyed the menu, aware that his was already closed, while he watched her with his hands folded.

"What do you like?" she asked him.

"I guess all of it."

"I don't usually eat a lot of meat, and I rarely get fish, so I think I might try the salmon."

"Good. If you like shellfish, you could consider getting the one that has the scallops and shrimp too."

"Oh no, that's okay. I'm not sure I could eat all of that."

Troy shrugged. "I eat a lot."

"I didn't mean to imply anything."

He shrugged again. "Occupational hazard."

Before Megan could ask what he meant by that, the waiter walked up, they placed their orders, and the chef followed up, firing up the grill for the show to begin.

CHAPTER 14

"What do you think?" Troy asked as he set down his fork next to the now empty plate where they had split a decadent chocolate lava cake.

"I'm stuffed, and I didn't even finish all of my food. I had no idea the portions would be so big. And I still have my drink that I have barely touched."

"I'm glad you enjoyed it. Take your time and finish the drink. They don't need the table."

Everything had been delicious, even the drinks Troy had ordered after the waitress had suggested something from the bar. It was clear Megan didn't drink or eat out much. Her eyes had closed when she sampled the sushi or sipped the drink as she savored. That she enjoyed what he shared with her made him want to share much more. In fact, the real feast was her. With her hair down, the red hue glowed in the light of the fire, making her look at home in the flames with a fire of her own. She hadn't worn much makeup, but the pink lips that pouted out invited him to stare and almost begged him to kiss her. He had requested a private table for that reason alone but was disappointed when the opportunity never presented itself.

They actually hadn't gotten much time to talk. Once the waitress had delivered drinks and water, the chef in a perfectly crisp, white hat and apron had arrived to deliver an artful display with his knife skills and spatula that danced on the hibachi grill in front of them.

Troy wasn't ready to give up the view of her across from him yet. She sipped her drink, which was a lemon drop he had suggested, and he watched the slender curve of her neck as she picked up the glass with a gentle touch and wiped her mouth afterward with the napkin from her lap.

"I'm surprised you made that drink last this whole time."

"I'm savoring," she said with a genuine smile in his direction. "How did you learn so much about food?"

Troy shrugged. "My mom was a great cook. I hung out with her a lot since my older brother was always with my dad on the ranch. Plus, it helps I like to eat."

"I think that's sweet."

"Do you like to cook?"

Megan shook her head. "I keep trying though. I like the idea of it, but either get lost in the details or hung up on the directions."

Troy let out a laugh and brought his after-dinner coffee to his lips. "Like what details?"

"Like how much is a pinch anyway? How brown is golden-brown?"

She flicked her hair behind her, showing off the jewel-encrusted peacock pin on her black dress. Just like everything else about her, it was understated and elegant. Her whole demeanor had a gentleness and poise that he hadn't seen before. Most women he had dated loved to be the one to do the talking, but Megan let him lead and seemed to relax when he continued to speak.

"With cooking, there's no right or wrong answers. It's whatever you want to do."

"I always second-guess myself." Her eyes glanced down as she ran her finger along the smooth stem of the martini glass on the table.

"You just have to see where it goes, and there's nothing wrong with that."

Her eyes met his. "Are you talking about cooking or something else? "

Troy's smile widened to a full grin, and he fought the urge to slide over to her in the booth.

"Both. I like to live my life like that. I mean, what else can we do but live in the moment? Enjoy what's in front of us." He tilted his head to one side.

"I've heard that before, but I have a hard time letting go."

"Of what?"

Megan paused, trying to find the correct word. "Fear."

Troy sucked in a breath and leaned forward on the table. "That's understandable. I remember the first time I went to Airborne school. I'm afraid of heights. Well, I used to be."

Her puzzled expression nearly undid him with her genuine concern. "That doesn't sound like a good fit."

"Well, the army has a pretty good system of beating it down and making everything idiot proof."

"How did they fix it? The fear, that is?"

Troy looked up at the ceiling and let out a laugh. "My drill sergeant had us get up on this pole, and it was crazy high, but basically it was a test and we were all strapped in, to get us to trust our gear, you know? Also, we scaled up. So first was rappelling, then it was jumping out of a fake plane with the gear, and then a helicopter, until the big day."

"I wish there was training like that for other fears."

"My sergeant major told me that we all have fear, but it's what we do with that fear that matters." He looked at her again. "I'm sure you know all about that in your line of work."

Megan pulled a tight smile and shrugged.

"You're right. Training helps. We're also never alone."

"The army is the same way."

"Like a family," they both said at the same time.

"Your dad told me you joined right out of school." Her spine straightened a little as she spoke, and she tilted her head to the side, considering his response.

He nodded. "I wanted a change and something to call my own. After my brother died, I had a lot of anger. I had lost my mom already, and it didn't seem fair."

"You still had your dad."

"That's true, but at eighteen I needed a fresh start. Dad and I talked it over after the recruiter came to school. At first, he wasn't that big of a fan, but after we talked it over he said it might be good for me."

"You didn't feel bad leaving him alone?"

"We talk regularly on the phone."

"Not regularly enough these days," she said without attitude, but the truth of her words stung.

Troy blew out a breath and took the hit. "You're right. I've gotten wrapped up at work and let my focus drift away from what's important. This has been a good reset. Seeing him lose almost everything brought back a lot of perspective. I needed that."

"It sounds like it."

"I appreciate everything you did for him. I know I've said that before, but it never feels like enough. I didn't even know you, and you were helping me all along."

Megan drew in a breath. "I lost my grandmother when I was in college. She raised me. My whole family died in a fire when I was an infant."

"Holy shit. I had no idea. I'm so sorry."

"Thank you," came the response that seemed almost automatic. Megan swallowed and continued like she wanted to get away from the subject as fast as possible. "I know what loss feels like, and I enjoyed talking with him. In a lot of ways, it was nice to have someone to talk with."

"He enjoyed it too."

"I guess that's why he tried to set us up," she said, letting out a laugh and brightening back up.

Troy followed her lead, even though he was desperate to know more about her past. No wonder she had become a firefighter and had such a powerful inner strength.

"Dad was thrilled today when I was getting ready. Actually, he was happier than I've seen him in a long time."

"I'll bet. He got what he wanted."

"He also told me I'm not allowed back in the house until late."

"Oh?"

"I was hoping to spend more time with you." He raised an eyebrow and grinned when she blushed.

Megan laughed and looked down before tucking her hair back behind her ear. "I don't know what it is about you. I keep trying to be annoyed with you, and it's not working."

"That's because of my devilish good looks and my rapier wit," he offered.

"Okay, you're still irritating, but that earns a point."

"Points are always good coming from a beautiful woman, who I'd like to get to know even better. How about we go for a drive?"

Megan paused and seemed to be on the verge of saying no.

"I know a great place we can see the stars and talk. It's a full moon tonight, so we'll have plenty of light."

She narrowed her eyes at him. "He told you all about me, didn't he?"

Troy felt himself grin. "He's a great wingman."

CHAPTER 15

Megan sat in Troy's truck as he navigated the winding road up to some overlook, which she had Googled on her phone during the drive just to make sure it was legit. According to him—and her quick research—not only was it legit, but the views were stellar.

"Keep an eye out for deer," he said as he watched the road with a laser-like focus. The moonlight washed over him and his powerful arms as he gripped the wheel and turned up another climb.

"I'm feeling a little sick."

"Hang on, let me pull over."

"No, it's okay. It's not much farther, right?"

He shook his head and continued up two more turns until the sign read scenic overlook, and the road thankfully leveled off into a parking lot that overlooked Goldvein.

Troy pulled up right into the front spot, the only car around.

He opened the door and hopped down, jogging to the other side not fast enough to get her door, but she still took the hand he offered to help get her down.

"This is breathtaking," she said as she walked forward to the picnic tables in the grassy area.

The city below them glimmered with golden lights.

"I agree."

Of course when she looked at him, he wasn't looking at the city but right at her. Megan quickly turned away and felt her cheeks redden with his eyes on her face.

He started to laugh softly next to her.

"What?"

"You know, I realize why my dad likes you so much."

"Because he had someone to talk to that listened when he was going through a crisis and didn't have family nearby?"

"Ouch. I deserved that, but I don't think that's it. My dad's a tough one, and he's lived in this town for his whole life."

"So you're saying he didn't need me?"

"Not at all. I think he enjoys having a smart, funny, beautiful woman around."

Megan looked back at him and didn't respond.

"I have to say, I agree."

Megan drew in a breath and opened her mouth to speak when a piercing scream shattered the night around them.

Troy jumped to his feet, and his head spun around toward the sound.

Megan was right behind as he took off in the direction, an unspoken agreement between them.

The screaming echoed through the pine forest around them, bouncing from tree to tree and echoing from farther down the road. Troy's stride was longer, and he pulled farther away from her down the hill toward the road, clearly driven by instinct. Megan was behind, but pulled out her phone, hitting the emergency button three times to start dialing for help.

The dispatcher's voice came through right as Troy slid on

the pine needles around the corner, before jumping up and sprinting out of her sight.

"911. What's your emergency?"

Megan rounded the bend and saw a smoking compact car smashed against the tree with all of the airbags deployed. The screaming pierced the air, loud and clear, punctuated with a dog barking somewhere.

Megan rattled off the location to the dispatch with quick details of the situation.

Troy was leaning against an open window talking to the woman inside, who was still screaming. He stepped aside when Megan reached the window and held his hand out to accept the phone she was already handing him, to take over the call to the dispatcher.

A brown lab in the back kept barking and whining. She shouted over it to make herself heard.

"My name is Megan. I'm an EMT and a firefighter. I'm here to help. Are you okay?"

A sheen of sweat covered the woman's pale skin, and her eyes, stretched with fear, landed on Megan's face but didn't register her presence. She looked to be in her late teens at most. She would've been considered pretty, but the terror made her look gaunt and thin. Her blonde hair looked like she had straightened it earlier that day, but now was frizzy, with flyaways trying to break loose from the static electricity. Behind her, the dog kept barking and whining, trying to escape the vehicle.

"It's okay. It's okay," she said in a failed attempt to reassure the dog. "We're going to get you both out of the car. Can you move?"

The woman was shaking now, her hands trembling by her chest, shoved back from the wheel by the airbag.

Megan reached in over the broken glass, threw the latch to the door from the inside, and mercifully it swung open.

Shoving the airbag out of the way, she fought to free the seat-belt and blew out a breath of relief when she heard the click releasing the belt away from the girl's lap.

"Can you walk? I want to help you out of the car."

The woman nodded through the shakes, and Megan took the woman's thin arm over her shoulders and braced her weight as she helped her out. The deadweight lightened as Troy lifted the other woman's arm. Limp from exhaustion, or maybe shock, the woman didn't walk but allowed herself to be carried to the edge of the road, where they lowered her down. She was wearing a thin T-shirt and would need something to keep her warm in the cold night.

As if he could read Megan's mind, Troy was already taking his coat off and draping it around the girl's trembling shoulders where she sat on the edge of the road away from the car. With him there, Megan turned back to the car where the dog was in hysterics and snaked her arm through the front window, her fingers working to find the latch for the back door. The dog's barking echoed in her head as she felt her fingers close on the smooth metal and pop the door. The dog limped out and stumbled, which led to more panic.

"Okay, okay, okay. Come here, calm down. Let's go see her." Megan tried to get the dog's collar, but felt a tug with weight as it collapsed again. With sirens in the background, Megan lifted up the lab and carried the quivering body across the road to where the woman sat staring in their direction.

As soon as she laid the dog down next to the girl, the snout found its way into her lap, snuggling down while big brown eyes took in the sight of its owner, who after a moment, started stroking the boxy head.

"Can you tell us if you're hurt?"

Troy turned on the light on his cellphone and flashed a pool of white light over the woman and dog. The woman looked even more like a girl than Megan had realized. Her hazel glassy eyes still stared ahead unseeing, and Megan could see the pulse fluttering underneath her skin, next to the collarbone where she was breathing short, rapid breaths.

"I don't know if she's in shock, but she might be having a panic attack."

The sound of the sirens grew in the night, and a glow from the flashing blue lights traveled from the road below.

"Must have been a deer or something she saw."

"Yeah, maybe."

A scream tore from the girl again, and she tried to scramble back from where she was pointing. Megan's head spun around to see a fully naked man emerge from the woods, bolting right in her direction, his eyes crazed and teeth bared.

CHAPTER 16

A scream ripped from her own mouth, and Megan threw her arms out in front of the girl and shielded her eyes from the impact.

It never came.

Instead, there was a grunt, thump, and scuffle over gravel, followed by a tangle of frantic pants that were drowned out by the approaching police car.

"Get to the ground now!" Ash yelled while exiting her cruiser.

Troy had the man around the shoulders, but was straining to keep his grip as Ash's words barely registered.

Ash and her new partner, Officer Wilson, stood over Troy, helping to restrain the man who continued to struggle against them, trying to lash out. Between the three of them, they got him handcuffed and sitting upright just as red lights started to mix with the blue when the fire engine and ambulance arrived.

Jordan and Buzz hopped out and jogged over to get the 411 on the girl driver, but quickly detoured to where Troy was still panting from wrestling the naked man, now under a thermal foil.

The engineer headed right over to the car with a dry chemical grade extinguisher.

"What in God's name is going on here?" Buzz asked anyone who would listen.

Ash was trying to talk to the man who was still straining against the restraints with odd jerking movements, so Megan took the lead.

"We don't know. Just heard screaming and ran down to see the car smoking. Driver hasn't said anything, but no visible signs of injuries, and this man just leaped out of the woods screaming at us."

"Thank God Laura is on tonight to check them both out."

"Pup's in bad shape too. Maybe a leg injury."

"Alright, well, let's call a tow truck and get another ambulance up here."

"On it," said Wilson who already had his radio up to his mouth. He and Buzz exchanged a greeting, having known each other in high school, and went right back into the work.

Laura jogged over and took a look at the girl. They handed Troy back his jacket, which he draped over his shoulder, and got her a foil blanket also before asking her questions and performing an exam.

Jordan took the man, who appeared to be in psychosis. His dilated pupils and involuntary head movements led Jordan to call the hospital and request a social worker to intervene for an assessment. After a few moments, the other ambulance arrived to take the man to the hospital, and the girl started talking to Laura and used her phone to call her dad to come and get the dog and give her information to the police.

While they waited for him to arrive, the tow truck also

came and started the process of extracting the car from the tree. By that time, Ash had taken statements from Troy and Megan, meaning all official business had been conducted.

"Did she talk to you about what happened?" Megan asked Ash when they were done.

"No, but she told Laura she was driving with her dog to meet friends, and the guy ran out into the middle of the road. When she swerved and hit the tree, he started beating the hood of her car and ran off when you two arrived."

"Had she ever seen him before?"

"Guess who one of the friends was."

Megan winced. "Ouch. Drugs?"

"We don't know, but she said she had never seen him like this before. Like he had a breakdown or something. Called his family too. They're going to meet him at the hospital."

"Damn," said Troy. "He came out of nowhere and packed a punch I'll be feeling for a while." He rubbed a spot under his ribs.

"Want to press charges?"

He shook his head. "I don't know what he's going through right now, but it's something and I don't want to add to it. I'll be okay."

Ash nodded and sent a small smile of approval toward Megan. "I'll hang out until the girl's family comes. Laura's on the clock too, but you're not, so you two are free to go if you want."

Megan exchanged a glance with Troy.

"Whatever you want to do is fine with me," he said with a shrug. "I didn't mean for this evening to end this way."

"I feel like that's a common theme." She blew out a breath and waved to Laura who gave her a thumbs-up from where she stood next to the ambulance where the girl was sitting. A gust of wind climbed the side of the overlook and rattled the foil blanket. Megan hugged her arms against herself and felt Troy's coat cover her shoulders.

It was warm and, despite having been on the girl, smelled like his cologne and gave her a sense of peace she didn't realize she needed. He wrapped one arm around her shoulders and steered her up the hill back toward his truck.

"Want me to pick you up down here?"

"No, the walk will be fine. I need to work off the adrenaline."

Troy looked relieved as they walked away from the accident, leaving the flashing lights behind them. "I'm glad you feel the same way. I'm not going to get her screaming out of my head for a while."

Megan nodded. "Thank you for stopping him."

Her mind flashed back to seeing Troy tangled up with the crazed naked man, fighting to restrain him from hurting the girl or herself.

"Training and instinct," he said in a casual voice, but his eyes were cold and distant as he watched the dark road in front of them.

"You could've gotten hurt. Someone out of their mind like that can do some serious damage."

Troy stayed silent except for the crunch of the gravel beneath them as they walked in step with each other, which felt like the most natural thing in the world.

"I wonder what caused that," Troy said at last. "I'm glad I could help."

"You did great. Oh, look at that."

Megan pointed to the sky where the trees had opened up, exposing the bright full moon in the sparkling night sky.

"I guess you were right about the full moon after all."

He let out a rueful laugh. "Maybe that's what's going on with that guy." He shook himself and looked at her for a brief second before wrapping his arms around her. It was only then that she realized he was shaking.

"Are you okay?"

The shaking dialed back to a tremble, and she held on tight and gave him a squeeze before letting her head fall onto his chest. She drank in the scent of him and his warmth all around her. She could feel his strength through his shirt and his jacket she still wore, but for all his strength, she felt him weigh down on her while she held him steady as the moments ticked by to the sound of the night.

Troy looked up at her and gave her a true smile that warmed her chest. "I know this was a setup and a thank you dinner, but I wanted you to have a nice time."

Megan searched his eyes, finding nothing but kindness. "I did."

In the dark, his deep brown eyes dilated into dark pools like the sky. Megan's lips parted on their own as he tilted his head to the side and closed the gap, pressing a tender kiss on her lips.

The only thought she had was this felt like home, and everything in her body wanted to scream when he pulled away, and the cold night air chilled her lips in his absence.

"Tonight didn't end like I planned. Would it be okay if I see you again?"

CHAPTER 17

"Son of a bitch," Troy called out, throwing the hammer down.

"You shouldn't have held it like that. You'll feel it in your elbow when you're my age," his dad called from down in the front yard of the house where he was supervising, which in his case was really just criticizing everything Troy did.

The past few days were a whirlwind. Megan was at work, so other than a few texts with various jokes, she had been quiet, and he had been tied up on his end as well.

Once the insurance paperwork came through, the checks were deposited and plans were drawn up for repairing the old ranch house while also bringing it into the new decade. While some of the work would be hired out—like expanding the HVAC system—the framing, electric, plumbing, and finishes would all require a heavy dose of sweat equity.

Troy didn't mind putting in the effort, but working with Dad was a lesson in patience. The same was true for Dad. He knew what to do, but age and doctor's orders to take it easy meant his body didn't allow him to work as he wanted. To add insult to injury, when he did want to get his hands dirty, his recovery time frustrated him to no end.

Troy pounded the nail into the stud and finished the wall to frame out the addition onto the new kitchen.

"When I go into town tonight, I'm getting a nail gun."

"Your grandfather built this whole house with nails and a hammer."

"He also didn't have a choice."

Hank spit out into the gravel and threw his hands up. "Fine, do what you want."

"I'm looking forward to it."

"That's not what you're really looking forward to." His dad gave him a knowing smile that made Troy roll his eyes despite breaking into a grin. "She's a good woman. Where are you taking her?"

"I let her know we're trying to update the house, so she agreed to help pick out colors at the hardware store and go look at countertops."

"Sounds romantic."

"Hardly, but she was excited. Then we'll grab dinner."

Troy was hoping for more. After their kiss, he hadn't been able to stop thinking about her. She tasted like summertime. Megan was warm and soft, but the strength within her drew him to her like a magnet. Seeing her in action at the crash had only deepened his fascination.

A shiver passed over him at the memory of the fear in her eyes when the lunatic had come barreling toward her out of nowhere. Troy had plowed into the guy before he could even think. He hadn't hurt him, but it was an exercise in complete restraint. He couldn't imagine if he hadn't been there in time and Megan had gotten hurt.

He had plenty of bad memories that lived in his head rent free, but he couldn't get her out of his mind, and he didn't hate it.

"Maybe she'll pick out something she likes for the kitchen."

"My leave only is approved for six weeks. I doubt it will turn into anything serious."

His dad spit again. "You always say that. Your mother was way out of my league, but you have to try. Can't let fear stand in the way of your life. What if she's the one, and you're too stubborn to see it?"

"Things aren't like that anymore. People don't live in the same town forever like around here."

"That's what you think. The right relationship can overcome a lot."

Troy shook his head. "I've been best man at enough second and third weddings to have my doubts."

"That's your generation and the military."

"So we agree then? Good."

"I know you like to keep things casual."

"It's easy—"

"It's the easy way out."

Troy threw down the hammer and crossed his arms to level a glare at his dad.

"If you would just invest a little time and have a little faith, you'd be amazed at what could happen."

"And if it doesn't work then I've wasted a little time and what little faith I have."

His dad shook his head. "I know you've been through a lot."

Troy hated the softness in his dad's voice. It made him feel vulnerable that someone knew about everything that had happened. No one really knew all of it, other than his therapist. His dad knew a lot though, and Troy hated when he brought it up.

"But you have to have hope. If you can't have faith, you have to have hope that it will work out." His dad walked up and clapped a hand on his shoulder. "Take her somewhere nice tonight. See where it goes. Who knows? She could be the one."

They picked up the tools and shut down the project for the night. Troy and his dad rode back to the small house, and after Hank had showered, Troy got him settled in the chair for the trifecta of news, *Jeopardy*, and *Wheel*, complete with a peanut butter and jelly sandwich and glass of milk by request.

Then it was time to get ready to go. Troy showered and put on some new jeans, a blue button-down shirt, and a sweater. He grabbed his coat, which was a replica of a WWII bomber jacket—his birthday present to himself last year—and headed out for the night.

He was picking her up this time, which made him smile. Before, he had respected her meeting him there, but there was something nice about being trusted to travel in the same car. Most of the girls he had been with over the years preferred to drive themselves. Dating apps and being safe played a huge role, so Troy understood, but it made picking her up feel so personal.

He checked her address again but didn't bother popping it into the GPS since it said she lived right on the main street through town. Troy set off, anticipating all that might happen this evening.

His dad wasn't wrong. He was starting to get obsessed. By now in any other city he would've checked out the local girls on the dating apps who were like him, looking for some quick casual fun, but he hadn't even bothered. He had gotten a few messages from girls back near post whom he had been chatting with before he had left so abruptly. Troy knew he only had a few more weeks of leave, so he had exchanged quick messages last night to let them know he wasn't ghosting them, to keep his options open when he got home.

But it didn't feel the same.

Before it would have been nothing to chat online all night while listening to his latest audiobook, but now it was an annoyance to give them an update. He had typed out a quick message, explaining the family emergency, and just copied and pasted it four different times, which didn't make him feel great. The whole thing had gone from feeling playful and fun to something he really didn't want to do. All he wanted to do was text funny cat pictures to Megan.

How in the hell had *that* happened? Usually when girls sent him funny little pictures throughout the day, he might give them a quick thumbs-up if he really liked them. Otherwise, he would just say he was too busy at work and ignore them. How the tables had turned. Over the past few days when he would text her, he kept checking to see if she had opened his message and started low-key getting nervous when she left him on read and didn't reply.

Troy had never felt like this before. Late night anxiety had started a few days ago. At first he was just tossing and turning while wondering who she worked with. There was that EMT. What did she call him? Jordan. He looked about their age? Where they a thing? What about that guy that drove the fire engine? He never talked, but waved back when Megan had said hi. How would they handle a fire?

He saw her hair, the color of fire, blend in with the surrounding flames. He hadn't known where they were, but there was fire everywhere. The roar of the flames and popping obscured everything he could hear, and the smoke blinded him.

He was trying to ground himself at night, but then the anxiety had shifted back to the familiar places he dreaded.

Fire. There was fire everywhere. He could see the outline of the Humvee and the flailing of arms and legs inside, clawing against an enemy that wasn't there. That's when the screaming started.

Troy had woken up and reached for the glass of water he habitually kept by the bed. He was blind and clumsy, but after the third time, he plunged his hand into the water, snapping himself back to the present.

This was a trick his therapist had taught him a while back. First water, then lights, next look at the clock on his phone—not the time, but what year it was. Deep breath in, deep breath out, start tapping. First right next to his eye, then under it, next under the nose, then the chin. He went through the routine on autopilot, coming back to present.

Right now, riding in the truck, Troy could feel the anxiety clawing into him, the memories he didn't want fighting for control of what he was seeing and experiencing. He reached down below and grabbed the icy cold can of Coke. He rarely drank it, but always had something there. The cold, smooth metal pulled his attention and he started his breathing exercises again.

The lights illuminated the main street of Goldvein, just as they had when he had been young back when his nightmares were just about his mom and brother. Everything looked the same, but the feelings where sharper. Sadder.

He pulled into an open spot in front of what he knew to be the original bank and sat for a few moments, breathing and tapping to bring his mind back to the present.

His name was Troy Chapman. He was here in Goldvein, his hometown. He was in his car driving to pick up Megan.

Like a lightning rod, her name and face calmed him. Megan. He was going to be with Megan and pick out paint colors.

The anxiety tried to outrun him. Paint colors because the house burned down with the memories of his dead brother and mother who he would never see again. The house almost burned down and killed his dad meaning he would be all alone and no one would ever care about him or what he did on this planet again. The dad he couldn't even get to quickly and hadn't seen in a year because he was such a shit son. Adam would've been better, but he died and Troy was nothing but a big disappointment. A mistake. His dad had everything, and Troy couldn't keep up—

"Breathe in. Breathe out."

He started again. Tapping under his eye, under his chin. Eight here and eight here. Breathing. A little less now. Okay. Another deep breath.

He reached down for the soda can, trying to focus on the cold metal. Not enough this time, he popped the tab and heard the familiar fizz, bringing it to his lips and feeling the tingly sweetness, tasting it as he swallowed.

He took a deep breath, had another sip, and looked around at the sights. It was dark now, and she'd be waiting. They were supposed to meet at 6:30.

He was a few minutes early.

Another deep breath and he unbuckled and hopped down from the car, welcoming the cold against his face that brought him back to the here and now. With every step toward her apartment, his mood lifted and a smile grew on his face.

He reached the old building, then hit the buzzer for her apartment and was overwhelmed by a wave of comfort when she answered.

CHAPTER 18

Megan hopped down the steps feeling more excited than she cared to admit. She had been thinking about Troy and the kiss they had shared over the past few days. Every time he sent her a funny video to make her laugh, she got all nervous that he wouldn't like her and panicked on how to respond.

One time she had waited too long to come up with a response and then had to run a call to a retirement home when she noticed he had texted three more times making sure she was okay.

Laura had pointed out she had it bad and shouldn't think too much. Ash had texted she liked the looks of him and appreciated a good takedown. Despite her friends both giving the green light, Megan had butterflies in the shower.

What if he wanted more? The pressure felt like too much. She was a hopeless romantic and wanted that real deal love. The kind that swept you off your feet and kept you warm in an ice storm. The kind that lasted seventy years and then couldn't end with death.

The problem was when she led with that it scared off her

dates. Of course, being so sheltered didn't help, which meant now she was caught between wanting a romance with the highest standards but being afraid to commit so she didn't get hurt. Last night she had tossed and turned, and today was anything but productive as she vacillated between panic and excitement about what to do for tonight. Would she know what to talk about? What if he wanted to kiss again? Should they kiss when he arrived? Last time it was simple. No pressure. Thank you dinner and goodbye.

The car accident had ruined all of that though. Now they were on a new level, and Megan felt very out of her league.

Her phone buzzed as she reached the last step. It was a text from her group chat with Laura and Ash.

"Have fun tonight!" followed by three heart emojis.

As if they were talking about her, Ash texted immediately after with a thumbs-up and a sly smiley face. "You got this! Have a great time with Troy!"

Megan rolled her eyes, feeling love for her friends and low-key panic at the pressure of letting them down if tonight was a total fail.

"Thanks! Talk to you later."

"Details, please!" Laura answered.

Ash sent a GIF of a dog with a sly smile and "Ditto."

Megan could see Troy's outline through the frosted glass windows and broke into a wide smile. When she ripped the door open, all of the anxiety went away until she saw his face.

Megan felt her smile falter. He looked like hell.

"Hey!" she said in an attempt to recover. "I'm glad you're here."

He gave her a tired smile, and before she could think, she stepped forward and closed the gap, enveloping him in a tight squeeze of a hug. His arms closed around her and he rested his chin on her head, and again she felt him tremble against her.

Megan pulled him tighter still and held on until she felt him let out an exhale. It was the kind of hug her grandmother had always given her when she was anxious or overwhelmed.

Megan had no idea what he was going through, but clearly something had gone wrong. He wasn't the smooth talking, cocky guy now. Instead he looked...eroded was the only word that came to mind. He looked like he was so tired he could fall into bed and sleep for days. What could've happened?

Troy drew in a breath and pulled back with a cough like he was overwhelmed. "Wow, um. Thanks for that."

"You looked like you needed it."

Ouch...that was probably a terrible thing to say to someone on a date.

Troy let out a laugh and rubbed the back of his neck. "Yeah, it's been rough. Sorry about that. I tried to look presentable."

Tried to look presentable? Troy looked down and smoothed out his soft blue sweater that folded perfectly over dark jeans. He had on polished brown shoes and had covered it all with a leather jacket that, of course, smelled like him. Maybe it was bad, but she could see herself wearing that jacket in the future.

Megan smiled. "That's not what I meant. You look great."

"Thanks. You set the bar high."

She had tried pairing jeans with a stretchy blouse that she had always loved and thought looked nice. It was a soft blue color, which she had been told went with her eyes. Of course, he couldn't see it under her coat, but would later.

Troy leaned in and planted a chaste kiss on her lips,

which was long enough to send her heart all aflutter, but not nearly long enough for her.

"Ready to go?"

She nodded, followed him to his truck, and felt her cheeks warm as he opened the door like a perfect gentleman. As much as she had wanted to hate his truck when they first met, the inside was comfortable and clean. The cabin was spacious enough for other activities like getting tangled up with more kisses that she probably shouldn't even be thinking about now.

He sat beside her in the warm glow from the cabin light and took a sip from an already opened Coke can in the cupholder before seamlessly pulling out into the light evening traffic.

"Thanks again for agreeing to come with me. I know this isn't the most exciting date, but I never trust myself with paint colors."

"How come?"

"Colorblind."

"Oh! I had no idea."

"It's not too bad. Just green hues all look the same to me. Never could be an electrician, which is why Dad is doing most of the wiring."

"I think it's great you're rebuilding."

"It's the country way. When Mom died, my dad got up the next day and started cleaning around the family plot at the local cemetery. Adam went out and bought a bunch of new plants to add. He knew the director really well, so he said it was okay."

Megan smiled and relaxed into the seat. "I think that's very sweet."

Troy shrugged. "I guess that's how we grieve. I planted a tree."

"Awww. What kind?"

"Red maple. Mom's favorite season was fall. She loved Thanksgiving, so it made sense."

Megan's eyes watered, and she swiped at them really quick in the dark while he continued.

"I didn't know what to do, so I just went and did that."

"That's your love language."

"Love language?"

"You know, there are five ways to show love. Yours is acts of service, like how you cooked for your dad."

"I guess that makes sense. What's yours?"

Megan sat back and watched the road. "I'm not sure. I never really thought about it."

"Acts of service makes sense with what you do for a living, but what about with, you know, others?"

"W-what do you mean others?" Ugh, stutter. Smooth.

"Boyfriends?"

Crap. What did she say? She hadn't been with the same guy for more than three dates? Hadn't gotten that far yet. Was that okay? Would he think that was weird?

"You know what, it's cool. We don't have to get into that. You haven't asked for my history. I didn't mean to overstep."

"No, um, no…it's fine. I just don't have much to talk about."

"That's surprising."

Okay. That was a nice compliment but made her feel weird like she should have more. Better to avoid.

"When I think of my love language, I think of my grandmother."

"I remember you said she raised you."

"Yeah, it was just the two of us. She was a true lady. Very old-fashioned, so when she died I organized all the arrangements with that in mind. That part was stressful, but I think the part that meant the most to me was when I stayed the whole time. She was old school, so I think she would've appreciated it. It helped me too."

"The whole time? Like you didn't leave the body?"

Megan shook her head. "I didn't. Paid extra to have the funeral home open it all up for others to join in as well. It was a long day." She thought about the memory for a moment and drew in a long breath to center herself.

"What language is that?"

"Quality time."

"I like that. What else is there?"

"Gifts, words of affirmation, and physical touch. People usually are a mix from what I've read."

"So you'd be acts of service, quality time, and physical touch?"

"How did you know?"

"You're a good hugger."

Megan smiled. "I think you're a great hugger, and a great cook. Does that mean you're the same?"

"Look at that, we match." Troy reached over and took her hand in his. "Just so you know, I can do a lot more than hug."

And boy, that alone sent a shiver of promise down Megan's body.

CHAPTER 19

The first stop was the hardware store. Troy parked the truck right up front since there weren't too many people there around dinner time. He came around to get her door and smiled when she had already hopped out. Whatever had happened earlier seemed a distant memory as his confident lopsided sexy grin was back on his too-handsome-to-be-real face. That jaw almost undid her, and Megan had to stay focused on walking when he slid his arm around her shoulders while they walked to the store.

She hadn't lied when she said she didn't have a lot of experience in hardware stores. In fact, other than showing up with Buzz to get random brushes to clean different parts of the fire engine and very specific lightbulbs for the station, she'd never been in one. The space had a tendency to overwhelm her. Where others might see possibilities, she saw a multitude of things she had no clue about. Hell, she couldn't even decipher what the loudspeaker was saying in the echo of the cavernous space.

They headed over to their destination, and rather than get overwhelmed, she found the paint section calming. All of the perfectly symmetrical colors fanned out in a rainbow display brought a sense of order. They found the interior paint wall, and each picked up a book on different rooms. He took bathrooms and she took kitchens.

"What looks good to you?"

"Well it really depends what you like. Unless you're hoping to open it up."

"How do you mean?"

"You could do a Bed and Breakfast someday. The house is big enough, but that might be a lot to take on."

Troy thought it over to himself while checking out the book of his own.

"It's not a bad idea for down the road. It would be awhile."

Megan nodded while flipping the pages. "That seems smart. You said you were expanding it."

"Yeah, farms are in right now. Dad's out of the ranching business, and we need to figure out what to do with the land. Besides, people like farmhouses. I don't know what I'd do with it, but maybe it'd be cool to rent it out."

"Like for weddings?"

"I don't know. I guess maybe everything's on the table. It's a five-bedroom house if you count the office, and we're expanding the kitchen. Adding a sunroom. It all needs to be redone anyway, so this is the time to grow."

"That's a really positive attitude."

"Sometimes it's a stretch for me," he said with a laugh.

"I get that. This is a nice option," she said, showing him a picture of a kitchen with cream walls and dark countertops. The cabinets were white with matching black hardware, and the whole thing was staged as a farmhouse kitchen on a bright sunny morning.

"It looks awesome. Can't go wrong with black and white, right?"

"Nope, but they are all pretty. I'd have a hard time choosing if it was me."

"What would you pick if it was yours?"

Megan tilted her head to one side and considered the other pages. "I don't think I have strong feelings. I guess as long as it looks nice. My friend Ash is all into feng shui, but I like things to be kind of funky and fun. Too serious and it feels stiff, but as long as you're happy that's all that matters."

"Eventually," he said. "When I retire."

Troy pulled a tight smile and kept flipping through bathrooms, settling on a black and white number that matched the kitchen Megan had picked. They ordered a few samples, and while they were mixed, they wandered over to the kitchen and bathroom section each taking turns trying out the models.

"You're a great cook so you need a good oven." Megan touched one of the red knobs.

"I've cooked on a lot cheaper things than this and come out fine. This is the top of the line. I've seen this on the network channels."

"Oh, I thought it just looked cool—never mind. I've never bought appliances."

"No, maybe you're right. I'll need to look at the budget and go from there, but yeah, I guess anything's possible now."

"Do you watch a lot of cooking shows?"

"A little. I mostly watch online these days."

"Oh yeah?"

"Yeah, I like cooking, don't get me wrong, but I really love to watch anything with history."

"Really? What kind of history?"

"Military mostly. World War II but I'm interested in a lot of different types. Ancient less so, but I'll never pass up a chance to read about Alexander the Great."

"That's pretty cool."

"Do you like to read?" he asked while leaning against a pantry cabinet.

"Yeah, but mostly romance." She shrugged. "It's not as cerebral, but I've always liked them. I used to sneak them into my house past my grandma and stay up way too late to finish them. I've tried to read other stuff, but I always come back to romance." She tapped her fingers in a farmhouse sink. "This is a nice piece."

"What do you like to read in romance novels?" Troy asked, his voice closer than she expected. She felt him step closer still. He wasn't crowding her, but having him so close felt nice. More than nice actually. There was warmth, security, and a sense of heat between them.

Megan drew in a low breath and kept tracing the grain of the granite in front of her.

"I like the happy ending. I also like when the guy rescues the girl. I know that's corny, but I guess in my line of work I like to read something that's always going to work out, you know?"

She turned to see him nod. "I feel that way with history. I know how it ends. I like the details but not the surprises."

"Oh my God, same!"

"I didn't realize we had so much in common," Troy said before he threaded his arm around the small of her back as they walked back toward the paint counter, taking a detour through the bathroom fixtures.

"I guess this must be a pretty terrible date compared to romance novels," he said when they passed the toilets.

Megan burst out laughing and couldn't help it when a snort came out, which only made her laugh more.

"It's very"—she paused while trying to find the right word —"comfortable."

Was she imagining it or did his cheeks get pink?

Troy reached around and rubbed the back of his neck. "Noted. I'll do better next time. It's not over yet, so don't count me out, and I did need help with this renovation. It's been a about a million choices."

"I bet your dad has been having fun with it."

"If you mean throwing his hands up and saying, 'fine, do what you want' before he launches into a story about someone who built the farm from the ground up while fighting off a bear at the same time."

"Sounds like he's taking it well," Megan said with an easy smile, picturing Mr. Chapman doing just that in his overalls. "His health is still good?"

"Right as rain, as long as he listens. That's the hard part. I came back from meeting the window people and he was trying to get on the roof."

"Wow. That's pretty terrifying."

"He was fine, said he had done it for sixty years and had more business than me being up there."

"I guess you can't argue with that. My grandma was the same about a lot of things. Never went on the roof though." Just the idea made Megan snort a little.

"You said she was a prim and proper lady?"

"To a tee. Hat in church, gloves when she drove, teatime at four. You should've seen her as my scout leader."

"Oh yeah?" He sent another one of those lopsided grins her way.

"Yep. Ironed everything and kept cotton handkerchiefs in her pocket. She was good at it though. She could cook a mean beef stew over the fire, and her sleeping bag was always perfectly folded. Weirdly, she was also good at tying knots and could out-hike all of us."

"Sounds like she had some spirit."

"She did. One day I asked her why she would bother with all that when she insisted on hiring help for any 'man's work' at home. She said that just because a man *should* do it, didn't mean a lady shouldn't know how."

Troy cleared his throat. "So what would she have said about our date to pick out paint?"

Megan's smile bloomed at the thought while she tilted her head toward his, nearly resting on his shoulder as they walked down the aisles. "She'd be happy I had a gentleman caller."

"But?"

"She would not be impressed."

"Ouch. I'm zero for two."

"Well. I loved her dearly, and miss her so much I can't even tell you, especially around the holidays. Working at the firehouse makes it easier, since I'm not home alone or looking to be the extra chair at someone's table, but I'm not like her, and I'm glad to be helping you pick out paint colors."

Troy planted a kiss on her upturned face. "I'm glad you're with me. Let's go grab the samples and then head to dinner."

As it was, tonight's feast was at Joe's Diner, which was familiar and comforting. The red leather banquettes squeaked as they laughed through shakes and two roast-chicken plates with mashed potatoes.

"I didn't realize you knew so much about raising chickens, but I guess it makes sense with you on a ranch."

"I'm hoping to get some more back eventually. Dad let most of that go a few years ago when it, ah, got to be too much."

Megan noticed he looked away, but didn't pry.

"I'm interested to know more about you," he said, sipping his coffee, which was black and smelled divine.

"I think I told you everything. There's not much."

It was so much easier to keep the conversation off her and on him, but clearly he knew that trick too. His smile deepened into one corner of his mouth—was that a dimple? He knew what he was doing when he flicked an eyebrow up in inquiry.

"I have a lot of pets."

That got his attention. "That explains your interest in the chicken coop conversation. What do you have?"

"Well, I have two cats, one turtle, and two birds, but I'd really like a dog, and yeah, I'd love chickens. I want to be a vet someday, so I hope maybe I could have something like your ranch with horses, pigs, and goats."

"I guess your grandma wasn't a fan of animals and you're getting it out now?"

"Yes and no. She didn't like them in the house, so anything had to stay outside. We had an old gray tabby cat who lived under the porch for a long time. She didn't shoo him away when he came up to her while she would rock, so I took that as high praise."

Megan twisted her hands in her lap and fought against her vulnerability. "I had a stutter and was very shy. As you might have picked up, Grandma was very overprotective, which was great, and I can't blame her, but I didn't have a lot of close friends growing up."

"I'm sorry to hear that."

Megan nodded and continued while blowing out a breath. "Animals make sense to me. I never know if I'm saying the right thing or talking too little or too much, and they always seem so appreciative, like they're really listening and can understand. It also makes me feel not as alone."

The second the last word was out, she wanted to reach out into the air and pluck it back, but there was no such way to do that.

She felt her cheeks redden with color, and to avoid his eyes she took a long sip of her shake and pretended to be nonchalant.

"She was all you had."

Megan licked her lips and nodded. "I guess you see why helping your dad wasn't as altruistic as you made it seem. He was good company."

"You have a lot of friends now. The cop and the other one—"

"Paramedic. That's Laura."

"Right, and you said you're the only female in your station."

He sniffed as he said it and took another sip of coffee.

"It's not like that. They're a bunch of brothers who don't really talk to me. I went out with one, but only twice. It didn't really go anywhere. Like I said earlier, I don't have a lot of experience with..." She waved her hand in the air between them.

"What do you mean?"

Megan took a breath and decided to come clean. "I've never had a boyfriend."

CHAPTER 20

Troy froze.

Megan put down her tea and kept talking in a rush of words he was trying to cling to and digest, grabbing bits and pieces. For someone who didn't like talking, she was doing a lot right now, like it had been pent-up and she was waiting to release it all.

"Grandma was very protective… I was very shy… Prom was so awkward… I'm a pretty late bloomer, but have always wanted the real deal, so maybe it's best."

Was Megan a virgin?

While his brain tried to catch up and put the pieces in the right place, he nodded because it felt like the right thing to do. How was this possible? She was drop-dead gorgeous.

Sitting across from him now, her red hair—a color he was so thankful he *could* see—shimmered in the light. Her ivory hands were slim but strong and darted nervously here and there. First they were in her lap, then by her earring, then she was straightening the spoon she hadn't used.

He watched the slender column of her throat as she swallowed and looked up at him with those big eyes.

"If this changes things, I'm okay with just being friends."

Troy coughed again trying to collect himself and bring back a casual air about him. He gave a slight frown and tried to process all of this. "Why would that change things?"

"A lot of guys aren't looking to be with someone like me. They like to keep it casual and just have fun. Someone like me, who wants more and doesn't have a lot of experience, can feel like too much pressure."

She could be a sharpshooter with that bullseye.

"Oh really?" he asked as if he had never heard of the concept.

"Oh yeah. I've tried a few dating apps before."

Oh boy…

Megan wrinkled her nose. "At first it seemed like a nice way to meet some people—no phone calls, just texting, but they were all about getting something quick and fun and weren't really interested in texting back or meeting up for coffee."

She let out a quick laugh, which sounded like music, and looked down to play with the edge of the paper placemat she had been folding and unfolding for most of the meal. "There was this one guy, and we were going to meet up since he had been pretty sweet, but then I've learned the hard way, you know, so I let him know I'm pretty new and like to get to know people before considering anything serious. Just like an FYI, you know? Let him know where I stand in case he was looking for something physical right out of the gate."

"And?"

"All of a sudden he had a test come up for this class he had never mentioned that he,"—she flashed her fingers in air quotes—"completely forgot about." She shrugged. "Never heard from him again."

"What a jerk."

Even Troy wasn't *that* bad. He had been close, but now didn't seem like a great time to bring that up.

"Yeah, my friends—we had just met at that time— they said it was a red flag and I dodged a bullet."

"Sounds like it."

"Yeah, but that was two years ago now."

"Have you met anyone else since then or tried any more apps?"

Megan shrugged. "I go back and forth. There are some new ones every now and then, but it's exhausting. I'm on a break now."

That gave him a boost, which he wasn't expecting. He tried not to think of his current profile status, which was very clearly still active, and smiled with interest. If anything it was fascinating to hear it from her perspective. It was clear this evening was not going to go the way he had planned until she stopped playing with the placemat and looked up at him.

"What do you think?" she asked.

"Is men are pigs the right answer?"

Megan laughed again, which was like a wind chime on a summer afternoon.

"No, I mean about the whole idea. Have you tried apps?"

Never mind a sharpshooter. Try sniper, with beginner's luck.

"A few." Liar.

"Are you on any now?"

"Nope. Taking a break, like you said." Sort of a lie. He wasn't as active as he *had been.* Especially since he had met her. Funny thing was that with everything she had said, she would've been a total swipe left, but there was something about Megan that drew him in and made him want to show her everything she was missing. It was like she called him to be better. Be more.

She opened her mouth and closed it.

"What are you thinking?"

"Nothing. I d-don't even know what I was going to say."

"I want you to know I don't think of you any differently. You don't have to be nervous around me."

Megan looked at him and sniffed. "It's nice to know that."

Troy reached across the table and held his hand open, palm up. She stopped folding the placemat and put hers in his. Of course they fit like a perfect match. Her hands were beautiful. Long, slender fingers with short nails that had the barest amount of polish on them. Perfect and natural. Just like her.

"I mean it. I'm glad you've told me so I don't overstep."

"It's a relief really. I was worried you wouldn't want to hang out anymore."

Troy had considered it for a moment, and that would have been the case two weeks ago in Kentucky, but Megan was different.

"Well, I guess I better come clean too."

Megan's smile went away but she didn't frown. "Is this the part where you let me down easy?"

Actually, yes it would've been. The thought wounded him. "No, no, nothing like that. I'm in the military. I'm only here on leave for a short time. I figured you knew that though."

Megan blew out a breath and smiled. "I figured as much, but didn't want to ask."

"So just so you know, I won't be around, and long distance is hard with my work schedule."

Why did he feel so sad saying that? Megan pulled a tight smile and nodded as well.

"Are you disappointed?" he asked. Troy must have lost his damn mind, because he sure felt like it.

Megan smiled sweetly and gave a half shrug. "I'm glad you didn't say you were suddenly gay."

Troy let out a bark of laughter. "Or that I had a test come up out of nowhere?"

"Yep. That was good. At least this is legit."

"Uncle Sam is very legit. I'll show you my papers if you want. I had a girl ask me that on a dating app before. I guess she had been with a lot of guys who used to lie about that sort of thing."

Megan nodded, impressed. "Wow. Good for her. Getting it out in the open from the jump. No, your dad told me. I knew. I just didn't know how long you'd be here for."

"Yeah, I had some leave to use up anyway, so it works out. I need to get back eventually for…you know, work stuff." Troy swallowed the word therapy and started to bounce his leg under the table. Not ready for that yet, even if it was Megan.

He rubbed the top of her hand with his thumb.

"I'd still like to see you."

"I'm glad. I'd still like to see you too." Her shy smile bloomed into her cheeks as her blue eyes left their hands and met his own.

"Then it's settled. No pressure."

"None. Just fun and good company for now."

The *for now* intrigued him.

"Unless it turns into more."

Megan gave a quick nod. "Of course."

"So you're open?"

Megan considered that for a second and watched his finger run slowly up to her wrist following the delicate bones under her fine skin.

"I am. Actually, I was recently thinking that it'd be nice to branch out and try some new things. I've always wanted the real deal, and I'm too scared to try with someone I don't know because I'm worried it'll fall apart, so why try, you know?"

"Are you proposing something?"

Megan bit her lip and blew out a breath so a lock of her red hair flew away from her face. "I'm very comfortable with you. I like you a lot. You said you're leaving anyway, so I know there's no pressure, so maybe we could make this..." she trailed off, struggling to find the words.

Troy was more than happy to oblige her. "Fun and casual?"

"I guess I can see the appeal after all."

He nodded. "A lot of people are afraid to commit. They want the experience but don't want to get hurt."

"I've lost enough people," she said, staring hard into their intertwined hands, before glancing up as if to see if he heard something that clearly wasn't meant to be said out loud.

It was funny, wasn't it? He wasn't looking for anyone serious. Was actually dead set on avoiding it for the very reason she spelled out. And yet, she was doing the opposite thing for the same exact reason. He felt bad even comparing. He had lost his mom and his brother and then his friends in that awful fire, but she had lost her whole family, twice. It didn't seem fair.

He understood why she wanted to help his dad. Not only was she generous with her time, but family was everything to her, since she didn't have one. It also made sense why she would hold it against him for the time it took to get home.

Everything about her from her past, her job, and her fears was the same as his. Never before had he met someone who understood so perfectly.

"Me too. I get it."

"Is it easier being intimate with someone that you know will leave? I've always thought about it as being harder."

Troy tilted his head to one side and considered her question, trying to choose his words carefully. He had never thought so much about his reasonings or been asked to explain. "I think it can be. At some point you get attached, but I think the way to do it is to take it day by day."

Boy, would his therapist be proud to hear him now.

"Day by day?"

"Yeah," he spoke and sounded more confident to his own ears. "None of this is guaranteed. All we have is today. We don't know what will happen tomorrow, so I think in a way it's easy just to focus on what's right in front of you instead of worrying or overthinking about the future. None of us know if we'll even be here at all."

Megan's eyes narrowed but not out of malice. She digested his words and started to nod slowly. "I've never thought about it that way before."

"You must be a remarkable firefighter."

Fire scared the shit out of him ever since that roadside bomb hit the convoy. The smell of burning flesh still haunted him.

Megan shook her head emphatically. "Not really."

"I beg to differ."

"You wouldn't understand."

She tried to pull her hand away from his, but he brought his other one over top of hers, gently keeping it still.

"You know, I've seen some stuff, and of course, there was Mom and Adam, so for a long time I became hyperaware. Like if I could imagine every possible terrible thing that could go wrong, I could somehow prevent it from happening."

"That's not possible."

"Exactly. I still have a hard time. And don't think I didn't think about putting Dad in a home where someone would cook his meals."

Megan's blue eyes widened at the mental image of his dad no doubt giving hell to some poor nurse just trying to do her job. "He would hate that."

"Oh, it would kill him, so…" Troy shrugged. "I let it go. We'll rebuild and move on. He feels bad enough about it. Tells me at night. He's already beating himself up about it, so I doubt he'll ever touch a gas stove again."

"I figured that's why the plans you showed me looked ADA compliant."

Troy nodded once. "Bingo. Microwave will be lower in the new island for easy access.

He drew in a breath and continued. "The point is, I can't predict what's going to happen, as much as I try, and I still have some hang-ups."

"What are those?"

Troy shook his head, not wanting to get into it. "Little things, but with people I just try to meet them as they come and take each day one at a time. Just because I won't be here forever doesn't mean I'm not sitting here holding your hand."

Megan smiled and looked down so that a lock of her red curls fell in front of her face. "I guess that's true."

Troy picked up her hand in his own and brought it to his lips, planting a delicate, gentle kiss on her soft skin.

Megan looked up and pulled her bottom lip under her perfect white teeth before giving her other hand to him.

"So tell me what happens next."

CHAPTER 21

Megan's pulse hammered in her chest as Troy navigated his truck out of the parking space and drove toward her apartment.

This was new territory.

She wasn't a child and knew what she was getting into and knew this had been a possibility, which meant she had taken care to clean up her apartment just in case he came back. Of course, she hadn't had the same anticipation as she did now.

She watched him as he drove, alternating between dark and illuminated as the streetlights cast their glow when they passed before plunging him back into darkness. In the few moments she could see him, she tried to memorize as many of his features as she could. He had a strong jaw but was clean-shaven, and his dark brown hair was cut short. In the dark, his brown eyes looked black and were clear and alert as he drove. While his eyes were alert, his body language was relaxed, with one hand on the bottom of the wheel and the other relaxed in his lap. If she didn't know better, she would think he was super chill, but his eyes gave him away.

She could see the anxiety. He didn't fidget like she did, or stutter like when she got nervous. His hand on the wheel didn't have any raw edges or chewed cuticles, but what he said resonated with her. He knew what it meant to be anxious and yet it didn't manifest in him. She would've thought he was placating her, but it all rang true.

To lose a brother during an accident and a parent to cancer would impact someone, but he had said there was more. It didn't seem fair to see that much hardship. In her own job, Megan saw terrible things.

She did her best to fix them, helping people whenever she could—not just in their emergency, but after, just like Mr. Chapman. Whether it was collecting cans at Thanksgiving, toys at Christmas, or collecting money at the annual station pancake breakfast, she wanted to help those who had experienced tragedy. Her thoughts went to the wreck on the mountain and the man in the woods. She would call Ash in the morning to see what had happened.

She was glad Troy had been there with her. He had known how to act, but to her surprise hadn't tried to stop her from running to help like she had first expected his male ego to do. When the chips were down, he had let her help and protected her from the attack.

Megan shuddered with the memory of the wide staring eyes of the crazed man. Like a shark, there was nothing behind them to stop him from attacking. Like all his humanity was gone.

"What's on your mind?"

"Nothing much."

Troy slid her a glance and a sly smile. "Sounds like over-thinking."

"Not really. I was thinking about work actually."

"Hopefully not an accident."

"Guilty as charged."

"Am I that bad of a driver?"

"No, of course not. It's just an occupational hazard." Megan knew better than to spoil the mood, and besides, he was already parking outside the old bank building where she lived. She might not have a lot of experience, but even she knew getting heavy on a date was a no-no.

As before, Troy was out in a flash and heading for her door when she opened it. She gave him a smile as she stepped down and got out her key.

The wind ramped up just as she unlocked the door where they had met earlier, and once up the steps, she fumbled with the key at the door, feeling her heart race.

She had never made it this far before. This was her personal space, welcome to only her closest friends, and now she stood here with Troy behind her. She could feel his presence, his strength.

Feeling like she was on some invisible precipice and guarding herself against overthinking, she opened the door and stepped inside.

Troy was tall, probably around six feet, but he might as well have been a giant in her narrow entryway.

"I have an extra hanger if you'd like to hang up your coat," she said, relying on good manners to get her through the overwhelming awkwardness she felt.

She went to shrug out of her own and felt his hands peel back the puffy nylon from her shoulders, in a move that felt so intimate and normal at the same time.

Good Lord, if she felt this way now about him taking off a coat, it was going to be a long evening.

She hung them up together in the microscopic hall closet, trying not to overthink the sight of them both together. Out of the corner of her eye, she saw Troy check the door handle, then the deadbolt.

A soft bump at her ankle let her know the welcoming committee had arrived.

"Well hello, you," Troy said, already leaning down and letting Popsicle sniff his knuckles before he scratched behind her ears.

Lincoln wasn't that far behind. His low, annoyed meow followed a blinking, one eye at a time, meaning he had just been rousted from a nap and wasn't pleased at the intrusion.

"You're a big boy, aren't you?"

Troy was right. The yellow tabby was a solid nineteen pounds and one of the longest cats the vet treated. He and Popsicle, who was a chocolate, runt of the litter pipsqueak, were best friends but total opposites.

"He doesn't warm up to anyone unless there's treats involved."

"Doesn't suffer fools? I like that in a man."

"Nope. Come into the kitchen. That's where I keep the kitty crunchies. You'll have a friend for life in no time. Can I get you a cup of tea?"

"That sounds nice. Thank you."

Megan pulled two cups down from the cabinet. They were mismatched and made by a local artist. Hers was her favorite go-to mug with blue swirls that fanned into flowers. His was taller, painted in greens with a leaf pattern that swirled into a tree canopy at the top.

Not being fancy, she filled both cups and nuked them in the microwave, as she always did for herself, and pulled out the various teas.

"Pick your poison?" she asked, turning to find him sprawled out on the floor handing out crunchies one at time, always in a different place to Popsicle's delight and Lincoln's annoyance. Popsicle was darting all over the floor, while Lincoln sat back and glared at the crunchy Troy placed just out of his paw's reach.

"What you got?"

"Black, green, mint, oolong, Darjeeling, and a mishmash of a few others."

"Darjeeling, please."

"Excellent choice." She plopped the bags in the mugs and went to the fridge. "Honey, lemon, cream, sugar?" She wasn't fancy with heating the water, but tea demanded to have various toppings.

"Black, please."

She slid a dramatic smile at him, impressed. "A purist. I like it."

"I like tea. Granted I get coffee more, but I like the flavor."

"That's not a surprise given that you're a foodie. Speaking of, I'm not a great cook, but I do have some cookies around here. They're cinnamon."

"Perfect for dipping."

Grandma would've frowned to know her Brown Betty teapot sat up on the high shelf, unused when a gentleman caller was present, but Megan hoped using the saucers, a tray, and lining it with a crisp white tea towel would ingratiate her again.

She walked over to the living room and placed the tray on her thankfully clear coffee table. Troy followed suit, trailed by the cats—Popsicle dying for more affection, Lincoln resigned to entertaining unexpected company.

"You have a nice place here. It's cozy."

That was the nice word for small, but it suited her. Of course, to him it probably seemed like a closet compared to his ranch. It really was just her bedroom, bathroom, kitchen and living room, both of which were combined into one open space. She loved the exposed brick, but the water pressure in the bathroom was an area of concern. Actually, all of the fixtures could do with replacing, a fact which had been painfully obvious when Laura had come to stay with Holden and tried to bathe him.

"Thanks. I picked it out because of the location when I moved here," she said, walking over to the birdcage she had covered when she left. Both birds were asleep.

Troy walked over to peek through the old towel she held open for him.

"The one with the white and hint of blue is Salt, and the yellow green is Pepper. They're much more active in the morning."

She fumbled on the last sentence, wondering if she had just invited him to stay, but Troy didn't seem to have noticed her slipup. Instead he smiled and turned slowly around the room, taking in her mix of furniture and style.

Seeing him there looking at all of her things, with Popsicle rubbing his leg, made her breath catch.

"When did you move in?"

"After Grandma died. Five years ago. I was born here, but after the fire, the memories were too strong and Grandma wanted to go elsewhere. That's why we wouldn't have met in school or around town."

Troy nodded. "I had wondered about that."

"When she passed, I felt like this was the right move. I didn't know a soul here, but my parents and siblings are buried here."

"Your Grandma?"

"She's here too. Her family had a plot and that's how it went."

"Do you go visit?"

"From time to time. Grandma made me promise not to go too much as she got older. She wanted me to know life is for the living." Megan paused and picked up her tea before sitting down on the coach. It had been her Grandma's and was comfortable, neutral, and good quality. She patted the chenille fabric next to her, and Troy joined her, his thigh touching hers.

"Do you come back often?" she asked.

"It's hard when I don't live here, but my dad would've had a lot in common with your Grandma. He says the same thing."

"I wonder if our families knew each other," Megan said, and smiled at the thought.

"I'll ask. What was her name?"

"Matilda Mae White. Went by Mrs. Tillie Mae"

Troy picked up a cookie and dipped it, while Popsicle and Lincoln stared at them from the floor.

"I'm not used to kissing a beautiful woman while being stared at by a small panther and a medium-sized tiger."

Megan broke into a nervous laugh. "You're very sweet."

"You're very beautiful."

He pushed a lock of red hair away from her face and tucked it behind her ear before planting a tender kiss under her ear, which sent a wave of heat over her. With her fair skin, it probably showed too. Damn genetics.

"I like seeing you here. Seeing all of your things and animals. I'm just missing the turtle now."

"Leo's in the bathroom. He's not any trouble."

"I don't know a lot about turtles."

"Actually, me neither. I'm learning as I go. He belonged to a science teacher who needed to rehome him. Apparently they get huge, and he outgrew the tank at the school. He's a pretty new addition."

"You're going to be a great vet. Dad told me how good you were with Levi."

His hand slid across her shoulders to rest behind her on the top of the couch, while he sipped his tea in the other hand. He propped one ankle across his knee and was the picture of relaxation. Seeing him sprawled out on the couch was a picture in a dream. As he shifted, his weight moved the couch more, and her whole body melted into his side.

"I've always loved animals."

"You don't sound happy."

"It's complicated."

"Tell me more."

"It's just money, school, and I'll have to leave the fire station."

"So?"

Megan cradled her mug in her hands and stared into the dark liquid for answers. The exhaustion weighed on her with this decision followed by a heaping dose of guilt. "I want to be a vet, but I should be a firefighter."

"Because of your family?"

Ha. If only he knew. "Yeah, basically."

Troy nodded and sipped his tea. "I get it."

Megan looked up at him. "You do?"

"Yeah. The army's the same way. So is the ranch."

"What do you mean?"

"Have you ever heard of Cincinnatus?"

Megan shook her head and he continued. "Ancient Rome. Cincinnatus leaves his farm to fight for the empire, but when the war ends, he goes back home and serves his family by working on the farm.

"Actually, he was George Washington's inspiration to walk away from the presidency and to return to Mount Vernon. That action is what kept us from becoming another monarchy again. People would've gladly embraced him forever."

"Really? I had no idea."

"Yeah, in fact King George III at the time was quoted as saying that he's the greatest man who ever lived. It takes a lot to walk away from duty and go back home."

"Is that why you're still in?"

"Yes and no. I like it, but I know when the time comes for me to come home and take over the ranch, that's it. Farmers can't travel without getting someone to come check on the livestock and tend to everything. It's a bit more complicated than a pet sitter."

"Wow."

"Yeah, so I wanted to see the world while I can. Serve—but now, it's hard."

Troy's demeanor changed. His body was still relaxed, but his eyes stared at her floor, hard and distant.

"Why is it hard?" Megan asked in a small voice.

"It's a family. A responsibility. It can come to define you, and then if you leave, what will you be?"

"Cincinnatus?"

Troy smiled. "I'd like to think so, but it's hard to hang up the uniform and step back. I feel like I should stay."

"There's others though. You've done your job."

"I know."

"They can replace you, but your dad can't."

"Also true. I'd say the same to you."

"It's not that simple. I'm sorry. I wish I could get into it, but I can't."

"I respect that, but just remember at the end of the day, it's your life, and you have to decide what you want."

Troy leaned forward, put his mug back down on the tray, tilted her chin to him, and kissed her.

CHAPTER 22

Megan was overwhelmed by Troy in the best possible way. He tasted like tea and cinnamon, mixed with a hint of that cologne she would've bathed in. He was warm and strong, but didn't crowd her or push.

She had been kissed before, but all of it paled in comparison to his presence.

As it deepened, she felt him tease her lips with his tongue, and she let him in, to taste him more, finding the movement intoxicating. Megan didn't want it to end and was panting when he pulled back just enough to look at her through his heavy-lidded eyes. The brown warmth of his gaze was intense and focused on only her.

"What is it you want, Megan?"

"I don't know."

"Don't you?"

She paused. "Let me show you my room."

"Your wish is my command, but first, let's clean up."

He smiled again, his broad grin crossing his face and crinkling his eyes in the corners. He took her cup and put it on the tray next to his own and stood, taking it to the kitchen.

"You don't have… Okay, thank you." Megan twisted her hands in her lap, then stood, trying to figure out what to do next. She settled on plumping the pillows that had been smooshed beneath them.

Troy checked the front door again and walked back into her living room looking sexy as hell, his eyes locked on her. "To the bedchamber? Or do they call it something else in novels?"

"Um. Well, it really depends on what you're reading."

"Mhmmm." His hand was on the small of her back as she walked back toward her bedroom, which was thankfully clean. "What do you like to read?"

She eased onto the bed, and he took his eyes off her for only a moment to look at her room before he shut the door and sat down next to her, on top of the duvet.

Her lamp on the desk against the wall was one of her grandma's Tiffany styled lamps with the multicolored glass shade. When it was on, it turned her room into a kaleidoscope of color, with reds, golds, and greens. Right now, it was the only light on in the dark room, and it cast a red glow over Troy's features, which looked dark and even more handsome. His lips turned up at the sides, and one eyebrow arched above his dark brown eyes, which looked almost black in the dim light.

"Well, I started with reading Regency novels. That's like with dukes and stuff. Old-school England."

"You mean like with the Duke of Wellington after Waterloo?" He phrased it like a question, but it was clear by his smile he knew exactly what he was talking about.

"Right, I forgot you like history. I like historical romances, or a good western. I'll read contemporary with romantic suspense, but sometimes those are a little too close to work."

"So you don't mind reading something with edge."

"No violence and all that…" He planted a kiss right below her ear and dragged his teeth along the back of her neck, scrambling her brain.

"That's not the edge I'm talking about."

Megan felt a wave of heat wash over her body. If she could turn into one giant blush, she would've on the spot. What she really wanted was her bedroom floor to open up and swallow her right into the old bank vault below.

"Well?"

His teeth kept going, and her whole body erupted in shivers that she was sure he could feel as he ran his fingertips over her exposed arm.

Megan tried to think of something clever to say, but finally blurted out, "They're called b-bodice busters for a reason."

Troy threw back his head with a bark of laughter.

Relief swamped her that at least maybe he wouldn't make her talk about every single thing. She might die of embarrassment.

Her celebration was short-lived, as she saw the glint in his eye.

"Tell me what you like."

"Troy—" she started, but he shook his head.

"Let me just turn off the light."

"No, that's not necessary. I…I like seeing you."

Troy looked at her, and a new expression crossed his face for a moment. He nodded once and pulled back away from the light, but something tugged at her.

"Unless, that is, you'd like it better."

Troy surprised her by hesitating and looking back at the light.

"It makes it easier to talk about things sometimes."

That surprised her. In all of her books, lights, fires, and candles seemed to set the mood.

"I have an idea," she said, jumping up, excited to know what to do and confident in that knowledge.

She reached on her bedside table and pulled out a pack of matches. She always kept small votives in glass jars next to her bed, bath, and in her kitchen to help her relax. Ash had taught her that relaxation trick, and it wasn't like she was afraid of fire.

Megan struck the match, touched it to the wick, and doused it by pinching her fingertips, feeling nothing. She ducked into the bathroom and ran the match under the water before putting it in the empty metal trash can. She might not have reason to be afraid, but she wasn't dumb.

"How's that? Best of both worlds?"

Troy nodded and turned off the jewel-toned lamp, and the room went even darker than before, except for the small golden glow from the white votive.

She could just make out his shape as he stepped forward, sliding his arms around her waist and pulling her closer to him. He ran his lips along the column of her throat and murmured against her skin, the vibrations of his voice scrambling her mind again like popping the lid off a box only he had the key to.

"You like this?"

"Mhmm."

"Tell me what to do next."

Right now, she could barely keep herself upright, and he must have known it for he was supporting her with his arms, and Megan had no doubt he'd catch her if she went boneless right there on the spot.

"No comment?" he asked, laughing to himself, sending waves of hot breath along the sensitive spot behind her ear.

"I don't know what I like."

"You shouldn't lie to me."

He slid his hand from the small of her back, up her

spine, and toward the base of her skull to frame her head and tilt her mouth toward him, which he claimed with greed.

Like before on the couch, he tasted of cinnamon and tea, and her head swam with heat as he found her tongue and tugged on her lower lip with his teeth, just enough to pop a little bubble of pain, which inexplicably heightened her pleasure.

Feeling her sag, Troy eased her back on the bed and lay against her side, propping himself up on his elbows, framing her face with his free hand and cupping her chin with care. His thumb rubbed against her cheekbone as his dark eyes flickered in the light of the candle.

The heat raged inside her, demanding more fuel be added to the fire growing louder and burning hotter within her.

Megan tried to pull him down, but he arched one of those sinful eyebrows again and flashed a coy smile.

"Not until you tell me something you like."

"I like this."

"You said that already. Give me another one."

Megan closed her eyes against the red hot shame she felt, but the passion was hotter. "I like when they go for the chest."

"Excellent, one of my favorite parts."

Troy slid one hand down, but not as low as Megan wanted, stopping at her collarbone. He pressed his lips to her and claimed her mouth again while skittering the pads of his fingers just barely across the thin skin above her bone. The sensation was enough to drive her wild and not nearly enough to satisfy.

She tried to lean up and press into him more to steer his hands, but he would not be moved, biting her lip again when she tried.

"There's an art to this," he said against her lips as he

trailed kisses down her jaw, neck, and finally to her collar-bone. "You deserve to be savored."

His voice was low, barely above a growl, and Megan hadn't ever wanted anything more than for him to rip her top off right here and now and take her right there on the spot, but as if he could read her mind, he slowed even further, painstakingly playing with the edge of her blouse. When he would give it a tug, the cold air would hit a new spot of hot flesh, until he replaced the heat with his own mouth, sending her head spinning.

Her breasts, though small, screamed for his touch through the fabric of her bra and shirt, so that she arched her back, begging for more attention.

Troy answered the call, running his hand down over her, and through the fabric it only inspired more frustration. As if he sensed her plight, he slid his hand down her shirt, past her bra, and cupped her bare breast, sliding over her nipple, once, twice, then catching the peak and rolling it between his fingers, sending jolts of energy through her whole body. Megan squirmed beneath, her body with a mind of its own, first trying to get away then fighting for more, while Troy's lips returned to her neck.

His breath was ragged which made her feel good. She hadn't taken off a stitch of clothing, yet was ready to combust. It served him right that he was feeling some kind of way too.

The taunting continued, him building her up then backing off, until her head swam with desire and the need in her roared so much she could hear the blood pumping in her own ears. No longer afraid, all that mattered was that he give her what she needed. Right. Now. She arched again until Troy covered one of her tortured nipples with his mouth, licking it with his tongue, sending her head so far back, she thought she might break. He reached around and teased her nipple, while lapping at her and rolling the other around in his mouth, which meant one hand now rested on her thigh.

Megan's legs had gone from rubbing against him to each other and now had opened on their own, hot with need and a throbbing ache for him.

On a broken breath, she called out his name. "Please."

He tilted his head and caught her eyes, the dark pupils burning in the night as he brought the heel of his hand to the very spot where she needed him to be. Through her jeans, the pressure was still enough to send her skyrocketing over the edge or so she thought.

Troy's nimble hand found the waistband of her jeans and tugged them down, sliding in to gain access where one perfectly placed finger found its target, wet and ready.

As soon as he began a rhythmic stroking, her legs shook on their own accord, and all of the pressure morphed in her tight chest. She couldn't speak, couldn't breathe. All she knew was him and pleasure and the rising wave within her that didn't feel like it would break.

She panted, trying to draw breath, clawing at him and shifting to get any relief and find her highest point.

Sensing her struggle, Troy nuzzled behind her ear and bit her on the neck, sending her over the top into a dark pool of satisfied bliss.

CHAPTER 23

Troy clutched the steering wheel. In the pitch-black night he could only see the taillights ahead of him as he bumped along the road, keeping track of the vehicle in front. He didn't want to be too close, but in the blackness wanted to make sure his wheels were on the same path.

The glow of his own headlights gave him a short distance, but beyond the light there was nothing. The dust from the others clouded up, obscuring what little he could see in a fog.

There were no stars. Only headlights and brake lights in front of him, and then another set behind him. He was in the middle, doing his best to react to the quick juts and dips of the sorry excuse for a road in front of him.

The glow of the dash cast a light hue over him. He was told it was green, but all he knew was it was lighter in color than the rest. He could at least pick up on shades. Only a few more miles and he'd be safe.

He saw the flash first. A split second before he heard it, he saw the spark in the dark that erupted into total hell, engulfing the right side of the Humvee in front of him.

He threw the door open and rushed forward on foot, which he knew was stupid, but he had to get to them. His friends. Simon.

The fire was like the devil himself, the flames licking into the dark sky. In a cruel twist of fate, in the darkness he could see nothing but the towering blaze. A few people staggered out, stunned from the blast, but the passenger side door didn't open.

Simon.

He heard screaming. Was it him? Was it the flames? Troy reached forward, and strangely didn't feel the pain searing through his hand. He could see Simon, motionless, screaming in the flames, and he tried to reach in and grab him, pull him free.

More screaming. Louder.

He couldn't get him. Tried to reach in deeper. The flames were all around him, smoke burning his eyes.

Troy reached in again, the screaming piercing his head and the smell of smoke in his nose driving him crazy, trying to get to Simon, but he just couldn't get him.

Someone pulled him back. He shouted out and pulled against them, fighting. He had to get in there. They had made a promise. It wasn't supposed to end like this.

His arms stretched out, but he was being pulled back. Hands tugged at his shoulders, but he threw them off, trying to lunge back toward the flames. Screams bounced around inside his head.

"Troy! Troy!"

His eyes flew open and took in total darkness; he couldn't see. He threw his hands out searching for something. He didn't know what he needed, but he was supposed to touch something. Cold. Where was it? Where was the clock?

He smelled smoke, the acrid stench clawing through his

head. He bolted upright and felt something hard. Things clattered to the floor, sounded different.

His throat burned. He was blind. He couldn't see. Where was Simon? He had to get to him.

"Troy! Wake up!"

Hands were on him. A woman's voice. Why did he know that?

There was a click and red light everywhere in the room. Troy dropped to the floor and covered his head, shaking now. Something sharp bit into his knee, and panicked scratching came from somewhere to his left.

"Troy! It's me, Megan. You're in my room."

Megan? Megan. He knew that name.

His consciousness slowly grew inside him, pulling up stakes from the dangerous parts of his mind. The bad memories faded. The scream faded. The smoke lingered.

He tried to speak, but it came out like a croak.

"What was that? What's wrong?" she asked, worry in her voice.

"Fire! S-smoke!"

"What? Oh, shit. No, no, no. There's no fire. Let me get the smell out of here."

He felt her get up and pick something up before walking away and running water over something. The putrid smell still stank in the air. He hated the smell of smoke, and thankfully, the cold air came in like a breath from God himself.

"I opened the bathroom window. Let me get this one too."

A latch, pop, and slide welcomed in icy air that washed over him like a cold kiss of reality.

He unfolded himself and took in the room. Megan turned on another light, just white this time, and slowly the night before came back to him.

As awareness dawned, he shut his eyes and dropped his

head, a fresh wave of exhaustion crashing through him and pulling him down.

"Why don't you lie down?"

Troy shook his head. He stood and walked over to the open window, bracing himself against the panes, looking down at the darkness below. He couldn't see anything outside, but reveled in the dark air against his skin, which felt hot and damp. He pulled a hand over his face to wipe the clamminess away.

Megan padded up behind him, and to his credit, he didn't lunge at her, but kept practicing on his deep breathing.

He drew in. One. Two. Three. Four.

Held. One. Two. Three. Four.

Blew it out through his mouth, his throat stinging. One. Two. Three. Four.

Megan must have sensed the tension in him coiled like a spring because she just stood behind him watching for a few more rounds.

Echoes of the dream haunted him. The screams, smoke, fire, and hands pulling him back. Had that been her? That part was new. God, he hoped he hadn't hurt her. He wanted to take her in his arms and reassure her, or maybe deny whatever it was she saw or heard, but it was too much. Looking her in the eye with the new knowledge she had about him was too deep. He felt too vulnerable.

Megan stood by watching, and once his breath steadied, or maybe it steadied because she crept away, he didn't know, but he straightened himself and started tapping.

It was good to have the privacy to do this. First under the eye, eight taps, then under the nose, then the chin, chest, rib, then he started on the specific pattern on his hands.

He heard sounds coming from the kitchen. Mugs being pulled down. Water from a faucet. The beep of a microwave, heating it all up, and the gentle clink of a tin container, no doubt holding tea.

He could kiss her for it and waited as he felt her presence come back into the room, carrying a tray, which she placed on the foot of the rumpled bed where they had fallen asleep earlier.

"Here." Her voice still reminded him of summer, but there was a tenderness there that hadn't been, a sense of connection and deep understanding.

He looked at her hands as he couldn't bring himself to make eye contact, and he saw a small, rolled washcloth. He took it and felt the cold dampness, a welcome relief, which he wiped over his face and neck, bringing him back to present.

"I made some tea. Would you like to have some with me now?"

Troy nodded and followed her back to the bed, where she took her cup and cradled it in her palms, sipping carefully. She tucked her legs under her and leaned against the headboard, staring into the cup. She must have slipped out of her clothes silently while he was by the window, because instead of her jeans, she had on a light blue robe that looked well-loved with a little ruffle at the edge. Perfectly cozy and appealing as always.

Troy took his own mug and went to sit down on the bed.

"Why don't you take off your pants? I mean..." Her cheeks were bright pink. "You fell asleep in them with your belt on. It can't be comfortable."

Megan was right. As it was, he normally slept in the nude, so maybe that also brought on the trigger.

He pulled off his belt and stripped, letting his pants fall, then pulled off the sweater and shirt he had worn earlier, tossing them carelessly on her desk chair. He still had on a T-shirt, thank God, and his boxer briefs, but the cold felt welcome against his legs.

A low purr at his feet told him Popsicle had arrived to check on him, and Lincoln sat about a foot away, watching him with a slow blink.

He reached down and ran his hand over the soft head before walking over to shut and lock the window, then turned to her.

Troy felt awkward and hated it.

"I'll be right back."

Megan watched him and nodded without judgment, but he felt it and tried not to walk in shame as he checked the front door again, looking down when he came back into the room with a paper towel as a pretense.

"You don't have to lie, and you don't have to explain."

Good. He wasn't interested.

"I'm okay. You don't need to worry about me."

He shut his eyes against the shame and forced himself to be present as he picked up the mug of tea and sipped.

It wasn't the same flavor as before. He couldn't place it, but was sure it was deliberate. The last thing he wanted was to talk, but he found himself asking her.

"What is it?"

"Chamomile with a little lemon and honey. I'm sorry."

Troy sipped again and frowned. "Why are you sorry? I almost wrecked your room."

Looking now, he could see he had knocked a few knick-knacks from the shelf onto the floor. One where his knee probably had been was a large, spikey, purple crystal. No wonder his knee still stung.

"I'm sorry about the candle. I just always read in books and movies that it makes it romantic. I didn't mean to fall asleep with it. I didn't realize—"

"It's fine. It's not you."

"No, lots of people may not like it—"

"You're fine with it. Hell, you're a firefighter," he said with a bitterness he hated himself for hearing in his own voice. "Nothing about it scares you."

Megan looked pained in a way he hadn't seen before, and he regretted that comment and would've paid God himself a million dollars to take it back. How could he forget her family?

"I'm sorry. That was unfair and mean. I'm not in a good place right now."

"Let's get some sleep. We'll sort it out in the morning."

Well, hell, it was still three in the morning. The witching hour.

Troy always woke up at this time. He sat holding the mug and feeling the warmth radiate through his hands. Megan looked at him, considering him as if he was a puzzle, which he probably was to her.

Slowly and in plain sight, she gently put her hand on his shoulder, moving slowly enough not to surprise him, which he hated and appreciated at the same time.

Her touch was lighter than a butterfly and connected her to him in a way he previously hadn't realized he needed.

"Do you want to sleep?"

"Sometimes I can. You rest though. I might need to sit up and gather my thoughts."

"That's okay. I don't work tomorrow." She tucked one corner of her mouth up into her check and bit her lip. "Would you like company?"

Troy smiled. "That's nice of you to offer." He took another sip of tea, and then not knowing what to say, lamely added, "Tea is good."

"I'm glad. We can watch TV or just sit in the dark."

"They don't come more than once in the same night, just so you know." God, the idea that he had lashed out toward her made him want to dig a hole and fall inside, never to be heard from again.

Megan gave his hand a slight squeeze. "Thank you for telling me. I'm glad for you."

They finished their tea in silence, before slowly easing back into each other's arms. Megan's head cradled nicely in the crook of Troy's shoulder, and he let his own head rest on the top of hers. As if they had been made for each other, it was a perfect fit, which baffled him. Sometimes he felt crowded by cuddling, but not only was this easy, it was effortless. There was a sense of peace, calm, and true connection that filled a void deep in his soul.

After a while, Megan's breathing slowed to a steady rhythm which told him she had fallen asleep. Whether it was the tea or her, or both, he wasn't far behind and this time, sleep came blissfully without dreams.

CHAPTER 24

Megan woke up to the sun streaming through her window and a very handsome man in her bed, which was a first. She considered him for a moment and took notice of his lashes resting peacefully over his cheeks. There was a slight frown and wrinkle between his brows, but otherwise he looked calm. Far more calm than he had last night.

He was beautiful to look at as he rested. He looked younger than when he was awake with his dark eyes watching everything. That he had checked the door repeatedly to make sure it was locked had not been lost on her. Without the confidence and defensive nature, he looked so gentle.

To let him sleep and get the peace he so desperately deserved, Megan slipped out of the bed and tiptoed toward the kitchen, taking care to shut the door behind her without any noise so the cats wouldn't wake him.

She padded in bare feet over the wooden floor to the kitchen and started fixing a pot of coffee for them both. The act felt simple, domestic, and...natural.

The thought paused her hands.

Last night had been some of the best pleasure she had known. She hadn't realized how much she had to learn or how much she could want what had happened. It had been wonderful. She had craved him, and as she stood here, she wanted even more.

She had thought it might be just physical, but that was before.

Megan had fallen asleep and was awakened by something jostling in her bed. At first she had thought he was awake—with how he was thrashing around, she had been sure of it.

He also was talking to someone, but Megan hadn't been able to make out the details. When he had started shouting and thrashing, she had tried to grab his shoulders and shake him awake, only to be thrown off.

That's when she knew not to touch him. He still hadn't been awake when his knee landed on her crystal, which had to hurt like hell.

It must have been the smoke from the candle. It hadn't caught on fire but had burned down to be extinguished naturally. The realization made her question what he had said at dinner, that *she* wasn't afraid of fire. Megan was too wrapped up in her own head to realize that maybe he was saying that because he was really afraid of fire. She was sure of that now.

His shouting echoed in her head. She could only imagine what he had seen that would cause that kind of nightmare.

Megan's lips thinned as she hit the button and heard Mr. Coffee get to work.

They hadn't even spent all that much time together, but she felt oddly protective of him, wanting to make sure he didn't have a nightmare again tonight.

Megan wondered if he tried therapy. She had never been, but Ash spoke glowingly about her time talking to someone—but then Ash was all about taking care of herself.

Lincoln nudged her foot and gave a low purr at her feet. As usual, Popsicle wasn't far behind, sitting by the cat bed behind the couch, yawning before washing his feet. Megan paid homage to both with a few kitty crunchies, pulled down a pair of coffee mugs, this time plain white, then followed the sound of fluttering from the birdcage.

"Shhhhh, we have company." Salt and Pepper's heads twitched in her direction, taking in her words with their black eyes, before hopping onto the side of the cage and starting to tweet. So much for silence, she thought. She folded up the towel and tucked it under the table the cage was on.

Thus began the morning routine. She refilled water and food, changed newspaper and litter, all as quietly as possible, and by the time she had slid open the curtains to let the morning sun stream in, the coffee maker announced it was done with a pleasant beep.

The doorknob clicked as it opened, and Troy walked through looking disheveled and slightly groggy.

"Morning," Megan said, walking over to the coffee pot. What did people do when they greeted someone who stayed over? Deciding just to act like she would if it were Laura or Ash, she smiled and started pouring coffee.

"How do you take it?"

Much to her surprise, strong arms slid around her stomach from behind, and Troy planted a rough kiss on her neck, scrambling her brain.

"I'm not picky. However you take it is fine."

"I know that's not true," Megan said.

"Fine. Just a little cream if you have it."

Indeed she did, but he held her still, breathing in deep as if he was almost still asleep. Megan watched the steam rise from the black coffee in the white mug for a moment, until she closed her own eyes and shifted her weight against him, letting him hold her.

This is what they both needed.

Seconds stretched into minutes, before he took a breath and she stepped back to open the fridge to grab the cream.

Hearing the tinkle of the spoon against her mug before passing it to him felt like the most natural thing in the world.

"Do you have to work today?"

Megan shook her head. "Tomorrow."

"Cool. Want to get breakfast? I'll need to get back to the house afterward."

More time with him? Sign her up. "That sounds great."

"Good. I don't want you to think I had planned this. I really didn't, but I keep some clothes in my truck. Can I use your shower if I go grab them?"

"Yeah, of course."

"Thanks, you go first though. I'm quick."

Megan put a piece of lettuce in Leo's tank and refreshed the water before she ducked into the shower and rinsed off. Had he not been waiting, she would've lingered as she enjoyed how relaxed she felt under the hot spray. An orgasm, shower, and coffee had done magic for her tense shoulders and back.

At first she was worried he would want to shower together. She wasn't ready for *that* yet. At least not this morning, when the main mission was getting cute for breakfast. She threw on some clean jeans and her favorite green jacket and took care with brushing her hair, letting it hang down except for a few pins holding it back from her face. To put in a little more effort, once she finished her coffee and brushed her teeth, she swiped on a little pink lipstick she had as a sample but rarely wore.

Emerging a new woman, she found her bed made neater than she had ever done. Her white and green striped duvet was taut like it had just been pressed, with the pillows fluffed and plump. Troy poked his head around the doorjamb and smiled, looking a lot more rested than he had previously. With the birds tweeting happily and the sun streaming in behind him, he looked like a literal gift from heaven.

"Hey, you look great," he said, giving her a slow up and down. Megan swore she could feel her skin shiver with his gaze.

His lopsided sexy smile was back, and he looked a lot more in control than he had last night, making her heart skip a beat.

"Thanks, I left you a fresh towel on the rack."

He gave her a smile and a wink, then shut the door. Megan stood and watched the closed door while waiting for her pulse to resume a normal rate. Now of course she was rethinking her privacy standards, because...

A low meow announced Lincoln's presence as he slunk around the door that was left open.

"You can say that again, buddy."

Megan cleaned the kitchen and sat down to check her emails, making a note of the upcoming interview with the vet school. It hadn't been that difficult to fit core college classes around her schedule earlier, when they were more general entry level, but the vet classes were very specific even in Bozeman's virtual program. Buzz had given her an ideal schedule to get what she needed in the fall, but running to and from class had been...a lot.

In fact, she had been sleeping so little in between work and labs that she had been irritable, tense, and so tired she had almost gotten in an accident when she swerved into another lane coming back from the station. Since then she had taken a semester off. It wasn't that she didn't want the job—she loved animals so much and wanted to do more with them in that field, but she just needed time. Still, taking more time away from school made her anxious and nervous. If she had gone straight through, she could've been in vet school by… Megan checked her math and groaned. She would've been one year from graduating.

She had enrolled right out of high school at Montana State University in Bozeman, but needed time off after her grandmother had passed away in her third year.

Now she was finally ready to revisit her dream, and after she had finished her four-year degree with a virtual program, was ready to apply for vet school.

"Hey, nice shower," Troy said, coming around the corner and planting a kiss right under her ear, making her giggle and sending a shiver of anticipation down her spine. He was dressed in jeans and a gray long-sleeve T-shirt that he pulled up to his elbows, which looked like a million dollars.

"Thanks. Ready to go?"

"Sure thing," he said as she shut her computer and grabbed her purse.

"Want to drive separate?"

Troy shook his head. "I can swing back around. What were you working on?"

Megan blew out a breath as she walked down the stairs with him behind her. "Grad school application for vet school. I just got an interview in a couple of weeks."

"Hey, that's great. You'll blow them away."

"Thanks. I have wanted to work with animals as long as I can remember, but it's complicated, you know? I always get nervous about interviews and if I'm saying the right thing. Plus, I'd hate to leave the fire station."

"Yeah, I get it."

If only he did. She smiled over her shoulder as he checked

the lock again, a move that made him give her a sheepish smile.

"Sometimes our lives change without our control. We just have to hang on," he said with a shrug.

Megan nodded and got in the truck when he opened the door for her. Troy leaned down and tucked her coat in the cab before shutting the door. It was such a gentle, thoughtful act that showed genuine concern.

"How about The Perfect Cup?"

"Sounds perfect," she said with a laugh, which he echoed as he reached over to hold her hand in his own before driving the short distance to one of her favorite places.

It all felt so easy, natural, and comfortable until she remembered he was leaving. The crack inside her was small, but she could feel the dark wave of disappointment sweep through her chest.

CHAPTER 25

Troy and Megan hadn't lingered at The Perfect Cup long. Neither of them was hungry, but the quiche and croissant breakfast sandwich were too good to pass up. They sat in Megan's favorite corner table while making quick work of the pastry and drinks, tea for her and coffee for him.

At one point, she wanted to ask him about the nightmare they still hadn't discussed but thought better about it. He would tell her when he was ready. He had started to open his mouth like he might say something, but then looked nervous, coughed, and started talking about the house remodel again.

She couldn't blame him. Whatever he had gone through had clearly been painful, and to have it thrust in front of someone else on a date would make her feel vulnerable enough to dive headfirst into an open grave.

Afterward, he had dropped her back at her apartment and pulled her to him for a long kiss that made her toes curl just thinking about it. Megan was no expert, but when he pulled back and looked at her through long dark lashes, she would've bet everything she had he didn't want to leave any more than she did. Of course, she had melted a little more when he winked, waved, and then texted that he missed her after driving away.

In his absence, the apartment which had been cozy now was cavernous and too quiet despite Salt and Pepper taking turns clacking their toys against the cage and ringing the bell she had gotten them.

"I know, I know. Maybe he'll come back," she said to Lincoln and Popsicle, who sat in stony silence in the kitchen.

Not wanting to dwell on his absence, Megan checked her phone to find a dozen missed texts from Ash and Laura. She answered giving them the proof of life they so desperately craved and laughed when the emojis came flying through begging for details.

Rather than text the whole thing, they arranged for a coffee date later in the afternoon that lined up with Ash's break.

With that settled, Megan spent the rest of the morning struggling to get into her normal day-off routine. Cleaning and doing laundry didn't hold the same appeal when her mind kept wandering back to the night before and the feel of Troy's hands on her. When it came time to change her sheets, she pressed her head into Troy's pillow and inhaled, letting his scent wash over her again and bringing a smile to her face. Unable to part with it yet, she left it there and stripped the rest of the bed, smiling at the unmatched pillowcase.

By the time she had done laundry and packed a few lunches for her upcoming shifts, it was time to leave. One of the nice things about living in town was that it didn't take her long to go anywhere. Today they had agreed to meet at SubZero, a no-frills sandwich shop near the police station.

Megan parked and waved to Ash who was texting on her phone.

"Laura texted while you were driving. Holden has a fever, so she's heading to pick him up from school now."

"Oh, I hope he's okay," Megan said and pulled out her phone to say just that in their group chat. "Carter must still be on his trip?"

"Yeah, he's in California for the rest of the week."

"I'll swing by later and see if they need anything," Megan said, knowing how much Laura did on her own. Before Carter was in the picture, she and Ash had always been willing to pitch in to help out like a family, which is where the friendship had really grown into a sisterhood.

While Ash came from a large family, Laura only had her mom, so the three of them had started traditions around birthdays, holidays, and other events, planning around their busy work schedules.

They each walked in and ordered. Megan wasn't too hungry so settled for a root beer and small turkey sub. She smiled to herself and wondered what Troy would have to say about it, knowing full well he would've been more impressed with Ash's concoction of artisan cheese, bread, sprouts, and all sorts of peppers.

"What are you smiling at?"

Megan tried to hide her smile but did such a poor job it only deepened at the corners of her mouth. "Nothing. Just thinking about your sandwich."

Ash gave her a peculiar look as they sat down and began to eat. "You shouldn't lie to your friend."

"Yeah, I know—sorry. You can always tell when I'm lying."

Ash didn't look up. "Yep. So what gives? You get lucky?"

Megan shook her head. Ash studied her with a raised brow.

"No, for real. He stayed over and there was a lot of kissing." She figured it was better to withhold than lie. "He's a foodie. I think you'd like him."

"I'm glad my opinion matters."

Megan looked up indignantly with an eye roll. "Are you kidding? You're an excellent judge of character."

"And have access to state databases," Ash pointed out without missing a beat.

"That's not what I mean. I just trust people more if you and Laura like them. I know I can trust you two."

"Like a council of war."

Megan laughed. "As usual you have such a way with words. Besides, if you approve, that means he's a safe bet."

Ash shrugged and wiped her mouth. "I placed Carter under arrest and I still like him, so I don't know what you make out of that, but he turned out great."

Carter Price, Laura's new husband, had gotten a DUI, trapping him in the state which was the perfect time for him and Laura to reconnect after being high school sweethearts. Now a very successful business owner with a tech start-up that went public, Carter had turned out to be a very good bet indeed, even if he had a rocky start.

"Yeah, that's true."

"So spill the deets."

Megan told her about the date at the hardware store, which made Ash roll her eyes. "He brought you on errands?"

"No, it wasn't like that; we also went out to eat. It was nice to be chill."

"Are you sure you're not just making excuses?"

"Positive. Just listen to this." Megan filled Ash in on everything they had talked about, shared, and how they had ended tangled up back in her bed.

"And?"

Megan blushed and remembered the no lying rule. "It was really nice." Until it wasn't.

Ash looked up with that peculiar look she always got when there was more to the story. "So what went wrong?"

Sure enough, Ash always knew. She was the best listener. "He had this nightmare."

As Megan laid out the story, Ash's eyes narrowed and she nodded occasionally. "He didn't get into it?"

"I don't think he wanted to."

"Given that he was deployed, it sounds like we can put the pieces together."

"Yeah, I just felt so bad for him. I wished I could fix it, you know?"

Ash nodded. "It'll take time. Maybe he should talk to someone. They do something similar at the police department whenever someone has to discharge a weapon, even if there is no injury on either party."

"That's good."

"Yeah, shit like that can take a toll on people."

"You still seeing Marj?"

"Yep. Every Wednesday. The offer stands if you ever want me to ask her for a recommendation or if she has an opening."

Megan smiled but shook her head. "You're so good at taking care of yourself."

"I have to."

"Being a firefighter isn't the same."

Ash raised an eyebrow, and Megan knew what she meant but didn't want to get into it, which was precisely why she didn't want a therapist right now. She was fine. She was good. She didn't enjoy talking about her past. Even the idea of it was exhausting.

Ash shrugged and smiled, knowing they'd had this talk before and clearly taking the hint today. "You don't want to… burn out."

"Ha ha ha. Noted."

"Tea and candles are great."

"I have you to thank for both."

"You're welcome," Ash said, nodding with a regal flair. "At least join me for yoga."

Megan groaned. "You know how I feel about gyms." She hated weights but fought through to meet the requirements for her physical fitness test. Her favorite thing was to put on some music and run. She wasn't very good at it, sweated like a pig, and had to stop to guzzle water frequently, but still it was the lesser of the evils available to her. Sitting still in the same position for sixty seconds at a clip sounded like torture. She was just too twitchy.

"Which is precisely why you should come," Ash said, slapping both hands on the table for emphasis.

"You are the most new-age cop there is."

Ash tipped her all natural fruit smoothie in a toast. "You have to take care of number one."

"And you do a great job of it."

"I have to or I'll go insane."

Ash laughed, but the truth was it was how she was raised. On a commune in California, Ash had grown up with crystal-wearing, vegetarian parents who lived off the grid on a solar powered farm, with raised garden beds and meditation practices after homeschool lessons. How they ended up with their oldest of six kids leaving to go to the police academy was beyond Megan and Laura, but it somehow worked. Ash didn't go home often but was friendly with her parents, calling home once a week and sharing a stellar tomato sauce recipe whenever she came back from a visit. Laura and Megan had been interested in visiting, but with shift work it hadn't lined up very easily, but they all hoped to get together out there one day soon.

The bitterness in Ash's voice caught Megan's attention.

"What's going on?"

"There have been two more accidents with other people like the one you and Troy found."

"Really? Any connection?"

Ash shook her head. "None that I can find yet."

"How's the man?"

"He's in the hospital now. His family and friends said they have no idea why he's acting like that."

"Bad batch?" Megan asked.

Ash shook her head. "No reported history and besides, he's clean right now. It's like he had a breakdown and it's spreading."

"But that can't be contagious."

Ash shrugged again. "It's bothering me."

"I can tell."

"People don't go from normal to crazy with no notice. Something sets them off."

"I agree."

"But I can't find the link."

"What are the other guys like?"

"Well, for starters they're all male, in their twenties and thirties."

"Okay, healthy? Employed?" Megan was familiar with quizzing Ash when she was on the hunt for answers as they liked to call it.

"Athletes. Prime of their life healthy. Employment varies, but they were involved in something that had to do with security of some kind."

"Any other cases in other localities?"

Ash shook her head. "I've put in a few calls. Nothing's popped yet."

"If there's a link, you'll find it."

Ash stared off into the distance while she turned over the case in her mind. "I'm trying. Different schools, families, socioeconomic status."

"What do you mean they all worked in security?"

"The first guy, the one you ran into—"

"You mean who almost ran into me."

"Right—until lover boy tackled him. He works as a security guard at the jewelry store."

"Okay and the others?"

"One is security officer at the local high school, and the last one is event security for when the fair comes to town."

"Oh, that is an odd mix."

"Yeah, so I don't know what to make of it, but it's bothering me."

Megan watched her and felt compelled to ask. "Do you think there will be another one?"

"I hope not. Be careful when you run calls."

"You don't have to tell me twice," Megan said with a laugh that Ash didn't return. "Is there something else going on?"

Ash's eyes had always been striking. A deep violet, like Elizabeth Taylor's, her eyes were clear, perceptive, and never seemed to miss anything. Never one for makeup, Ash's dark eyelashes naturally framed those eyes as she looked at Megan. Everything about her was natural and practical. She had short dark hair and clear, alabaster skin that was something to envy, but came with an intensity that matched her job. She chewed methodically on her sandwich, and her eyes shifted away to the table, staring at something invisible.

"So what is it?"

"I don't know if I can tell you yet."

Megan didn't get offended. She knew there were things that Ash couldn't share as part of her job. Even her anxiety didn't question that and besides, sometimes it was bliss to be ignorant. Still, she wanted more.

"Is it bad?"

Ash tilted her head to the side. "Not sure."

"Is it a today problem?"

"No. I don't think so."

"Will it change anything?"

Ash hesitated and thought for a moment, her usual clue that Megan had hit on something in their familiar game. "No, I don't think so."

"Can you do anything about it?"

Ash shook her head again, this time almost immediately.

"You always tell me that's the one to focus on."

"True. I'm glad you've been listening."

"I always do."

They chatted more about everything that had happened recently. One of Ash's siblings was going to be graduating from college to become a home economics teacher, so she was planning to take some time off for a visit back to the homestead. In other news, her parents had recently started raising goats to start a goat yoga farm and had been begging her to come home for a while.

"That sounds right up your alley."

"Yeah, we'll see. Mom saw it on Instagram and heard about it from one of her trips to the Ashram. Let me guess, now because there's animals you want in?" Ash asked.

"Maybe."

"What does lover boy think about animals?"

"He was cool with the cats and birds. I think he even said hi to Leo."

Ash smiled more and crumpled up the wrapping from her fancy-ass sandwich.

"You know, I'm glad you found him. I think he's good for you."

Megan smiled and felt her phone buzz in her pocket. Ash heard it too and nodded for her to check, laughing when she saw the name.

"Right on cue. I think he misses you."

CHAPTER 26

Troy smiled as he slid the phone in his pocket. Texting with Megan grounded him and kept him smiling as he worked to install new kitchen cabinets. It wasn't the install itself but the leveling that was going to drive him crazy. He knew he could be a perfectionist, but his dad treated that bubble in the level lines like it was the eye of God and turned perfection into an art form. It was particularly impressive considering there wasn't one plumb wall in what could be saved from the salvaged farmhouse.

Despite their pursuit of perfection, they did work together well, but that was once they got past the bickering and jabs. He smiled to himself every time his dad released a one-liner in his direction before throwing up his hands. Whatever it took to put spring back in his old man's step made him smile. It was lucky for him that they were building the house and memories at the same time. What was different this time compared to when they'd done projects together in the past was that his dad would have to go sit down out of breath after climbing the stairs to the house to check on the work.

His cellphone buzzed, flashing a familiar name from Kentucky. Troy answered with a smile.

"Hey Troy! How are ya?" Cervantez's laughing voice came through loud and clear over the phone.

"Not too bad, man. How are you doing?"

"Ha! You wish you were better than me. I'm doing well. Can't complain. Same old same old around here. How's the ranch?"

Troy eyed around him. "Getting things back in order, but it's going to be a while. Catch me up. What's going on?"

"Well, I only call when I want something."

"Figured as much." Damn, it was good to hear from his friend, so whatever the favor was, Troy was more than happy to oblige. They had two deployments together and more trainings than either wanted to think about.

"I got a call from a buddy of mine in Arlington yesterday."

"Oh shit."

"Nah, it's not that bad."

"Okay. What's up?"

"He's in the Old Guard, and one of their horses named Braxton is a real piece of work. Kicked someone again and acted up during a funeral, so he's being retired along with a few others."

"Oh damn."

"Yeah, he asked me if I knew anyone, but I just figured since they're offloading about half a dozen right now, that I'd give you a call first and see if you have some space on that big fancy farm. Apparently, Braxton's a dick, so they can't just let anyone have him."

The horses at Arlington National Cemetery were some of the most well-known and well trained. The Old Guard managed the stables, events, and the Tomb of the Unknown Soldier. Once upon a time, Troy had wanted that post, but it never had happened. Cervantez had been stationed at Fort

Belvoir nearby and befriended a few. Like any animal after army service, when they aged out they were put up for adoption after a rigorous vetting process.

"You'd still need to fill out the forms and whatnot, but you know we'd all rather them go to one of our own."

Troy had the space and the barn. Dad didn't have any farmhands, but that could be fixed with an ad in the paper. "Consider it done."

"Awesome. I'll send over the required paperwork and everything. Who knows, maybe I can even swing a bit of a road trip and see this place you talk so much about."

Troy's smile widened even further. "That'd be great."

"Perfect. Talk soon."

Troy looked at the phone with a small smile. He skimmed the emails from Cervantez and made quick work of the forms before starting a list of things to consider for the horses' care. Another hand and pair of eyes would come in handy for when he wasn't around. With that thought in his mind, he drummed the pencil on the notepad until a pang from his stomach drew his thoughts away from feed and trough heaters.

Troy stood and put away his tools for the night before checking his phone again for a reply from Megan, frowning a little when there wasn't any. He drove the short distance to the house, waved to his dad who was already in his chair, and pulled open the fridge to be blinded by the white light and vacant shelves.

"Alrighty, shopping it is."

"Whaddya say?"

"I'm going to the store to get some food. Want anything?"

"Get whatever you want, except for oatmeal."

"It's good for your heart."

"Fine, then get bacon too."

Smiling to himself, Troy pulled on his jacket and grabbed his keys, locking the door and checking it twice.

He made it to town after listening to a shuffled playlist that ranged from classic rock to nineties hip-hop, and ended with Bachata. Vibing, Troy grabbed a shopping cart from the corral before heading inside, thinking of everything from horses, to the house, his dad, and Megan.

He wondered what she was doing and checked his phone again, trying not to be worried that she hadn't texted. It wasn't unusual for her to be focused on work. Maybe she was in a meeting, but the feeling tugged on him and he couldn't place his finger on it when a familiar voice called out his name from the top of the aisle.

"Troy? Is that you?"

Keira McKinney with her familiar laugh came over and opened her arms for a hug, which he easily returned.

She was short, coming in well below five feet, which is why she had always called herself fun-sized as a joke back in high school. She had brown eyes and curly long hair, just like before, and the same bubbliness that always meant she was giggling in class. Despite that, every teacher loved her because she just lit up the room. They had dated for a few months when they both took multicultural literature, which she excelled in, coming alive with every passage. Honestly he would've been interested in continuing to see her, but she was deeply religious and wanted to get married and be a ranch wife. Troy had been seventeen at the time and wanted more out of life. Still, whenever he thought of her, he smiled.

"Oh my God, I haven't seen you in how long? Geez, it must be years now. Where are you? How have you been?"

"Good, yeah, I'm in Kentucky now."

"Wow. I tried to follow online how many times you've moved."

Troy smiled and scratched the back of his neck. "Yeah, it's

a lot, but you know, that's the army for you. How have you been?"

"Good. The kids are driving me crazy."

"Yeah, three boys under five. I don't know how you do it."

She blew out a breath, and when she let her smile falter, he could see the lines and weariness etched in her face. "I don't know either. They drive me nuts, so today I came to the grocery store by myself. I feel like I'm in heaven it's so quiet and peaceful."

She sighed, then continued. "So what brings you back to Goldvein?"

"Dad's ranch burned, so I'm here to help him rebuild and recover."

"Is he listening to you?"

"For the most part."

"That's impressive."

"You remember."

A warm glow hit her cheeks, bringing out the warm brown of her eyes like a deep honey color. To this day, whenever he heard "Brown Eyed Girl," he always thought of her. Some songs just stuck with people, playing on repeat in the mind on the mixtape of life.

"I do. Are you in town for a while?"

"I have a few more weeks of leave before I need to go back."

"Maybe we'll bump into each other again," she said with a smile.

"Yeah, that'd be nice. It was great to see you. I loved catching up."

Keira didn't hesitate with the hug which brought back so many good memories. She waved a few fingers in goodbye and walked back over to an overflowing cart filled with cookies, chips, cereal, and family-sized packs of meat, fruit, and veggies.

Troy watched her go and waited for a feeling. His therapist had coached him to see the feelings, not fear them or tamp them down but instead wait and observe. He expected to feel longing or sadness but was pleasantly surprised when all he felt was the appreciation for a warm memory of young love.

CHAPTER 27

M egan opened the door after what was an extremely long day at work to a very welcome face she had been missing. "Hello there," she said with a coy smile of anticipation.

"Hello, you're a sight for sore eyes," Troy said, leaning in for a kiss that melted her on the spot. "You look so cozy."

"Thank you. It's part of my postwork ritual."

"I love it."

She had showered the second she got home and thrown on her good robe. Part of her felt like dressing up when he had texted asking if she was finally off her shift and open to company, but the other devious part of her thought he might like seeing just her robe.

Of course when she had said as much, Troy very much affirmed her decision by requesting her to keep it on until he rushed over.

He stepped inside and greeted the cats who each walked to give rubs and head butts of affection to Troy's legs. "I missed you. How was work?" He walked in the kitchen and put a bag from The Perfect Cup on the counter.

"It was okay. One call. Laura wasn't working so I missed her. Mainly just worked out and helped Buzz get ready for some programs we're doing this summer."

"I brought huckleberry muffins."

Megan took a big sniff from the bag and exhaled in bliss. "Am I that easy to read?"

Troy took her by the hips and propped her against the counter, kissing her fully on the mouth, exploring, tasting, and looking for more. Knowing exactly what she needed, he trailed kisses down her chin and up toward her ear, making her giggle with delight, before making her burn with want when he hit that spot on her neck that melted her legs into jelly.

"So soft and warm," he murmured into her neck, the vibrations of his deep voice making the sensation that much stronger.

His hands ran up her back, sending thrills of excitement with them as they traveled, and he cupped her face while he planted kisses all over her including on her forehead, leaving his lips there for a few pounding heartbeats.

"What do you want to do?" he asked with his lips still on her head. He had asked before while they were texting.

"I want more of what we did last time. I loved it."

He pulled back and searched her eyes. His brown eyes were darker in the middle, but faded to a rich warmth that had flecks of gray around the outer edge.

"Are you sure?"

"Yes."

"You let me know if you want me to stop."

"I won't want you to."

"If you do."

"I appreciate that."

He leaned in for a kiss, and she met him willingly, giving so much of herself, wrapping her arms around his shoulders and lifting herself up on her tiptoes to reach more of him.

Troy's cologne enveloped her with the familiar sense of belonging she had loved before. She breathed in deeply while he went back to her neck, grounding herself in this moment with him and the smell of his hair and the feel of his slight stubble on her sensitive skin.

He slipped his arms down her shoulders and inside her robe, cupping her bare shoulders with his hands. The touch of him on her smooth skin sent a shiver over her body, and she knew it wasn't from the room temperature even though she was completely exposed.

He pulled back with a little line in between the eyebrows. "Are you cold out here?"

"Not really," she said, surprised he noticed, as another shiver of anticipation fluttered over her.

"Ready for bed?" he asked, his voice full of concern. "I don't want you cold."

The heat her body was giving off with his hands on her skin was enough to make her burst into flames on the kitchen floor.

"Let's go. I don't want an audience."

Troy smiled and glanced down to see Lincoln looking up at them with a bored, unimpressed expression.

She led him into the bedroom, taking care to close the door behind them for privacy, and started to move toward the light and candle when she remembered what happened last time and stopped short.

"Turn it off." Troy's voice was low and right next to her ear.

She clicked the switch on the multicolored lamp and plunged them into darkness. It was a full moon, so the moonlight pooled on the floor, illuminating the shadow of the windowpanes, giving just enough light for her to see the silhouette of the man in front of her walking forward, slow and deliberate.

With a tug, he pulled down the short zipper at his neck, pulled it over his head, and tossed it somewhere in the dark. His belt made a slight rattling and clattered gently to the floor in a rush of heavy denim.

Megan felt his arms come around from behind her, rubbing her arms before snaking their way to the bun she had thrown her hair into when she was in the shower. With quick work from his hands, her hair tumbled down in a mass of curls. His fingers teased the tendrils apart with a gentle touch before he ran his hands through it, giving her another shiver. Still behind her, he gathered it up in one hand and placed it in front of her shoulder, taking care to run soft kisses where her neck met her shoulder.

Megan felt her knees go weak from him knowing that one spot could drive her wild, and she blew out a breath of satisfaction through her lips as he ran his mouth on the column of her neck.

His hands rubbed the knots in her shoulders, kneading away tension, a touch she hadn't expected which made her want to melt into him more. As if he read her mind, he stepped closer, ready to brace against her weight.

He pushed the fabric of her robe to the side, sliding it down her arms, again exposing her skin to the chill of the room, giving her goosebumps with every inch.

"Chilly?" he said, behind her ear.

She made a noise in her throat that she hoped he knew was a no and almost levitated when he ran his hands over her exposed breasts, much to his amusement.

"Jumpy or excited?"

"Excited."

He laughed low and quiet and nipped at her shoulder from behind her.

Megan leaned back against him, resting her head on his shoulder and closing her eyes in bliss, content to let his hands work her into a frenzy and for his shoulder to hold her up.

The sensations of him all over her skin made her head spin and her knees buckle with desire, and of course, he was ready to catch her.

Megan slipped the knot free on her robe, letting it fall to the floor, then stood before him in the pale moonlight.

A wave of chilled air rushed over her body, and she tried to fight the feelings of embarrassment that bubbled up.

In the dark, she could see Troy's head sweep slowly down her naked body, taking it all in. With every inch, she could feel his gaze on her.

"You're breathtaking."

Megan smiled and felt her cheeks warm with pleasure. She wished she could see more of him in detail in the dark, but as he was backlit by the window, all she could see was the outline of his powerful frame. Just the muscles around his shoulders made her ache to know more.

"I want to see you too."

She stretched out her fingers to run them across his shoulders, and he caught them, pressing them to his lips. Holding both her hands, he steered her to sit on the bed and somehow eased her back while sliding next to her, pressing kisses to her lips, collarbone, and working his way down to her breasts.

When his mouth reached his targeted destination, Megan's eyes snapped open and her back arched to meet him.

His low laugh vibrated across her skin while his mouth and hand worked her into a frenzy of want. Megan let out a gasp followed by a small moan when his hand circled lower, parting her and pressing one finger exactly where she needed him.

He worked her like that, alternating the tapping and rubbing, before exploring deeper inside, making her oscillate between it being too much and being desperate for more. Somehow Troy knew her body and adjusted right before she lost her mind, giving her exactly what she needed.

It didn't take long for her to be panting in rhythm with him—every muscle in her body tense and wanting more—and when Troy drove her over, it sent thrills of pleasure through her body.

He propped himself up on his elbow and watched her recover, running his hand gently around the curve of her hip, warming her with his body.

When her breathing resumed a normal rate, Megan leaned up and pressed her lips to his, kissing him and wrapping her hand around his neck. She wasn't fully satisfied and had never wanted anything more in her entire life.

Her hands raked down his chest, exploring an odd texture, raised from the skin in no pattern.

Troy moved her hands off and shifted away so he was lying partially on top of her, taking care to prop himself up with his elbows on either side of her. He was so gentle, but she burned. What he had given her so far was only enough to stoke her appetite for exploration.

Troy pulled back from her hungry kisses, and she smiled when she heard his own breathing was ragged and labored.

"What do you want?"

On an exhale that sounded more confident than she had known, Megan cupped his cheek in her hand and smiled. "You. All of you."

He didn't hesitate. Troy dove back into kissing her, his hands roaming her body like a starving man desperate for food. She felt the weight of his erection against her but needed it closer, ached for him to be inside her.

Megan reached down and stroked him once. She had no idea what she was doing but grinned when he groaned somewhere between pleasure and pain.

He planted a hard kiss on her, pressing her into the bed, and rolled off to grab his jeans.

God bless the moon, because she could see his silhouette. *All* of him.

Megan heard a wrapper and shifted herself onto the pillows with her elbows propped up. Troy maneuvered the condom on and crawled toward her on the bed, kissing the soles of her feet as he spread them apart.

"God, you're so beautiful."

He pushed her legs apart with a nudge, and Megan spread them, feeling excited and vulnerable at the same time. Troy straightened up onto his knees and looked down at her.

It was only then that Megan realized the moon was on her like a spotlight.

He ran his hands along the sides of her body down from her breasts to her ankles, before bending down to kiss the inside of her leg, lifting it to his mouth, trailing kisses up toward where she wanted him to be.

An eternity passed, and Megan let her head fall back into the pillows as she tracked his kisses in her mind, getting closer an inch at a time, making her wallow in anticipation.

There was no mistaking when he arrived. Just seeing his head dip in the dim light made her toes curl, but when his tongue touched her most sensitive area, every nerve in her body lit up with attention.

He was tender, but he was determined and pleasured her until her head swiveled on the pillows and her legs stretched out on their own, wanting more from him and overwhelmed by everything that wicked tongue did.

She clawed into his thick dark hair and held on tight as he took her to new heights, sending waves of pleasure through her body. He sent her higher and higher before stopping just before she crossed over the edge again and looked up with those dark eyes that looked like the blackest night. His eyes bored into her own, and the message was clear.

Megan let out a "please" that sounded like a moan and felt her arms stretch toward him in invitation.

Troy propped up and came closer, positioning himself over her and lining up where she wanted him most. Megan was panting with need and drenched with want.

"Troy, please…"

He pressed in, filling and stretching, taking his time to let her accommodate.

The sensation was new, and she wrapped her arms around his shoulders as he filled her completely. She expected it to hurt, but this was what she had wanted so badly. She no longer felt empty and wanting.

She let out an exhale of relief that matched his own and felt him start to thrust inside her. At first he was slow and gentle, but then he sped up and the thrusts became more powerful. All the while he watched her, kissed her, and took the time to nibble the spot on her neck that drove her crazy.

The depth of wanting more drove them both as they clung to each other, her gripping his hips, driving him as he pistoned up and down faster and harder, hitting a spot that sent waves of building pleasure through her body. A rising tide that she couldn't control brought her higher and higher. Every muscle in her body tensed so hard she thought she could break before the wave of pleasure crested her defense, and she collapsed back onto the bed in complete bliss and relaxation. With a final pulse, Troy was right behind her, and they tumbled into the darkness in each other's arms.

CHAPTER 28

"Welp, that'll do it," the driver said as he offloaded the last of the horses. The six animals were beautiful and strong with clean coats, perfectly fitted for the services at Arlington. As Cervantez had promised, Braxton was a complete ass already, tossing his head around his stall and snorting up a storm, but the rest had the air of military discipline that Troy appreciated.

"Thanks again for bringing them all the way." He shook the hand of the drivers from the equine transport company. The journey from Virginia all the way out here had taken several days with enough stops to ensure the animals' comfort, but everything was done to perfection, and he was satisfied.

"Sure thing. Give us a call if you ever take on more."

Troy nodded and waved to the driver as he cranked the semi's diesel engine.

"They did a good job. Weight looks good and no scratches in the coats," his dad said, walking up with Levi beside him to wave to them as well. Still a rancher at heart, he had come down to inspect the new livestock with a critical eye after a damn near transcontinental transport.

"Yeah, I was worried."

His dad shrugged it off as if he hadn't been pacing all day yesterday jingling the change in his pocket with a nervous energy. "Racehorses do it all the time, but normally they have someone travel with them."

Troy nodded and listened while his dad went on about the price of hay and alfalfa, and which vet in town was worth a damn these days because all of the good ones had retired, of course. It was good to see him this animated. His dad had been working in the barn for over a week since Troy had shared the news that it would be occupied again. Light duty, but still it was good for his mind, body, and soul. Even though the horses were retired and would amass the steep vet bills of aging animals, his dad had a spring in his step and had personally replaced three of the stall doors and hinges prior to the arrival.

The barn was old but in good condition. A wood structure with a metal roof, the newest feature was a trough heater from the seventies that kept the water from freezing in the dead of winter. The tack room had been a total disaster, but his dad had taken his time and brought everything outside, going through what was salvageable and what needed to go before sweeping the whole thing out. The last cowboys had been good, hard workers but as the bills crept up and the stock dwindled, they got overwhelmed by the work and things fell through the cracks and into disrepair.

His dad would never say, but it must have been a certain kind of hell to watch something you love decay. Especially when you knew what needed to be done but didn't have the resources to make it happen. It was all too much for one person.

The new arrivals had put a purpose back into his step,

and while his recovery was going to take a little longer, and tasks took a bit more time than they had in the past, the work was being done and being done right.

Even now, he went again and inspected his work with a broom in his hand to make everything as tidy as possible, while Levi walked alongside him and sat in front of the first stall. A big bay's head came down and eyed Levi, who leaned up against the door, lifted a paw, and panted with his classic golden retriever smile.

"Down, Levi," his dad said, and Levi dropped like a stone to his butt, yellow fluffy tail sweeping the floor with restrained joy.

"We're going to need to add an extra bolt on Braxton's door. He's a kicker."

Troy eyed the beautiful black horse, who was big at seventeen hands, unsettled and looking like he was ready for a fight, snorting and pawing at the ground.

"Yeah, Cervantez said as much." He had sent the records over early so they knew what they were getting into and could prepare. Only one was on a prescription and all had seen a farrier recently, thank God. That would save some money in the short term. Of course coming from the Old Guard, they were groomed to perfection and had the healthiest shiny coats.

"He wants to run. It's too cold to turn them out tonight, but tomorrow morning we'll take them to the east paddock. Young grass is coming up there, and the fence is strong."

"Sounds like a plan. I'm going to bring Megan out to see them too."

"Good, she'll love that. Get her to stay for lunch. Levi misses her."

Troy smiled, knowing full well it wasn't just Levi who felt that way.

Troy watched as Megan held out her hand, palm up, enticing one of the big bays to come forward and take the apple. The joy on her face was palpable and contagious.

He couldn't help but grin as her own face split into a wide smile of complete joy as the horse ate and offered the side of his neck for scratches. Megan was happy to oblige, murmuring sweet words of complete adoration to the animal, so much so that Troy would've been jealous had he not gotten the same attention for the past several nights.

It was easy to see what attracted her to being a vet. Her touch was comforting and gentle, while her eyes assessed everything with a curious and intent nature. All of it was natural and compassionate. He could feel the true empathy she had for this animal. Watching them both like this, they were kindred spirits, sharing something secret he wasn't privy to. Underneath it all, Troy had the strange sensation of isolation. As if Megan had secret sorrows she shared with these animals who understood and offered her a solace no one else could.

There was something about her that relaxed when she

was with animals. Her shoulders uncoiled. Her breath eased. Without the weight of tension and anxiety, her neck extended and her demeanor was less guarded and afraid. She hadn't stuttered once around them, and it hadn't taken him long to realize it was worse with stress. But here in the barn, her entire disposition had changed. Troy flattered himself to think that she had relaxed around him, but that was nothing compared to watching her bloom when she was around the horses.

She stood straighter, brighter, more confident, and at peace. The barn was still cold this early in the day, but the morning sun was strong and glinting through a space between the boards. In the light, he could see the variations of her hair with the red and gold curls moving with a life of their own, highlighted not with ornaments or styling, but flecks of hay that had been drawn to her.

She checked each animal, speaking to them as if she was a gentle nurse speaking to a young child at the doctor as she got acquainted and checked them over personally before turning them out into the fenced paddock.

He stepped forward on instinct as she approached the last one.

"Watch him. He's the one I was telling you about."

"Braxton? I hear you have a lot of personality," she said as she walked up to the door. The black mane shone in the light as he came toward her with an indignant head toss looking down from his height, assessing her.

Megan stood still, letting him look. After a while she spoke, slowly, deliberately, never moving or flinching under his annoyed jerks and impatient snorts. Little by little, they waned until Braxton brought his nose down to sniff her, looking for treats. Finding what he wanted, he stilled and allowed her to pet him with a very watchful eye.

"There you go. You're just a big, strong guy, aren't you?

Let's get you out with your friends. I can tell you don't want to be away from them. Oh, there's two bolts. You are strong, aren't you then?"

"Dad insisted. He was already testing the strength of the door and starting to kick."

"Gotcha. Welp, let's get you out of here," she said, throwing the other latch and letting him trot out toward the others. Megan clapped her hands together to get the hay off before shoving them in the pockets of her barn jacket. With an arrogant toss of his head, Braxton was off like a shot to meet his counterparts in the paddock, leaving the two of them alone with the rest of Megan's day off ahead of them.

"They're beautiful. I can see why you wanted to take them. Especially with the military connection."

"I didn't appreciate them until I wasn't around them. It feels good to be back to that."

"Like you were missing a part of you?"

"Exactly." Troy smiled and shoved his hands in his pockets to match her stance. "You're really good with animals."

Megan shrugged. "I'm not the best with people. And before you say otherwise, I went through a long time where I had a hard time connecting. Sometimes I still do. I have to think about it."

"Well, you're a natural with them."

"They're good listeners. I just try to listen back."

Troy watched her gentleness as she folded back into herself with his praise, unsure of what to say or how to act. Her shyness was still there along with her stutter—a part of her but one she had worked to hide from the world.

Since there were no more treats, the horses ambled off to graze as the morning sun crested over the mountains. The view was peaceful but far more beautiful with Megan in it. As the sun hit her hair, bringing out all of the different colors as it moved on the breeze almost with a life of its own, his breath caught in his chest at how in this moment, for once he had no thought of the past or the future. All he needed was to stay here in the present and appreciate the beauty around him.

A rumbling of a distant truck broke the soft birdsong.

"Looks like the flooring is here," Megan said, turning to him with a smile.

"Good, I was hoping to get your opinion."

"Did you go with the one I liked?"

"Sure did, so all of the credit and all of the blame is yours."

"Oh God," she said as she laughed. "I hope I didn't disappoint. I can't wait to see it."

"Do you have any other plans for today?"

Troy smiled when Megan shook her head.

"Good, because I didn't order installation, so I may need an extra hand."

"Seriously?"

"You don't have to if you don't want to, but seeing as you did pick it out—Ow!" he said in mock pain when she smacked his arm with a grin.

"The only experience I have with flooring is walking on one."

"You're hired," he said and grinned when she laughed again.

Two hours later, Troy was on his knees trying not to bash his thumb again like he had several times each time he got distracted by Megan bending over. The floor was easy enough once they got going and sorted through all of the directions. Since it was a laminate, it was going to float over the vapor barrier without any glue or thin-set.

Megan had proven to be a huge help and a quick study. Once they had centered the room with the chalk line and got the first few pieces together, they had made quick work and had most of the center of the room finished. The progress would slow down when they needed to cut the edges, but still it felt good to see the project coming together.

"I told you it would look good," Megan had said with a smile when they laid out the first few pieces, and she hadn't been wrong. It was just the right shade with the right amount of grain to show off the history of the house while keeping the space fresh.

After a full morning, it was early afternoon by the time the floor was in, and Megan was starting to sweep up after all of the cuts were made. Troy dusted off his hands before he walked back in.

"That's the last of the trash."

"Perfect. Let me just finish up here with this dustpan. You got the other trashcan?"

"Right here." He brought it over and helped her make quick work of the last of the dust from their cuts before they stood back to admire their work.

"It really does look incredible."

The sun came streaming in through the new windows, bouncing off the fresh coat of paint, letting the floor shine. But none of that was what captured his attention.

He shifted until he was behind her, cupping her hair and tucking it out of the way around her shoulders before he began to knead the knots that were forming in her strong back.

Megan let out a sound that nearly undid him. She pressed herself back against him, letting him take some of her weight.

The side of her neck, exposed without her hair, invited him to leave a trail of kisses up and down the smooth column of her perfect skin.

It wasn't long before his hands moved to her arms, stomach, and other places.

"There aren't any curtains, you know," Megan whispered after a few minutes, breaking away from their kiss.

"Isn't it exciting? Besides, I like the look of you in the house. In my house."

Megan smiled and edged down against him more, rubbing into an area that sent an electric shock of desire through him. Her smile was an invitation that he gladly accepted.

A hell of a quickie later, she laid her head on his shirt, with her red hair over him like the softest blanket he could ever know. He almost wished he had taken off his shirt—he'd somehow avoided that every night they'd spent together so far—but he wasn't ready for that yet.

His phone buzzed over in the corner where he had thrown it when things had started to heat up. Hopefully it wasn't broken, but in the moment, a cracked screen was very far down the priority list.

"You should probably get that," Megan said, not moving an inch on his chest. Her breath had slowed from the panting, as she melted into him.

"All I need to do right now is stay with you right here on this floor."

"Your dad could come by any minute."

"Yep, he sure could."

Neither of them moved. Megan took a big breath in, like she was getting an idea, so Troy brought his hand to her back and kept stroking it, stilling her from moving away.

The sun streamed in through the windows with the passing of the day. Even though he was flat on his back on the new floor they had just broken in, he was more comfortable than he had been in years. He could only see the top of her head, but somehow knew her eyes were closed and at peace with her breathing. He kept stroking her back, memorizing her hair and the variations in the colors. One curl danced with every breath he took, proving every inch of her was vital, real, and filled with joy. Troy soaked up every perfect moment, committing it all to a memory he would cherish forever.

The buzz of the phone interrupted him again.

Megan pulled up again, and this time he let her.

"Next time I'm not throwing it that far, so I can end every call that comes through."

Megan laughed. "Next time?" she asked with a raised eyebrow over her bright blue eyes.

He pulled her down for a kiss and then stood and grabbed the phone to see who in the hell was calling.

"Oh, that makes sense." Shit. He had totally forgotten about the antique guy.

"What's wrong?"

"Nothing, it's fine. I just forgot I had scheduled a time to go check out an antique tub and a few doors from this guy that does salvage work from old houses. Want to come ride over?"

"I'd love to, but I have to meet Ash and Laura later."

"We could drive separately. I'd like you to see what kind of stuff he's got. Maybe you could even help me pick a few things out, since you've helped with everything else."

Megan brightened and straightened her shirt which was now sadly back in place. "Yeah, sounds good. Where is it?"

Troy rattled off the address, and Megan shifted. "I'm not the best with directions, and I'm out of data on my phone so I can't do GPS now."

"I'll make a mental note not to text you so many pictures and FaceTime so much," Troy said with a smile while she blushed.

"No, it's fine, I just need to adjust my plan. I'm not used to this."

Troy gazed at her while a slow smile grew across his face. "I love that about you."

Megan blushed some more and looked down.

"I could follow you, but you should know I get really nervous about that sort of thing."

"How do you mean?"

"I just get worried if I can't follow exactly or a car gets cut off. I'm also super bad with directions." She started to shift from one foot to the other and twist her hands in front of her, already clearly agitated at the idea.

"They don't let you drive the firetruck, do they?" Troy joked, hoping to lighten the mood and put her back on firmer footing.

"Oh God, no, I'd be terrible. The engineer does that. They're in charge of the drive and everything that has to do with the truck. I go in."

Horrible memories popped into his head at that, but he pushed them to the edge of his mind and focused on her. He might have put her at ease, but the image of her running into a fire did not relax him at all.

"Gotcha. Look, I'll give you the address and here, you can track my phone. I know you're out of data, but this way if you lose me, you can find my location right here in the app. Does that make you feel a little better?"

Megan smiled and watched him type it in. "Yeah, actually. That helps a lot. You're okay with this though?"

Troy waved a hand through the air. "You can follow me wherever. I mean, I'm mostly here, so it won't be interesting. I'll try to go to the grocery store more often to spice things up for you."

Megan smiled again and put the phone back in her pocket.

"Let's roll."

CHAPTER 30

Three hours later, Megan pulled into the driveway down at Laura's house for dinner and parked behind Ash's cruiser. The antique store had been exactly what she had expected—a dusty warehouse full of nooks and crannies with stacks of treasures, loosely categorized. The owner was an older retiree named Mac who was versed in local history and accompanied by a golden retriever named Lucy. The pair of them delicately wound through the narrow paths toward the back warehouse.

Megan had never been one for antiquing but had marveled at all of the trinkets, eyeing the perfume bottles and music boxes carefully in hopes of finding a match to the one she had, to no avail. It was easy to see what someone would love about it. The scent of once-loved books on the shelf, mixed with wool of old military uniforms, with notes of silver polish—it was like walking into a memory you had long forgotten and had suddenly recalled from deep storage.

Troy had bought several doorknobs, placed a hold on a bathtub, and even had checked out a few pieces of furniture. It had been another day of shopping with him, which was easy and natural. Troy asked her about everything he looked at and listened with interest to what she had to say. If she stopped to admire something, he stopped and listened to her memory. She returned the favor when they reached a stack of World War II war bond posters. She knew how much he liked history, but hadn't realized how much he had studied.

It had been interesting, lighthearted, and fun. With a kiss goodnight, he had shut her door and waved her off as she headed to Laura's, thinking of him for the whole drive.

She knocked on the door, which swung open immediately.

"Hey, there you are! We were about to call you."

"Sorry, am I that late?"

"For me? No. For you? Yes. Come on in. We'll be ready in about ten minutes. Ash is in the dining room."

Megan walked in carrying the two-liters she had stashed in her car earlier, and put them in the fridge for later. Carter glanced up and waved from the kitchen stove, while Holden bounced around showing her all of his latest toys. Eager to see, Megan admired each one before he ran up to his room for the next round of show and tell.

Ash waved her over next to the empty chair in the dining room. She smiled but looked tired and more rundown than usual.

Typically, Ash was the calm, serene one who managed her body through a series of supplements, green juices, and fitness classes, but today, dark circles were under her eyes. If Megan hadn't known her, she wouldn't have thought twice, but immediately she was on guard.

"What's wrong?" she asked when Laura left to check on Carter and the food.

"I'm great; thanks for asking."

"Sorry. I forgot that part. You just look—"

"Like hell?"

"No, like you've been working overtime and then some."

Ash shook her head and took a drink of some sort of bottled juice Megan didn't know. Judging from the green color, she never would.

"Yeah, it's just these cases of weird attacks. None of it makes sense, and I'm trying to figure out the link."

Megan reached across the table and held her friend's hand. "You're doing a great job."

Ash wasn't one for too much emotion, but she looked up and smiled before closing her eyes in what appeared to be relief. "I did get one thread to pull on, but it's not getting me anywhere yet."

"How come?"

"One of the guys was on something. His mom had told me he had appointments, but she didn't know where. I poked around his house as much as I could and didn't find anything until there was an empty blister pack in the trashcan. It was unmarked, except for the company, which I thought was odd."

"If it's the one I saw, he definitely was using," Megan said.

"Yeah, but this company is legit. It was built about an hour from here."

"Can't you just ask him? He's still in custody, right?"

"That's the weird part. He has no memory of this."

"He's probably lying."

Ash leveled a gaze at her and shook her head. "He's not."

"Are you sure?"

"Yeah, I can't get into how I know. I just do."

"Gotcha."

"So yeah. All I have is a random blister pack from Borealis Pharmaceuticals. Couldn't even tell you what they look like."

"No medical records?"

"They don't mention it at all."

"What about calling the company?"

"They have been…less than helpful."

Megan frowned. "But if you have a warrant?"

Ash started to answer when a firetruck siren overtook the room as Holden came running back in to show her. Given who his mom and aunties were, they had fostered his love of all EMS vehicles and even knew the proper names for each.

"Alright, who's hungry?" asked Carter, walking in holding a platter of baked ziti in one hand and a basket of garlic bread in the other.

They all dished out their food and were eating in no time, while Holden dominated the conversation about his friend's birthday party, which had included a lizard show at the playground.

Megan kept stealing glances over at Ash, who had perked up with some good food and Holden's story. Whatever was going on, she had no doubt Ash would do whatever she needed to do to get to the bottom of it.

"So how's your cowboy?" Carter asked.

Laura choked on her ginger ale and went into a coughing fit, which saved Megan and her flaming pink cheeks a little embarrassment.

"You have a cowboy too? *Toy Story* is my FAVORITE," said Holden, while Laura was still gasping for air in between coughs, with Carter patting her on the back.

"Sorry, I told…him…not to…ask," Laura said in between coughs.

Ash looked like she was holding back a laugh, while studying Megan's response.

"Um, I don't know if he's mine exactly, but Troy's great. He's rebuilding his family's ranch. I went with him to pick out some stuff and met the new horses. They're retired from Arlington, and he's keeping them in his barn."

"It sounds like you guys are spending a lot of time

together. What? That's a good thing!" Carter added when Laura gave him a look.

"Yeah, maybe a little."

In the past, she would've wanted to dive into her ziti and never come out, but something was different. She allowed herself to smile a little as Troy came to mind. There was nothing wrong, nothing to be ashamed of, and now that he was on her mind, she kind of wished he was sitting right next to her.

"I can't wait for you guys to meet him—Troy."

"You do look happy," Laura added with a smile.

"Thanks," she said with a shrug.

"So he's not Woody?" Holden asked with the wind taken out of his sails.

"No, and I don't think he has a snake in his boot either, but I like him anyway."

With that he shrugged, clearly questioning her taste, and went back to eating.

The rest of the dinner passed with a lot of laughs, talking about old calls and characters they had run into.

They took a break to clear the table and get ready for the board game when Holden started rubbing his eyes. Laura and Carter stepped away to put him to bed, while she and Ash set up Clue.

"We haven't played Monopoly in ages," Ash said, looking at the discarded box.

"You know it takes forever."

"Yeah, I guess. It's still my favorite."

"I guess it makes sense that after a day of investigation, you're not digging the candlestick with Colonel Mustard."

Ash smiled and dropped the envelope in the center of the board. "Maybe. I do still love it, but I like being a slumlord more. No mysteries. Everything's out in the open in Monopoly."

"Still thinking about work?"

"It's impossible for me not to."

"I know it's hard, but maybe you need a day off or a fresh angle."

"Yeah, maybe that's it. I'll keep plugging away tomorrow."

"Alright, ladies, you are going down," Laura said, coming back downstairs with an eager grin.

Ash's mask was back in place. With a determined edge in her smile, she grabbed her pencil, ready to make notes. "Bring it on."

Two days later, the sound of the whisk beating the eggs against the bowl was music to Troy's ears. It had been another great night with Megan and an even better morning when he had woken up next to her.

Instead of some glib remark about leaving, today he wanted to take his time making her breakfast and treating her to something special, so omelets were on the menu, along with bacon in the skillet and her favorite huckleberry muffins that were warming in the oven.

He had planted a kiss on her neck when she was making the coffee in her robe, right in that spot she loved, then set to work, making himself at home in the kitchen. Even the birds were chirping happily away.

It all felt so normal, from the eclectic styling of her apartment to the sounds of breakfast cooking with the TV on in the background. He had never really lingered long enough to cook breakfast for someone, and he loved the familiarity.

The scuffing of her slippers announced her arrival in the kitchen after making the bed and taking a quick shower. Her skin was pink from the shower, and her red hair was thrown up into some sort of bun but was wet at the edge of her neck. He hadn't lied when he said how much of a knockout she was, but seeing her in leggings and an oversized stretched-out Henley brought new meaning to the word cute.

God, that sleepy smile undid him.

"Breakfast is almost ready."

"It smells delicious. I'll set the table."

The sounds of the bacon sizzling mixing with a clang of silverware brought him back to being in Mom's kitchen as a child. The smells and feel of the cast iron in his hand invoked a muscle memory that filled him with joy. He finished his own omelet, which was not as good as the ones his mom had made, and set it to rest under a plate as a cover, before putting the bacon on a paper towel to drain.

Now warmed up, Troy poured the eggs into the hot pan for Megan. He ran the spatula around the outside edge of the pan when the eggs had firmed enough and sprinkled in the cooked peppers and onions before adding the cheese and folding the eggs around everything. With a flick of the wrist he slid it out onto the plate. He plated everything and brought the dishes over to the table. Megan sat with one leg tucked under and was checking her email on her phone, looking cozy and cuddly.

"Breakfast is served," he said, placing it down in front of her with a flourish.

Megan looked up, and he closed the gap to kiss her on the lips before sitting down to eat.

The news came back on the TV, and the reporter looked grim. "A local woman is recovering in the hospital in stable condition after being attacked on a run in Dury Park last night, and police are asking for your help. Keira McKinney, a thirty-year-old mom, went for a run yesterday afternoon, but never returned home."

"Oh my God!" The sound of Troy's chair hitting the floor made him realize he had jumped up.

"You know her?" Megan asked, leaning forward to see if there was more to the story.

His mouth went dry, and a wave of heat flooded over him as the blood pounded in his ears. "We used to date in high school. I bumped into her about a week and a half ago at the store."

The TV cut to a park scene, which looked like an empty path. "Keira McKinney's family noticed something was wrong when the mom of three did not return from her evening run. After two hours with no word, the woman's husband, Steve McKinney, dropped their children at his mother's house and drove to the park using the location services he had enabled on her phone. It was then he found her unconscious in a dry creek bed in the woods."

Troy wanted to act. To do something. His hands itched to grab his phone and try to contact her, but he didn't have her number or any business reaching out to her. He had just seen her. How could this happen?

"Troy?"

His head snapped in Megan's direction, and he tried to use the expression on her face to judge how long he had been standing.

"Are you okay?"

No. He was not okay. He was anything but okay. Keira McKinney was one of the kindest, sweetest people with the best heart. She was a mother, a wife, a daughter, and she was fucking attacked.

The newscaster continued. "McKinney called 911, and first responders transported her to the hospital for treatment for her injuries. Police noted her wallet, jewelry, and headphones were all taken from the scene in what appears to be a robbery. They believe no technology was taken due to the tracking ability. As of our last update, police are asking anyone in the community with information to come forward."

Images of terrible things came back to him in a rapid, horrific slideshow of worst-case scenarios. Did they grab her hair? She had beautiful hair. Dark and curled in ringlets. In high school it went all of the way down her back. Her laugh was so light, and she was so excited by everything in life. Would that optimism dim? Would the light go out of her eyes? He had seen that before.

"Troy? Come sit down."

He nodded, and Megan steered him toward the couch.

"I'll call Ash and see if she's heard anything. The news isn't always the whole story, especially with something active."

"True." He sat watching the TV, hoping for more information or simple answers, but there were none. "Thank you," he added to her, but she was already on the phone in the kitchen. He could hear her soft voice in a hushed tone so as to not upset him, which he hated. Judging by the disappointment in her voice, he could tell there was no new information. How could there be? He had just watched the news.

Anger at nothing came from deep inside. She was a mom of three boys at home. One of the best people with the kindest heart. She probably made cookies and crafts and took pictures of terrible drawings and hung them on the fridge. He saw someone grabbing her hair, the classic takedown, bashing her head and tossing her limp body in the ditch. They took her wedding ring, probably already pawned it for quick cash. Poof. Gone. Just like that. No one cared.

Absently, he wondered who would tuck the boys in while she was in the hospital? How did Kiera's husband tell the children why their mother wouldn't be home that night? Did they sleep? How could they? The world wasn't safe.

He knew this to be true, and that little children had to know that so young brought on a deep feeling of sorrow and rage.

It shouldn't be this way.

Visions of Adam, his mom, and the fire in Iraq flashed through his head, looping faster and faster. He couldn't see where he was; all he could see was smoke and fire and death, as one after the other, smiling faces were extinguished.

CHAPTER 32

"Okay, thanks," Megan said, while pacing. "Yeah, keep us posted. Alright, sounds good."

She ended the call with Ash and went back to find Troy standing again, starting to tremble.

"I talked with Ash."

"No new information." It wasn't a question. His tone was flat and distant. Megan wondered if it was intentional. Megan made sure she was in his line of sight and slowly stretched out her hand to touch him with plenty of warning. He knew she was there and didn't flinch when she touched his shoulder. Was it intentional to keep his feelings at bay?

His eyes were flat, cold.

"I'm sorry this happened. I'm glad they found her when they did."

"Her husband found her."

Megan nodded. "I'm glad."

"They didn't catch him or stop it. He had to go get her out of the ditch."

"She's going to be okay. They're treating her for non-life-threatening injuries. It's going to be okay. She's stable. It's terrible, but sometimes bad things happen to good people. The good news is she'll be okay."

He glanced at her, and his eyes chilled her to the bone with the depth of their sorrow. He looked haunted. That's when he started pacing and rubbing the back of his neck as if he was trying to hold off a headache. Megan wasn't surprised when he checked the doors again.

"Troy, I'm sorry—"

"Don't be sorry. It's not you, but I'll be damned if I let it happen to you. I've lost almost every single person I care about. You said bad things happen to good people, then why do I have more than my fair share? It's not right. Besides it's getting worse. There's some nut or something going on right now—"

"They said they're looking for—"

"One of the best people I've ever met was attacked and could've been killed. I've lost my mom, I lost Adam, I lost Simon." He squeezed his eyes shut and pressed his fingers to the corners. "I almost lost Dad. I can't lose you." He let out a choked sob. "This world isn't safe, and...and—I just want to fix it."

Megan's heart swelled. She stepped forward and wrapped her arms around him, relieved when he let his weight lean into her. He was shaking. It was so slight she hadn't noticed, but she could feel it. He was quite literally holding himself together.

She didn't have to ask if Simon was the one he was trying to get to in his nightmare. She just knew and clearly now was not the time.

Megan held on to the man she loved. He was so strong. So powerful, but had so much pain and worry inside him. All of this grief and rage had nowhere to go. It was all from a place of great love. She knew that to be true.

"Oh Troy."

He jerked back and sucked in a breath, visibly tamping down all of the emotion.

"I want to enable your location on my app. We already did it on yours."

"What?"

"I know you can't always stop what you're doing to text me that you're safe, but,"—he took her shoulders in his hands and brought her close to him before wrapping her in a big hug and pressing his lips to her forehead—"I won't be able to sleep at night unless I know you're okay and I can get to you if something goes wrong, no matter how far away I am."

Megan was overwhelmed with emotion. For so long she relied on herself to stay safe, but now she had someone who worried about her other than her friends. He truly cared for her, not just when she was with him, but when she wasn't. There was a warmth in her chest that hadn't been there in a long time.

"So you'll be able to see my location the way I can see yours?"

He nodded. "There's too many crazies out right now. I don't know what's going on, but when I saw that guy coming at you, something in me just took over, and it wasn't just the training. I thought it might have been that, and it certainly helped, but thinking that you may have been hurt..." He stopped and shook his head. "I just can't lose you."

"I don't want to lose you either."

Troy looked down and smiled and kissed her. "Let me get your phone and we can set it up."

"You okay?"

He sighed. "I'm getting there."

Megan looked at him as he walked into the other room. He was so strong on the outside but was coiled like a spring. Even now she could see the tension under his eyes. The conflict inside him was like an animal poised for fight or flight, but with nowhere to go, trapped and fearful.

His arms were powerful and muscled, stretching his T-shirt so tight. She remembered the strength in him. His dark hair was tousled and her fingers remembered the feel of his thick hair between her hands as she had clung to him during their passionate nights.

Troy was always so gentle and understanding, putting her needs above his own. To see him like this with the emotion he had been carrying and the anxiety of yet another tragedy, she could see his reality of waiting for the next shoe to drop. The story had been terrible, but it had a happy ending, and he couldn't even see that.

As much bad in the world as Megan had seen herself, she saw plenty of good too. Neighbors helping neighbors when fires broke out. Strangers risking themselves to stop and help others during a car accident. People coming out of the woodwork for the station's canned food drive and toy donations. There were good Samaritans everywhere. There were bad things, accidents, and sickness too, but she truly believed the world was mostly good. Troy didn't.

He came back in the room still wearing his boxer briefs, which showed off excellent legs. The muscles on his chest stretched the T-shirt, and as she admired him, her fingers itched to know what was under his T-shirt that she felt every time they were together.

Megan realized now why he always felt so strongly about the light being off and had controlled where her hands had been. When she had felt the scars, he had shifted away so she couldn't reach him, but seeing the physical evidence of the pain he was suffering from, Megan wanted to know every inch to try and understand. Maybe then she could know and help him in some small way. Even if it was terrible, she wanted to know everything he had gone through, because it was him and a part of his story. Megan wanted all of it. The good and the bad.

"Here. Check on my phone to be sure it works." He punched in a long passcode to his phone so fast she couldn't see it, then held it out to her.

"You don't want to do it?"

Troy shook his head. "No, I need to get up and move around or something. I'll clean the kitchen. Did you finish your food?"

Megan nodded, and he whisked away the dirty dishes and started scraping the little bits they hadn't eaten into the trash while the hot water ran.

It was all so domestic, and she loved him for it. Seeing him in his underwear, lathering up a sponge in hot soapy water while her two cats looked on, made her heart swell in places she hadn't known it could.

With a few swipes she enabled location settings in the app on both of their phones and did a quick check to make sure they could each see the other from where they were. Until now, she had only done this with Laura and Ash, so having Troy join her inner circle made her smile.

Troy's phone buzzed in her hand as a message alert popped up.

When are you free? I miss you! We need to catch up soon. Xoxo Samantha

Megan frowned and hit the notification banner on instinct, revealing one of the new dating apps she had heard about. Samantha's profile picture came up showing a pretty blonde with short hair in a beanie hugging a dog.

Three dots appeared before a kissing face emoji.

I see you're there, so don't leave me on read again. I've been so fired up while you've been gone. Can't wait to meet up again when you get home.

A low heat fell throughout Megan's body from the top of

her head down through her chest and into the pit of her stomach. Hitting the back button, she held her breath and let it out in a rush of shock and pain when she saw dozens of open chats, some of them with recent new messages.

She clicked on the profile picture, seeing Troy's picture, a brief description, and a recent update saying he was looking for quick, casual fun.

CHAPTER 33

Ice ran through Megan's fingers as she looked at the phone in her hand, trying to make sense of what everything meant. It wasn't damning, was it? Maybe he had just forgotten to disable it.

Not wanting to see any more, Megan swiped up for the home screen, and saw not just one, but several dating apps. His carefully crafted breakfast felt like a brick in her gut, and her breathing picked up in shallow spurts as the wave of heat washed over her.

She blinked and tried to look up at him, the man who had been so attentive each night and held her as they fell asleep.

The phone buzzed again. Megan peeked down and saw another message, but this time from a new girl. She didn't want details but could see from the preview text that it was sexual.

Everything in her went hollow. It had been special. She thought they were special.

"I can't believe he let her out that late," Troy said, still talking about the attack they had seen on the news. He seemed to have calmed a little. He wasn't shaking with anger anymore but was still slapping that sponge around in her sink. She could see the muscle pulse in his jaw, and a vein was raised on his temple.

"You know? It's too dark and she was running alone, probably with headphones. I can't believe her husband allowed that."

Megan blinked a few times and tried to reconcile what had happened last night with what he was saying and the phone in her hand. Why was he acting like this? "She had no reason to think it wasn't safe. I'm sure she had done it a bunch of times. And, it's not like he didn't know where she was."

He glared at her from where he was elbow deep in the suds. "So, you think it's fine?"

"No, I'm not saying that. I'm saying I don't like your tone. Her husband trusted her and knew where she was, not that he needed to."

"What is that supposed to mean?"

"She's a grown woman. She can make her own choices. That's part of a *healthy* relationship, isn't it?" Megan emphasized healthy relationship and hated herself for it.

"Look, I'm just saying that it's weird times, and people need to watch out for each other. It's hard to know people these days—"

"Boy, you got that right."

Troy paused and shook his head, too deep in his own shit to realize what she meant.

"Exactly. And women are weaker so they're more likely to be outrun or overpowered—"

Megan felt something in her crack. She had been barely holding it together, but as he talked, he kept digging himself deeper and deeper into a shit hole.

"Weaker?"

"You know what I mean. It's nature—"

"I'm sorry. Who's the one that ran into your dad's house?"

Troy turned slowly, wiping his hands with the dishtowel, his stormy expression at odds with the cheerful floral pattern in his hands.

"You know what I meant. Besides, you said yourself that you have backup at all times."

"If you think I can run through fire because I have a man behind me, you couldn't be more wrong."

"So you'd run into fire without a team? That's crazy."

"So you think I'm crazy now?" Megan could feel her voice rising and rose out of her chair with it.

"I didn't say you're crazy, but willfully putting yourself in danger is fucking nuts."

Megan ground out her answer through gritted teeth, fueled with rage on every level. "That's. What. I. Do. *It's my job.*"

He threw the towel in the empty sink and propped his hands on his hips. "Are you saying you're better than me?"

Megan's head almost snapped back from the shock. "What the hell does that mean? All I'm saying is I'm a firefighter."

"And someone who rescued my dad. I bet you love to lord that shit around."

"It's a fucking fact! I'll say it again. It's my job!"

"And you think it makes you better than me!" His face was red again, and she could see the muscles in his jaw working as he folded his arms and stood his ground. God, the thought that she had clung to him last night made her eyes sting with anger and frustration and not just at him.

"This has literally nothing to do with you."

"Oh, come the fuck on. Lighting the candle like some badass and putting out the flame with your fingers. It's not a fucking game to me! My friend died in a fire, and my shoulder is all fucked up because of it. Got it?!"

Megan could see him starting to shake again, trying to hold himself and his emotions together. As much as she hated what was happening between them, she didn't want him to suffer. Megan blew out a breath and tried to collect herself.

"Troy—"

"Don't spout off some bullshit to me. I've heard it all, and it's all a worthless fucking lie."

"I can't get burned."

He smirked and sucked his teeth. "What the fuck does that mean? Trying to rub shit in my face?"

"No." Megan swallowed and closed her eyes for a moment to steady herself. "I legit cannot get burned. That's how I survived."

"That's insane."

Megan glared at him. "That's the truth. You could set this whole place on fire, and it won't hurt my skin. The smoke irritates my lungs, but that's it. How do you think I got Levi out? Pets don't like the helmets. I had to take it off, and my gloves too. I could walk in there stark naked and be fine."

"And this is supposed to make me feel better? That you *allegedly* can't get burned?"

"I can't."

"And I'm the one who can. I'm the weak one?!"

"You think you know everything, but you don't have a damn clue! I'm stronger than you think!"

"And what about the rest of the team? Do they know? What about them? What if the building goes down because you're too cocky and stay in too long? What if someone follows you? Then what, huh? What if one day you think you can't get burned, and then surprise! You die." He waved his hands around, mocking her.

Megan crossed her arms, now standing opposite him,

containing her own rage. Of course he would find the things that haunted her the most and exploit them.

"Fine. If you can't deal with your own feelings, then be angry forever. It won't change what happened. It won't bring back anyone. You'll just keep hurting the ones around you and cutting yourself off."

"You don't know—"

"I've lost my whole fucking family too!" Megan's voice shook, but not with a stutter. "You think it was some picnic growing up knowing I'm the one that lived? At least you got to meet your family! Not that you even give a shit about your dad. Pretty soon you'll head right back. Got to get to Samantha and the other one, huh? I guess they're more important. Until they get too close and then, you know, got to cut them out and move on to the next. God forbid you allow yourself to be vulnerable."

Troy's face changed, the lines in between his brows vanishing along with the anger. He frowned and looked at her with recognition in his eyes. "What?" At least he had snapped out of it.

Megan's full body was shaking now. She spoke slowly so she wouldn't stutter. "She misses you." Flashing air quotes, she mimicked, *"Looking forward to hooking up."*

Troy's whole demeanor changed. Cool distance replaced the hot anger as he walked over to get his phone from her. She put it on the table between them so they wouldn't touch. He picked it up, watching her.

"Seems you're popular. Someone else is looking forward to hooking up and getting some of that tongue when you get back."

Troy closed his eyes with a grimace. "I haven't seen—"

"What? Like you're not going to text them back the second you leave?"

"I told you I like things casual. I've seen too much divorce and don't want to put anyone through that."

Now it was her turn to pace. "God, I'm such an idiot! It was all a fucking lie. A game to you. Just a way to kill time."

"Megan…"

"It's my fault. You told me. You said casual. Now I know that's code for manwhore."

Troy winced at her language, but she was past caring. "I trusted you! I wanted you to be the first. I hoped this would be special. I told you everything about me. Congratulations! You know it all, but I guess you have a bunch of secrets you don't want to share. So it's my fault for trusting the first guy who comes around and takes an interest. I thought you actually cared. It was all a lie. A way to kill time until you get back to whoever else is texting you now."

"Megan, it's not like—"

"Bullshit." She looked at him, now seeing him for what he was. Behind all of that strength was a web he had built around his pain.

"You know what your problem is? You're too afraid to care about people. Too afraid to let people in and be vulnerable."

"That's not true." But his face clearly said she had hit a bullseye.

"Faceless sex is a lot easier when you don't have to give a shit if they get killed in a car accident wearing the same clothes they picked up off the floor of your room."

He winced and jerked back. "Megan, c'mon, that's not what this is."

Megan's eyes started to burn with hot tears that she so did not want to deal with right now.

"Get out of my apartment. "

"I—"

"I said get out!"

Troy winced again and turned around to look in the kitchen as if he was unsure what to do with himself. Megan was struck by how awkward he looked as he ambled around her place removing all evidence he had ever been there. She stayed rooted to the spot and forced herself to watch him go. Everything in her body wanted to run and turn from him, especially when he looked up and his eyes met hers on his way to the door. The sadness in them made her want to crumble on the spot. Megan stood her ground. Until the door clicked closed.

As she hugged herself, the tears spilled down her face and didn't stop.

CHAPTER 34

Troy hadn't been able to sleep in two days. Every time he lay down, he tossed and turned while his mind ran away with anxious thoughts.

Last night was the worst. He didn't think he was asleep, but maybe he was in that space in between when his mind was his own while he still was aware of his old mattress and thin pillow in the small bedroom.

It started the same. Her blue eyes brimming with tears and the hot shame burning in his chest for lying to her. He tried to reach out to her, to cry out and explain, but she wouldn't listen, running away from him and into the burning ranch house.

Flames shot through the upper windows, licking the siding. A thick black smoke billowed out, blocking all of the stars, mixing with the purple night sky. He tried to call to her, but she ran inside, out of his reach. The choking chemicals suffocated him, burning his throat. He had no voice. As much as Troy called out, the howling of the flames roared in his ears.

He lost sight of Megan, now replaced with the shadows of

someone in front of him. First it was Adam, then it was his mom. Both of them stood side by side in the burning kitchen with distant smiles, waving to him as if he had just come home from school, unaware they were in a literal hell. His voice screamed in a muffled, painful cry. His mom opened her mouth to speak. Adam was saying something too.

What? What? Get out of there!

Neither moved, but instead got up and turned away to walk from him. He tried to reach them, but they turned around and walked through the flames deeper into the house.

Troy tried to follow but was paralyzed. The weight of his legs held him welded to the spot as the flames edged closer to his boots, taking over until he was not in the ranch house anymore.

That's when the smell came.

Burning flesh lingered on the soul and in the mind. It was one of those smells that you couldn't forget, as if the body knew it was fundamentally wrong and got stuck trying to process the sin against its nature.

It was Simon. His eyes peeled back wide with fear from within the window, too weak to fight back but still present to understand. The look in those eyes would've cured anyone of a love for war.

Troy clawed at the door's searing metal, trying to wrench it open, paying no mind to the flames crawling up his arms, chest, and shoulders.

There was screaming everywhere. He couldn't tell if it was his own or Simon's or the roar of the flames, but Troy would've paid God himself a million dollars to make the screaming stop.

But Troy didn't have a million dollars, and if God was real, he'd stopped listening a long time ago.

Troy wasn't asleep now, but nothing was working. He had

lost control of his thoughts. They just kept looping over and over.

Sometimes he would try to do the dishes at the start of his dad watching *Jeopardy* and find himself still standing in front of the sink when the show was over and *Wheel*'s theme had started. By then the water was cold, and he wondered where he had gone for that time.

Troy's dad knew something was up, but only asked a few times about Megan before he dropped it. He couldn't remember what he had said when they had been painting—the color she had picked out— but clearly his tone or face or whatever he had said had been enough.

Troy had tried grounding techniques, switching from tapping to stretching. The Coke can wasn't working, and looking at the clock just reminded him of death. He wasn't an idiot. He recognized he needed help.

One more week. In seven days he would be back on post and he could get back with his therapist. It had happened before, and treatment had helped.

At first he hadn't thought he needed help, that he could handle it, but the nightmares had been regular companions. He had joined every dating site and had found a new person to chat with at least once a week to keep the looping thoughts at bay. It didn't affect him at work. If anything, it was nice to have something else to focus on, until he had a bad day at work. He barely held it together until he got home, then while cooking he got lost in his thoughts, burned a steak, and beat the shit out of the counter with a sheet pan. That was when he realized he might need some help.

Last night, Troy had messaged his therapist to set up the appointment for next week, only to find out they were on emergency leave for the next month.

Megan had been right. He didn't want to be vulnerable and would rather hedge his bets than risk losing everyone. In the process he had lost her along with any interest in other women. Troy lay awake at night trying to reconcile everything she had said.

He tried the lonely man's way to put himself to sleep and work out the kinks, but only found himself wanting her more, lying awake alone with his thoughts.

During the day, he pushed himself at the ranch house until his back was sore and his arms trembled. Today was no different.

"You're going to go blind if you keep painting the trim with your eyes that close."

"Gotta get it done before I leave. Aren't you always the one that said not to do a job unless you're going to do it right?"

"That's true, so that's why you should call her."

"Gotta love that blunt honesty."

His dad must have shrugged, because next he heard the telltale sound of his hands slapping the thighs.

"I'm right."

"Not about this. She doesn't want to talk to me."

"What did you do?"

Troy didn't answer, hoping it would go away like when he and Adam would ask Dad a question that Dad never acknowledged.

"You know what your problem is?"

"I'm leaving in a week and this house still isn't done."

"Nope. Minor. You'll be back. This place is your birthright."

Troy winced. It should've been Adam's.

"Are you going to see her again before you leave?"

"Probably not."

"Then that's it?"

Troy closed his eyes, grateful he was facing the wall, so his dad wouldn't see his pain. "Yep."

"When will you be back?"

"Not sure, maybe Thanksgiving. Depends on where I head next. Probably will get new orders next spring. Not sure where I'll go next. Germany was on the list. I think it might come through this time." Troy focused on his paintbrush.

"You've been wanting that for a while. A lot of history. I know how much you love that."

"Maybe you could come visit if the doctor says you're doing okay."

"Gah, I'm fine. Tip-top, and I'd like that. I've never been that far away. I'll need to get someone to watch your horses while I go."

Troy winced again.

"They've missed you. That big one always perks up when you go in there."

"How do you know?"

"I see you go down in the morning and stay a little longer than you need to. They're going to miss you when you're gone. This whole place will. Won't be the same without you here. Megan will miss you too."

"Doubtful. And you know how it is. I have to go."

"You'll miss it too."

God, more than he wanted to admit. The thought had plagued him for a while now, but he had to get back to treatment and see that whatever shit was stuck in his brain got out as fast as possible. He wanted to stay. He wanted to crawl back to Megan and beg for her forgiveness while her cats walked all over him. He burned for her. As much as his past was creeping up into his present life, she had been right. He hated feeling vulnerable, and as much as he wanted to avoid it, it had found him anyway.

"The circumstances weren't ideal, but coming home has been good for you. You fit here."

Troy opened his mouth to refute.

"You know the army isn't forever. You will have a life outside of your job. It's important to leave enough energy for that and think about what you will need with you when that time comes. You need to think about what really matters and who really matters too."

Troy blew out a breath and turned to face his dad. "I only have eight more years until I can retire. Then I'll come home. Having my pension will make it easier to run this place. Who knows? Maybe I'll turn it into a bed and breakfast or open it up for events."

Voicing Megan's suggestion without her in his life felt like the ultimate gut punch. God, to think he could come back and live here. Would Megan still be single? Again, doubtful. Even the idea of seeing her with someone else made him sick. No wonder she had thrown him out when she had seen the messages. Admitting that he had broken her heart made him crumble.

His dad nodded. "That'd be good. You love to cook. Always were good at it like your mom."

"Yeah, so that's the plan. The pension will make it easier to get it up and going, but yeah. That's the goal."

His dad smiled, but nothing in it made Troy feel any better.

CHAPTER 35

Megan had thought about cleaning her apartment for two days but couldn't bring herself to wash the pillowcase he had slept on. Instead, she spent most of her time lying on the bed, replaying all of their time together, trying to find the signs she had missed to suggest this sort of pain would happen.

Nothing had gotten done. The apartment was a mess, and if she was honest, she had barely checked her email and only replied to enough text messages to give her friends a proof of life until they were satisfied. Both had repeatedly offered to come over and invited her out numerous times, but Megan wasn't interested in visiting with them and rehashing everything.

It was barely enough for her to feed her pets and herself. She had even called in to work, which she hated to do since they were so short-staffed, but she'd had a migraine for days, probably due to the whole barely eating and sleeping thing.

Megan knew she had to pull it together. Soon, she would have to get ready for her vet school interviews and start the life she had always wanted. She had exchanged emails with

Traci, the administrative assistant in the admissions office, who had the sunniest personality. Maybe it was that she was stepping a foot in the right direction, but just by talking with her for a few minutes, Megan felt a little ray of hope that someday she could crawl out of this pit of emotion she was feeling.

The change of scenery couldn't come soon enough. Now all she had to do was wait until they were ready for her, then she would pack up everything and move away from Goldvein and toward her new life.

Megan flopped over and let her eyes roam over to the pictures of her family, all smiling and looking at the camera. Try as she might to not end up hurt and alone, she had arrived at her destination anyway. It was as if she and fate were locked in a battle, and she would forever be one step behind. Megan closed her eyes against the tears, but they came anyway.

Minutes or hours later, she didn't know, she pulled herself up toward the only comfort she knew, tugged out the chair she couldn't remember ever sitting in, and collapsed into it.

Sights, sounds, and smells were all so powerful, and her only connection to the love she had lost.

Megan turned on the Tiffany styled lamp, reveling in the jewel-toned lights. Admiring the colors, she wiped some nonexistent dust and turned it to catch the most perfect array of colors, letting them wash over her.

She reached out and picked up her favorite bottle of perfume, a black swirling work of art with an atomizer pump with a tassel. As she had since she was little, she pressed it and felt only air on her face. Her grandma had known she was fascinated with it and left it empty on purpose, giving it to her to play with. Now, Megan had them all to herself. She reached for the green one in the back. It was a glass onion bottle, with a hand blown leaf with a ladybug for a stopper. She popped it and brought it to her nose, not wanting to waste it on her skin, preferring to preserve it forever. The smell brought her back to the feel of her grandma's arms around her. She had worn the same scent for her entire life.

With this bottle in her hand and the smell wrapping around her senses, it was as if her grandmother was right behind her wearing diamonds, a scarf, and reading glasses on the bridge of her nose.

Megan's tears came faster now as she reached for the final item. The music box had once been white with gold trim, but the smoke from the fire had stained it. It was the only thing recovered from the ashes of her childhood home. Smoke had tarnished the outside, and inside, the red velvet had turned to pink, but the sound. Oh, the sound was still so perfect. Thank God.

Megan had heard it for so long, she hummed along, her voice matching the pitch on its own. The rise and fall of the tinkling music took her back to happier times she couldn't remember, but the proof in her hand showed her they had existed.

For so long she had wanted to know more. Craved the knowledge of the music, wondering what the song was and wanting to know the backstory. Had her mother bought it? Was it a gift? Who gave it and why?

Once again, the box offered no answers other than its tune.

Megan wound it up again, twisting the little knob until it would go no farther. She heard the song play again and again, the third time interrupted by a note that didn't belong.

Puzzled, she turned around and picked up her phone,

seeing a text from Laura checking in. Ash had called last night, but Megan had claimed she was just tired.

Megan stared at the home screen a few beats while hearing the music and nearly dropped her phone from shock when the realization hit that it could help her solve at least some of the mystery.

She opened the music recognition app and white-knuckled her phone while she watched the loading symbol, full of hope, only to be derailed when it came up empty.

Undeterred, she typed as much into the phone as she could. Getting frustrated, she tossed it to the side and opened her neglected laptop in a flurry of research, getting closer and closer until…success.

Megan sat back and looked at the page of what her music box used to look like on eBay. It was worn but still white and from what appeared to be a quality company, but that was for another time. She scanned the page, straining to find the end to a twenty-five-year-old mystery when she found it.

Memory. Of course. How ironic.

"Memory" by Andrew Lloyd Webber. Megan searched for the song and found the video from *Cats,* and with her heart in her throat clicked play.

As the lyrics washed over her for the first time, matching the tune she had grown up with, Megan wept.

It was the closest thing to hearing a ghost of a loved one. With the click of a button, the sound had matured from a sweet child's music box to a full orchestra of meaning and depth of understanding with a full spectrum of human emotion longing for something from another time. Wanting more. Wanting connection before it was too late.

Megan had heard this her whole life, and now, for the first time, she understood.

CHAPTER 36

Three days. He had three more days to get through until he would be in his truck on the way back to his apartment. His job. His therapists. His dating apps. His life before all of this had started.

He just had three more days.

Troy had made up his mind. He was going to spend as much time on the ranch house as he could. It was mostly done. The insurance money was spent and to great effect. There were a few things that would still take time and work, but at least they had gotten the basics done.

He had spent a lot of the week in the barn talking with the horses as well. Seeing them connected with him on a deeper level. He didn't know how or why, but that big one Braxton had taken a liking to him. So much so, that even though he hadn't ridden in forever, Troy saddled him up with some old tack left over from one of the cowboys and rode out onto the property toward the original homestead.

He remembered coming out here as a boy with Adam, each taking turns pretending to be the old miners hoping to strike it rich. Like their ancestors, they never did find any gold. Only a few artifacts like a button, belt buckle, and a couple of horseshoes.

Funny enough, all of those things he had kept and were safe in a box in his apartment back in Kentucky, waiting for him to come back so they could remind him of home.

It had become his ritual. Every morning and every evening, he would put Braxton through his paces, and gently ride him out onto the old pastures toward the foundation of the original house. Once there, he would let Braxton graze while he sat and admired the mountains he had memorized as a child. They looked almost blue, and when the right light hit with the clouds in a certain pattern, it was as if he was looking at the ocean.

All of it was peaceful, but nothing did anything to cure the aching pit in his chest or the memory of those blue eyes brimming with angry tears.

His dad didn't bring Megan up again, but took notice with a smile when Troy would go out and ride. Once he even gave a curt nod, the country way to say, "This is right and as it should be."

But it wasn't. Troy had to go. Had thought he wanted to go. But with each day, he was caught somewhere between wanting to do the next right thing and feeling let down by the disappointment of it.

He knew his job in the army. He was good at it. It was comfortable, honorable, and familiar. What more could he want? What more should he want?

Visions of red hair in the dim light came to him, making his chest ache with longing again. Never before had he felt this way. His path was obvious, wasn't it? He was going to go back and fulfill his mission. Get new orders. Make time for himself on the side and build a life that could support him coming back to the ranch later.

He pulled his lips tight as he brushed Braxton's black coat after one of their rides. "I'll be back, bud."

The big brown eye blinked once and stared into his soul. Troy didn't want to think about leaving his horse, Dad, or Megan, even though she didn't want him. God, he had been going to the coffee shop every day at nine to get a glimpse of her, but to no avail.

This was the longest time he had spent here since he had joined the army, and the ranch and the town tugged on his heart more than he could've expected.

Of course in a perfect world he would stay, but the world wasn't perfect. He knew that to be true more than most people.

Much to his surprise, he loved the quiet mornings, the little projects that added up over time to something larger. The way his blushing dad pretended not to notice the older lady flirting with him when he went to McDonald's once a week—with his doctor's blessing—to treat them both. He had gotten to know the coffee shop baristas, people at the hardware store, and the farrier and equine vet who had come out to do routine work on the horses.

He never expected to fit in, but the slow simple conversation felt more natural, and he started eyeing the baby chicks at the feed store every time he went.

But the work emails started trickling in, a reminder that this was all temporary and fading fast. If he was completely honest with himself, he was savoring every minute of these last three days. He just wished he could see Megan again and make it right.

With Braxton tended to, he patted his neck and went to clean up before heading into town. The knot in his stomach grew as he thought about the help-wanted ad up at the grocery store. There on the community bulletin board, in the local classifieds, and online, Troy had posted he was looking for a farm hand to take care of some retired caisson horses.

His replacement.

Troy closed his eyes against the confusing thoughts he had yet to sort out. It probably would've been easier if he was sleeping, but that wasn't going anywhere fast.

He needed to go somewhere to not think for a while. Literally get away from the looping thoughts, the what ifs, the hopes that couldn't happen. Lucky for him, a new gym had opened up downtown, and since he had to get a few things for his dad in town anyway, he threw some sneakers and shorts in a gym bag and headed there.

Thirty minutes later, he walked in to the welcoming smell of a new pool and fresh paint. He signed in at the sleek new desk and nodded when the attendant offered him a quick tour around the facility which had just opened up a week ago.

The overall vibe was a cool, sleek take on new industrial with spots for Instagram photos as well as top-notch equipment. He hadn't been a gym nut before—he went more as an obligation for work—but once he had started going, he found that running his body into the ground to ear-pounding music drowned out the looping thoughts until he was so exhausted he couldn't even think and had no choice but to sleep.

Troy thanked the employee and threw his stuff in one of the quick-rent lockers and started out by running on the treadmill to some old-school rock. The miles melted away under his pounding shoes as he got lost in the music, letting it take him out of his mind. He ran himself for almost five miles before he called it quits, hitting the end button and walking away on jelly legs to get the spray. He wiped down the equipment, not bothering to mess with the after workout cooldown or any of the fancy prompts that wanted to talk about heart rate.

He circled around the weight floor, taking everything in. They were usually his go-to, but lifting weights seemed too repetitive and allowed his mind to wander on its own, which was not a happy place right now. On his second lap around the gym he saw it in the corner. The punching bag suspended by a chain was perfectly still and untouched.

Troy smiled to himself and headed straight over, putting his water and phone down off to the side. He started with a few quick jabs, then a cross pattern, followed by a quick uppercut.

He was clumsy and out of practice, but as he settled back into the rhythm, he picked up the pace and fell into a pattern. He would go for a few rounds, still listening to the music blaring in his ears, strong enough to drown out the worst memory. He pushed himself harder and harder, wanting the bag to swing back against him, as he punished them both in this exercise of madness.

Sweat dripped off his nose as he kept up the punches. The satisfaction of having his knuckles make contact with the bag connected with his soul. Troy hadn't been a boxer or wrestler in high school, and never had a head for fighting, but alone with the bag, he kept pushing until every muscle in his body was spent with the energy all flooding out of him into the black leather. His shoulders and arms burned, while he couldn't feel his hands at all. His calves were seizing up as well from the run, and now from being on the balls of his feet as he hopped here and there.

He kept it up, pounding though his arms and getting lost in the movements. Taking out all of the anger. All of the pain. All of the things he couldn't fix. He couldn't be in the army and be here for his dad. He couldn't live on the ranch and travel the world. There was no way to reconcile what he wanted. Especially what he wanted most.

Megan.

Troy hadn't stopped thinking about her and was trying not to be super creepy, because going way out of his way to drive slowly past her work to make sure her car was there was...not good. Literally everything in him wanted to go straight there to check on her—scratch that—run inside and beg for her forgiveness. Just to see her again, hear her laugh, and feel her lips on his own one more time before he left.

He had probably typed out a hundred text messages only to delete them night after night. Really, he was trying to respect her wishes. She didn't want to see him, and as much as it hurt, he was trying hard to stay away.

It was karma in a way. Just like she had said. After all of that time avoiding commitment to avoid pain, here he was, dying inside without her. Craving her touch and the feel of her body against his own.

Troy kept going, hitting the bag again and again, wishing he could clock himself in the head for being such an idiot. He should've deleted those apps and gone all in. Shown up. Been there. Taken a risk and been vulnerable. Maybe then she would've been open to a long-distance relationship. But he had fucked it all up by getting too deep in his head. In the process of trying to protect himself, he had limited how much of himself he gave her, and that was the painful truth Megan had been trying to tell him before she threw him out.

Someone tapped him on the shoulder, and Troy nearly jumped out of his skin and almost clocked the poor attendant.

The look of total fear on the kid's face told Troy exactly what he must have looked like beating the shit out of a bag and then rounding on him.

His mouth was moving but Troy couldn't hear the words. He ripped the earbud from his ear.

"I'm sorry, what did you say?"

The kid's voice almost shook, and there was definitely a crack in it. "Sir, I'm sorry, we're closing now."

Oh shit. He checked the clock and did the quick math. No wonder he couldn't feel his hands. His knuckles were red, and some were cracked with a tinge of blood welling through the break in the skin.

"Thank you, uh, sorry. I guess I lost track of time. I'll wipe this up and get out of your hair."

He did just that and went to the locker to get his stuff, then waved to the kids at the front desk as they shut off most of the lights behind him. Through the windows, he could see the rain that must've started a while ago. The parking lot wasn't flooded yet, but water was pooling around the drains with more coming down.

Troy checked the temp, which had dipped, and unzipped his bag and shrugged into his Army Gore-Tex. Might as well get used to his uniform again. His truck was at the very end of the lot, alone under a streetlight like a sad spotlight on an empty stage. He would need a shower anyway, but didn't feeling like messing up his seats.

With a last wave, he forced a tight smile and headed out, not seeing when the two teens picked up the phone to dial the police.

CHAPTER 37

The call was a big one. Three alarm fire.

Megan knew the complex before they even left. Laura had lived there a while ago. It was one of the old apartment buildings downtown.

Muscle memory took over as she grabbed her gear and hopped up into the engine behind Buzz and next to Nick. The ride was quick through the dark, and the smoke billowing out of the window mixed with the night sky to obscure the stars.

It was the building next to where Laura and Holden had lived before, full of young families.

That was evident as couples stood around in the grass around the parking lot, holding little kids covered in blankets, still in pajama pants, clearly just having been pulled from their beds.

Megan headed for apartment 1C which dispatch had let them know was the start of the fire. In one hand she had the big silver fire extinguisher, rated C for chemical. Dispatch reported it to be the dryer.

She pushed through the open door and found an inferno.

A literal hell. She stepped inside a small corridor, pushing farther into the fire. The wind from the blaze taking the oxygen from the open door thrust her in more as she tried to find the source through the towering flames and thick black smoke. That's when she spotted it in the back corner of the little hall off to the side.

What once was a stackable unit was almost unrecognizable and had been consumed by the inferno.

A few shots with the fire extinguisher did little more than shoot a cloud of yellow dust into the blaze, but it was too far gone to handle with this tool. The flames had caught onto the wall and were ripping across the ceiling, firmly entrenched and spreading fast.

"Extinguisher won't do it. Spreading fast."

"Wind is high," answered Buzz. "Switch to recovery."

The objective was to search for anyone remaining in the apartments first and try to save the building second. At least here they had town water to draw a supply from.

They went in two by two like always, calling out and searching for people. Buzz radioed in her ear.

"Everyone is accounted for except for one. Thirty years old, last believed to be in his apartment. Has a sprained ankle and can't do stairs right now. Not answering calls."

"Which apartment?"

"3B"

"On it."

Megan turned from the kitchen she was in on the second floor and walked to the other side of the building, knocking on the still shut, pockmarked metal door.

No response. Megan tried again, and then a third time. The heat around her was rising. She could feel it in her suit as the fire raged around, climbing up toward the third and top floor.

"It's locked. I need to pry it open. K Tool and Halligan."

"K and Halligan bar coming."

Megan knocked a few more times while listening to Nick clear the ones behind her.

"Behind you," Nick said in her ear.

Megan reached and grabbed the tool, seeing how thick the smoke was getting. The steam from the hoses was making everything harder to see. It was a delicate balance of containing the fire so the building wouldn't collapse and keeping an exit clear for them to get out.

She jammed the K Tool in over the deadbolt and shoved in the forked edge.

"Hit."

Nick was right there with the axe, treating it like a sledge-hammer to jam it in farther. Two more times, and Megan pushed up, popping the deadbolt right out of place, revealing a key slot. She made quick work of that and jammed the fork in the doorjamb near the knob, which was locked as well.

"Hit."

"Hit."

She could tell the weight of the axe was getting to Nick, who had already climbed the stairs twice going back to get someone's family pet out as well.

Megan repositioned based on a gut feeling, plus training mixed with experience, and with a sharp crack the door broke in.

"We're in 3B," she radioed to Buzz, her eyes scanning for signs of life through the billowing smoke. It was everywhere, coming through the vents, filling the space. As it mixed with the rising heat from the inferno below, she knew it wouldn't be long before this apartment was ablaze too.

She pushed through each door, using a flashlight to try and find anyone. It was a two-bedroom with stairs heading up to a loft.

First bathroom empty, first bedroom empty.

"You guys have got to get out of there." Buzz had that tone of voice she really needed to listen to.

She could see Nick miss a step going up to the loft.

"Nick, get out now. I'll be behind you."

He didn't respond immediately. Shaking his head before hitting his radio, he said, "I ain't quitting you." The words came out with every other breath.

"I'm serious. Get out. I'll find him."

"Both of you need to GET OUT NOW." Buzz's voice thundered in her ear.

Megan went to the back hall with the last bedroom. Thankfully, Nick was coming back down from the loft.

"Kitchen's clear, living room too. Last bedroom now."

"GET OUT!"

"Nick, go!"

"Two in, two out."

There was a shearing moan echoing from behind them through the open door. Every firefighter knew the sound of steel framing started to bend. It was a sad, mournful sound as it failed slowly. Wood snapped, hard and fast, but metal creaked in a slow apologetic twist to all of the engineers and architects it was letting down. There was no collapse, not initially, but like a sinking ship it started to list to the side, as it slowly gave way to gravity, pulling everything down with it.

But not yet. The floor was still stable, but not for long. She just needed a few more—

"MEGAN—"

She punched through the last door, flashing her light to each corner, finding nothing. The bed was empty and even made.

"He isn't here!"

"EVACUATION! EVACUATION!"

Megan turned around to find Nick still behind her

starting to sway. Fire had broken through, now coming up from the vent from the second floor and through the outside windows.

Megan threw her arm around him and marched through the flames, prepared to carry him if needed, all the while praying the building wouldn't collapse.

"What in the fuck was that?" Megan could feel Buzz's eyes staring holes in the side of her head as she hung up her gear. Nick and a few of the guys looked on from a doorway, but heard Buzz's tone and got the hell out of dodge quick, shooting her a fleeting look of pity.

"I was looking for a person."

"The building was starting to fail."

"I just needed a few more seconds."

She hazarded a look in his direction. He was pinching the bridge of his nose, and a vein looked dangerously close to bursting on the side of his head.

"Megan…that's how people get killed."

"I know. I'm sorry. The information we had said there was someone else. Someone who needed help."

"Information is just that. And it was wrong. Once you breached the door and didn't hear someone coming, you could do a quick search instead of a full sweep."

He was right. Megan knew it but had been compelled to keep going. She didn't try to defend herself. She knew she had been pushing it even for her. She tried not to think of

Troy's voice echoing in the back of her mind. He had been right. She was pushing it in an attempt to try and prove her strength. None of it made any sense. She had never in her life been so wrapped up in someone else's shit that it affected her this way. Up until now, she had always found a way to block it out when on a call or in class. Able to compartmentalize her shit to when she was at home or meeting new people. At least, she *had* been good at that.

The fact was, she had been wrong. She had spent too much time there. Her judgment was off. What little confidence she had melted away. She stood and looked at the concrete floor.

Buzz propped his hands on his hips. "It's unacceptable. You're in violation of a direct order, and you know this isn't the first time. Nick just got certified. He's new—green—and supposed to be able to count on your judgment, which last night was questionable at best. No, it was downright dangerous."

Megan wanted the concrete to open up so she could shrink into the hole. Hot shame flooded through her chest as she fought the urge not to crumble.

"I'm sorry."

"Look, I know you've always liked to take risks, but this is getting out of hand. You're not invincible. None of us are. You need to remember that."

"I will."

"Until you do, I don't know if I can trust your decision-making."

"What does that mean?"

"I've been here more than twenty years. I've seen a lot of hotshots come in here thinking they're God with something to prove. I can't tolerate someone going rogue and blatantly working against policy. It's not safe. The stakes are too high."

He sighed and took a pause. Megan didn't fill the space, watching like a hawk to see where this was going.

"I have no doubt your heart is in the right place. And I looked away last time, but I can't let this go on. Usually when someone goes rogue, people notice, and unless leadership acts, people will end up hurt not just because someone is trying to help in the wrong way, but because of a failure of leadership."

Megan felt herself start to tear up and blinked fast to not let it come down in hot angry tears. His disappointment crushed her.

Buzz and the other guys at Station Three had always treated her like family. When she was hired, and they realized she didn't have any family, they made sure to pick up the slack. Buzz had come with her to sign her lease for her first apartment and even acted as a cosigner. Her grandma had left some money, but that hadn't been enough for the leasing office to trust a twenty-year-old with no credit. Nick had taught her how to change a tire and her oil, and Mike had taught her weird skills like basic self-defense.

Originally Buzz had tried to play matchmaker and wanted her to go out with one of them, but it hadn't worked. They all viewed each other more as siblings and well, that was that. Megan might not have her own blood family, but she had an oddball group of men acting as uncles and big brothers watching over her.

Now she wasn't so sure.

Megan eyed the older man and remembered all of the times when they would ride together on errands. He would always be behind the wheel, singing along to a country music station on the radio, off-key but not missing a single word. When he sang the old classics, Megan couldn't help but join in, especially when he sang "Jolene."

Today he was in uniform, but normally he preferred

casual clothes like his old Station Three sweatshirt under his tried-and-true Carhartt jacket. His skin was worn, and he looked every bit the seasoned firefighter that people would expect, unlike her.

She couldn't look him in the eyes, so she studied his hands. Thick like baseball gloves, they had a smattering of thin white scars, and there was a faded tattoo that peeked out from under his plain golden wedding band. Both were a testament to a lifetime of hard work and a strong marriage to his wife Judy, who was a secretary at a local doctor's office and was tough as old nails.

He looked gruff, a man worn by the harsh Montana winters and a hard life in the outdoors, but Megan knew from personal experience, he was a giant teddy bear who cared deeply for everyone at Station Three. She also knew he did not suffer fools.

"Am I b-being fired?" She cringed when the stutter came back and tried not to sniff, but figured it was better than a big ball of snot coming down. Pathetic. She was just pathetic.

"No. But you need to be honest with me. What in the hell is wrong?"

And that was when Megan burst into tears.

She held her head in her hands, but it did little to hide the gut-wrenching sobs. His arms came around her, smelling like a mix of stale coffee, Old Spice, and the occasional cigarette.

"Is it about your school applications…or that boy you were with that night?" Buzz's voice had taken on a different tone. Somewhere between gentle to her but with the vague promise of a threat toward whoever may have hurt her.

Megan stopped and let out a rueful laugh. "You always were a great shot."

He stepped back and looked her up and down. The look in his eye was disapproving and worried, but at least his ire wasn't directed at her anymore.

"Let's go in the office."

Megan followed him into his space in the back. There was wood paneling from the eighties when the station was last renovated. The whole space smelled like stale coffee and printer ink, which wasn't a surprise considering the paperwork that went through here.

"Now, pop a squat and cut the crap."

Megan sunk into the old wooden chair opposite his desk and took a deep sigh and looked at the linoleum floor. It was outdated, but waxed and clean, a testament to how hard they all worked to keep this place up.

There was so much to say, and she didn't know where to start.

When the fire had happened as a child, she was the only survivor. No one understood how. The local news referred to her as a miracle baby. Her mom, dad, and siblings had all died in a fire started by a Christmas tree. She had only been an infant at the time. All she had were the pictures, music box, and secondhand stories. She had always wanted to have a normal family, but never had gone without the love, support, and guidance that others might. Her grandma had been such a wonderful influence and raised her as her own without missing a beat. She had enrolled in music and dance lessons, tutoring, and scouts where she had gone on her first camping trip.

It was there Megan learned why she had survived.

A bunch of the girls sat around the campfire toasting marshmallows and making s'mores. Her grandma was off to the side talking with the other moms. Grandma had always insisted on chaperoning any overnight trips. Megan resented it during her teenage years, but always understood why. After so much loss, her grandma couldn't take any risks.

On that day, Megan and a bunch of the other seven-year-olds took turns running their hands through the flames of the campfire, each daring the others to get closer and closer until the smell of burned arm hair mixed with the caramelized sugar of the marshmallows.

Aware of fire safety—it was priority one for her grandma —Megan had eyed her grandma when the time had come for her turn. She put her hand near the fire and felt nothing. The other girls giggled and cheered her on in hushed whispers with squeals of disbelief when she put her hand in the coals and grabbed a log. Another girl, Lila, the bully of the group, was not to be outdone. She tried to pull the same stunt, screaming in pain when the fire burned her straight through. Of course she blamed Megan. At the time, Megan was too stunned from her own experience to defend herself.

Her grandma had freaked out. Absolutely lost it. She got the lecture of a lifetime on the way home. It wasn't more than a few months before Megan found an old birthday candle and smuggled it up to her room. Late at night with the window cracked so as to avoid setting off all of the smoke detectors—Grandma had one in every room—Megan practiced touching the flame over and over. When it was burned to the base and she could no longer light it, only then did she start to understand the impossible.

Fire didn't burn her. Or rather, she couldn't burn.

She had extinguished the flames with her thumb and forefinger so many times, but there was no evidence of pain or discoloration. The only sign she had touched it was the smear of black soot around her nail.

It was then she realized why she had been the only one who had survived the house fire. She didn't know why she had this ability, and never had told another soul until last year when she had told Laura after seeing her friend's ability for herself.

Laura had responded to Megan seeing her use her ability just like Megan would've if caught. She tried to leave in the dead of night, running away with her son, Holden, from everyone she had ever known because Megan had witnessed her ability to heal. As it was, revealing that secret had led to her now blissfully happy marriage.

Megan had shared her truth too as a show of understanding. She and Laura had been best of friends before, but the experience brought them closer than ever. Neither one knew how or why they had the powers they did, and both had chosen professions that allowed them to use their power to help others. Both of them also felt they could take more risks, but there was a darker side too.

During one of their talks at the tea shop, both Megan and Laura confided in each other the same sort of guilt and impostor syndrome. Their colleagues that did the same jobs without the same insurance were the real heroes. She was a fake with a secret up her sleeve.

On top of that, she had always dealt with survivor's guilt, but when she had started working, the feeling had morphed into a strange insecurity and feeling of being a fake. She was always rehearsing for the day when everyone found out she was a phony. She wasn't brave at all. She just couldn't burn. If she could, she'd already be dead. She never could've run into a burning building or cut someone out of a car on fire without that knowledge. Sure the equipment was good, but without her ability, there was no way Megan could take the same risks. The other firefighters and EMTs thought she was the bravest person there. It was a complete lie. She wasn't brave at all. And today was the day it all fell apart.

"You okay over there?" Buzz asked her while opening a drawer. He pulled out a legal pad and pen. For what, she didn't know, but she would've bet her chances on becoming a vet that whatever was coming was not good.

CHAPTER 39

Troy folded the last pair of pants and zipped up his duffle. The only things left that identified he had ever occupied the room were the clothes laid out for tomorrow morning and his toiletries. Everything else, he had already staged by the door.

Today he had spent most of the day cooking. Troy made everything his dad had loved while they had been together, including some new favorites he had snuck in on a whim and a hunch. Dad had always been a meat and potatoes guy, so of course there was pot roast, meatloaf, and beef stew. Troy had also made a lasagna, chicken Alfredo, and two pans of baked spaghetti. What surprised him was that his dad had enjoyed chicken tagine. The flavors were an exploration, along with pork carnitas, Caribbean jerk chicken, and jambalaya.

Troy had gone to the store and fixed pans of these meals, using every pan in the kitchen multiple times and wearing out the oven and crock pot. His mom had been a meal preparer too, and the proportioned container he held in his hand reminded him of her so much. Because work on the ranch had busy times, she made sure to plan ahead, always having something to pull out of the deep freezer so they could have a home-cooked meal on a short turnaround. Now he packed everything for two servings, taking care to label each one with the name and reheating instructions.

His dad didn't say too much all day, preferring to sit in his chair and read the paper while Levi lay on the braided rug in front of him. The new wood stove crackled while the morning news changed to daytime TV, then the evening roundup of primetime shows.

From where he had stood in the kitchen, Troy could see the TV and the back of his dad's chair, taking notice how he folded the newspaper when he did the crossword, spoke too loud on his cellphone when a friend called, and made a note in his date book on the end table when the doctor's office called to confirm an upcoming appointment.

Troy tried to memorize every detail and movement, while anticipating what else he could do to make his departure easier. He had ordered a cord of wood and tipped the guy to stack it right next to the house, which allowed for easy access for his dad. That would be plenty to get through the cold snaps of spring and the rest of the summer through the beginning of fall when he hoped to return for a visit.

He had taken the truck for a tune-up, making sure to update all of the paperwork. And of course, he had cooked all day.

He knew his dad was looking forward to the last part the most because during a commercial break he had asked, "Are you fixing that Cajun dish?"

"Yeah, just put it in."

"Good."

The minimalistic praise brought a smile to Troy's face even now as he thought about it. Home-cooked food had been one of the ways his mom had shown her love, and Troy was glad to be able to do something with his hands.

When he was finished, he cleaned the whole place top to bottom, finished laundry and bedding, and then called to make arrangements for someone to come and help deep clean the place on a regular basis. His dad had decided he liked his new house better now that he and Levi had settled in. There were fewer stairs and it was still home, with fewer memories in his face, and less change than what was happening at the ranch house. In his dad's words, "I don't need all that fancy new stuff going in."

Troy hadn't argued. It wasn't a surprise his dad didn't want to rush back to the place filled with so many memories. In a way, it was a new chapter for them both. His dad had leaned into that idea.

He also was incredibly practical too. There were two steps going up to the small, covered porch. This walk-in shower was much newer and had a little more space in the bathroom. The bedrooms were smaller, but the walls were tighter and it was easier to heat. The biggest thing he hadn't mentioned was the one story.

They had never spoken of the fact that he had to be carried downstairs in his own home, but Troy had known his father long enough to know that was a painful thing for the old cowboy, and pride wouldn't let him go back again. Of course, Troy knew there had been a lot of smoke and his dad was weakened in the moment, and this had little to do with his actual ability.

Of course all this meant the ranch house would sit empty until his return. Troy had balked when his ever-practical dad had suggested renting out the house to "a nice, young ranching family."

He didn't like the idea one bit, so his dad had dropped it. Still, they both knew the money from the insurance had run out. Taxes didn't pay for themselves, and even though Troy planned to send money back to help for the horses, more income would be a necessity. With him not here to manage the place, the B&B plan was as good as asking Uncle Sam to accept an IOU.

All of this wasn't even to mention his dad's medical bills, which had started to roll in. He was on Medicare, but not having a supplement was a real headache. Troy had learned far more about insurance than he ever wanted to in his life and had been on hold enough to be able to sing along to the bad hold music.

The reality was, in his time here, Troy had done everything he could, and despite it all, he still felt like shit.

Troy had paused to go out and visit with the horses, finding a now familiar peace in the smell of the hay bedding and dusty warmth of the barn. Seeing Braxton again made him want to stay, but what he wanted didn't matter. All he could do was his best with the time he had. At least he could take comfort in that.

It helped him as much as the new therapist had. He knew there was no way he could get trauma treatment without a rapport, history, and relationship, but in the absence of his treatment, all of the old habits had started to get the better of him, so he had made an appointment to at least go talk with someone.

The licensed counselor's office was downtown, and while he had only gone three times during his time here, she had helped reframe the short-term incidents he was having and a few of his feelings of inadequacy and fears about relationships. Of course, he had tried to steer them away from that. He didn't have enough time to unpack all of that shit here and now. While they both knew it wasn't a long-term thing, it felt good knowing he had support whenever he came to visit his dad.

Now, the truck was ready to go, and Dad was settled in. That was that. Troy had even reluctantly checked his email to find hundreds he had to sift through. In what seemed like a matter of minutes, *Wheel* was over and his dad kicked down the new La-Z-Boy's footrest.

"Big day tomorrow. Got to get some sleep."

"See you in the morning, Dad."

That was all that was said, and as Troy looked at the duffle in front of him, he recognized how shameful it was that there was so much left unsaid between the two of them. With his imminent departure, the distance had started to creep in again just like it had before. Work, time, and differences in day to day life crept in, pushing the gap wider, straining any conversation until they became two strangers who wanted to connect but couldn't speak the same language.

He couldn't let it happen again. He would call. Check in. Be the person Megan had inspired him to be.

He shut his eyes at the memory of her. That was the biggest regret. If only he could see her one last time. He had wanted to text. Just saying he was leaving and thanking her for everything. Hoping she would talk to him again. Even if she was mad, it was better than her absence.

But the pain of rejection had scared him away. He had kept hoping. Going into town and lingering just to see her. Hoping she might bump into him and—

The knock on the door almost had him tripping over himself to get down the hall. He didn't care what he looked like, only that she was here now and he could pick her up, wrap her in his arms, and press his mouth to hers in a hot kiss marking her as his.

Levi waited by the door, barking and walking back and forth in anticipation of who was on the other side. If Troy had been a four-legged animal, he would've been doing the same. God, he had missed her. He might fall on his knees right here and now and beg for forgiveness, asking her to stick with him while he was away, come visit every other month, and then move in together in the ranch house.

Troy wrapped his hand on the handle, threw the lock and ripped it open.

His smile faded to confusion, politeness, and then cool understanding as he processed what he saw on the porch looking back at him.

Two police officers stood at the door with paperwork in their hands.

"Mr. Troy Chapman, you're under arrest."

CHAPTER 40

The news was all over the papers, TV, and social media the next day. An arrest had been made matching the description of the perpetrator.

Megan sat on her couch where he had sat just a couple of weeks earlier and watched, holding a pillow to her chest as the newscaster undid her world one sharp-tongued sentence at a time.

"A man from Goldvein was arrested in the recent attack at Dury Park. Troy Chapman, age thirty, was taken into custody by police last night for attacking his one-time girl-friend, Keira McKinney, while she was on a run.

"Police believe the suspect picked his target after seeing her at the grocery store. Chapman is son of Hank Chapman, who recently had a house fire on his property six weeks ago. His son, Troy, was visiting here from Ft. Campbell, Kentucky, where is he a non-commissioned officer in the US Army."

Troy's mugshot showed up, and at the sight of him, Megan's stomach had done a belly flop into a pool of emotion. She hadn't been prepared at first.

Earlier today, she had woken up like normal and flopped over on her bed to scroll through her phone before joining the land of the living. That's when she had first seen the mugshot.

It was a blue background as was expected. He wasn't smiling, but he wasn't frowning either. He looked terrible. Like he was completely bone-tired, but those brown eyes looked back at her from the screen, and her traitorous heart had started hammering in her chest. Once she had made sense of what she was reading, she had jumped up and scrambled to the couch, hungry for any and all information about what had happened.

That had been three hours ago.

This was the first rerun of the news cycle, but she couldn't look away in case there was any new information.

The TV flashed to a clip of a man in a fitted gray suit with a purple pocket square that matched his tie and complemented his shirt. He sat in front of a fake plant in some cold office suite with a bookshelf behind him.

"Dr. David Lionel is here joining us." The newscaster flashed back on screen in a red dress that matched her lipstick. "Dr. Lionel is a psychologist who treats posttraumatic stress disorder in the surrounding area. Dr. Lionel, thank you for your time."

She sat back against the couch, feeling her shoulders fall from their position around her ears, filled with tension and anticipation. There was no new information, so they wanted to keep poking for a new angle to get airtime. Megan knew there was nothing but speculation, but didn't dare look away in case she missed some detail or kernel of truth.

The TV flashed back to Dr. Lionel in his office. "We believe this attack was brought on by psychosis from PTSD. When we looked at all of the recent attacks, we can see that there is a pattern of those who work in high pressure jobs in security of some capacity. It is not uncommon for people in these jobs to develop PTSD due to the nature of their work. While it does require a medical diagnosis, it can be treated through a variety of options by a medical professional."

"Are those treatments being offered to the other recent perpetrators in the similar attacks?"

"I can't discuss details of individual cases, but once those suspects are in custody, additional resources become available to get them the help they need."

The newscaster began to speak while a clip of people running in Dury Park ran in the corner of the screen. "Chapman has been charged with aggravated assault and robbery. Further charges may be coming. We will continue to update you as this story unfolds. Next, some local elementary students are getting a shock by going to a mining facility nearby—"

Megan's phone buzzed again. It was Laura and Ash offering to come by. They had texted earlier when they had heard the news. Megan appreciated the offer of company, but honestly just wanted to sink farther into the couch. There were so many questions. She had so many feelings.

No wonder he had freaked out when he had seen the news reports. His reaction still struck her as odd, and she played it over in her mind again and again looking for answers she hadn't seen. How could this be? Was this the same person who was so kind and gentle? It didn't make sense.

Visions flooded through her mind of how he had held her. Kissed her. Cooked for her. Once he had arrived, he'd cleaned his dad's house and cooked for him. He had told her how that day, they immediately went out to buy a new La-Z-Boy recliner to replace the one that had been lost in the fire. A new gift to replace the old. She could see Troy sitting there at the dining room table with Levi resting his head in Troy's lap, looking up at him with a knowing smile.

None of it made any sense. He was kind. He was attentive. Hell, his truck was cleaner than hers. Megan racked her brain to try to reconcile what she had missed.

There were odd things, but nothing that made him seem dangerous. The nightmare, the locks, even—God help her—his aversion to commitment could all be explained. He'd had a lot of trauma in his life, so much pain, but never responded with hate.

Megan forced herself to stand and get some water to try and clear the fog in her head. As she watched the water fill the glass, she thought of the tea she had made for him after his nightmare. There had been real fear. Real terror at whatever he was seeing. He didn't lash out at her. There was shame, and he'd pulled into himself when it was over, like an animal who didn't want to be seen retreating into a cave.

He didn't want a relationship so he could avoid the pain he had seen in others. He was trying to keep things happy and light and trying to get away from that pain and shame he knew too well. He wasn't going out to try and hurt women. He didn't prey on anyone. Other people could respond differently, but Troy didn't.

Even with that fear, though, he had checked the locks all of the time. Everything he did was defense not offense, so why did he get arrested?

Megan drained the glass, wishing—for one of the first times in her life—it was something stronger. Somewhere in the cushions of the couch, her phone buzzed again.

Megan closed her eyes, trying to avoid it all. Just like Troy, she didn't want the pain of having to explain to her friends how she had misjudged. Her anxiety bloomed from an ugly seed in her chest. She was never any good with people, and here was the proof. This is why her grandma had always sheltered her away from others. She didn't want her to get hurt. Wanted to save her the hot shame, the heartache, the longing.

Even her biggest secret hadn't been enough for him to stop and listen. To care. By some miracle, Megan had been given a gift, a chance at life. She had tried to pay back the universe by using her gift to help others, but she felt like a fraud. Now, she was putting the lives of others in danger. It was time to go. She couldn't do it anymore.

She should be dead. When she told him her greatest secret, Troy had flicked that off like an insignificant piece of dust. It was impossible, and therefore it didn't matter. None of it mattered to him. He had told her that, and she had been stupid enough to start to love—

Megan dropped the glass. The loud, hollow crash sent the cats running and the birds into a panic. A cold wave of dread washed over her as the tears fell. She had tried to avoid feeling close to anyone, yet here she was. She loved him; therefore he had gone.

CHAPTER 41

The rain was cold. It hit her face like pellets biting into her skin, somewhere between sleet and freezing rain. It wasn't that cold, but the gray overcast area made it seem darker, bleaker.

Then again, coming to the cemetery for some family time never had been a party.

Megan shoved her hands in her pockets, tugged the hood of her raincoat on, and marched uphill away from the parking lot. The cemetery was one of the oldest in Goldvein and somehow still had room. She didn't know much about the history of who was buried here, other than her family. Rumor had it that some of the graves were of Civil War veterans, which she believed as the town had been settled by miners looking to strike it rich and expand west.

Troy had lit up when he talked about history with her at one of their dinners. He had a few artifacts he had found on his family's property, and Megan wondered what the old foundation to the original house had looked like. She had wanted to see it. He had wanted to show it to her. But of course that was not going to happen.

To get her mind off him, she tried to focus on the cold, wet grass—new green growth as the beginnings of spring had started to peek through the biting frost. There would be another cold snap before the sunny days settled in to stay. That's how it always was.

Megan's family plot was toward the back. She knew she was close when she saw the tree. There was a maple the cemetery director had planted when her family had been buried there. Her grandmother always admired the tree's beautiful leaves on the few times they had visited. The memories had been painful, so they only made the trip back to Goldvein once a year. It seemed only fitting that she should lie under it when her time had come, and that's what Megan had done.

She looked up ahead and saw a figure sitting on the bench near the tree. They wore a dark coat and hat, despite holding an umbrella to stay dry.

Megan stopped and looked around her. No one else was present. All of the years she had come here, no one else had ever been visiting her family when she was. She stopped, watched, and waited.

They didn't move.

The rain continued a steady pattern of unhurried watering. It was cold, but gentle. A good reminder of the facts of life.

Megan stood from a distance and watched, trying to calm the anxiety racing through her. She knew she was in a vulnerable place. Her heart had been ripped out, then everything she thought she knew about Troy had turned into a lie. She wanted to know more. Craved the comfort of information and connection. Wanted to turn to the women in her family for comfort navigating the new feelings of wanting, despair, longing, and rejection. She had so much she wanted to understand.

Her body trembled with the cold and exhaustion. She hadn't slept properly in days. Couldn't focus and had no appetite. She knew she had lost weight again but couldn't make herself eat. This morning it had gotten so bad she had thrown up in the sink when brushing her teeth. That hadn't happened in years and wasn't a welcome return.

Coming here had always brought comfort, and now someone else was in her spot, on her bench, looking at her family.

Megan stood rooted to the spot, her heart hammering in her chest while her anxiety swirled in her stomach.

Should she turn around? Come back after waiting in her car? The rain picked up around her.

She didn't have time for this. Tomorrow was the first day of the rest of her life. If she nailed the vet school interview, she would be fulfilling everything she wanted. Finally back on her path to becoming what she knew she was meant to be.

This was it. She needed to see her family, get over herself, and move on.

Dread and guilt swamped her. If...no, *when* she left, she couldn't come back here as much. She would need to leave the station, leave Laura and Ash. And she wouldn't be able to help people as a firefighter anymore.

She had looked and there were stations near the university, but the program specifically stated it was full time, and attendance was compulsory.

Her ability—gift, power, whatever—would go unused. A life saved for nothing.

She tried to close her eyes against the visions of people dying that she couldn't save, telling herself there were others who could help. She wasn't good enough. Pictures of families ate at her, corroding her broken heart with visions of what she would never have.

She didn't have parents, siblings, grandparents, and her only lover was gone too.

There was no one, and she was completely alone.

The tears came, and she tried unsuccessfully to fight them off. They slid down, heating her cold damp cheeks as she stood halfway to her family.

Her thoughts started looping faster and faster now. All of her failings—what if she left and failed again? How could she do this to the station? When would she see her friends? What did it all mean? Would she still be alone?

Megan shook herself and looked around at all of the headstones around her. The granite was dark and gray with the rain. Literal marks on this world.

Each one of these people had been children, loved ones, cherished. Did they have children of their own? Well, that's how it went, didn't it? What legacy did they leave? One of kindness? Friendships? Family?

At her grandmother's funeral, a few locals had come by, but Megan didn't remember many of them. It had been a blur of well wishes in a numb shell of emotion. No one was close enough to hold her while she cried. Just like now, she had been alone.

Found alone in the ashes, alone to grieve, alone in love. Would she die alone? Did it matter?

She hugged herself as the thought chilled her to the bone. She had friends. How long would it take for them to realize she wasn't at home if she let go of the wheel on the ride back?

Enough. Megan pushed those thoughts away and stood tall.

Yes. She did matter. She had friends, and dreams, and goals. She had family and she didn't know if she was religious or not, but she believed she would see them again. She would be loved.

Megan tramped up the hill, focusing on her family and what she wanted to say this time, not on the person sitting there. She would say hello and that was it. Maybe they would leave after a time, even though they had an umbrella and she did not. She made sure to let her boots stamp on the ground so as not to scare whomever it was. They didn't flinch as she approached from behind, and she started to speak.

"Good afternoon..." She jumped when she recognized him. At the sound of her voice, a large yellow tail started thumping against the wet grass. Levi jumped up and bounded right over, muddy paws and all.

"Hello, Megan."

Mr. Chapman sat under a large black umbrella. "I was wondering if I would ever see you here."

CHAPTER 42

"Mr. Chapman? What are you doing here?" Megan asked through the drips of cold rain.

"Just visiting the family." He nodded his head toward the gravestones on the opposite side of the bench from her family plot and gave her an odd smile. "I like to keep in touch. Want to join me?"

"Sure." She sank down next to him on the cold granite bench.

They sat together like that, with the sounds of rain around them. Mr. Chapman's golf umbrella shielded them from the cold rain. They admired the graves through the drops of water like tears off the edge of the umbrella.

Levi snuggled down at their feet under the bench, which was presumably keeping him dry. Minutes ticked by before either one spoke. Mr. Chapman broke the silence first.

"I remember when Troy first met you."

Megan smiled, the sadness tugging at her heart. He must be heartbroken. In a way, he was losing his last family member too. Megan had thought about calling him to ask how he had been after the arrest, but never could bring herself to pick up the phone.

"He was interested in every little detail about you. He didn't want me to notice, but I could tell. Any chance he would get, he would ask me about you. About what you liked or what you didn't like. About your family."

Megan didn't move or speak, not sure of where this was going. Her heart was too tired to want to try and predict, having already bet the house and lost. If she didn't like him so much, she would've let him know about the bad breakup and shut him down. Given everything he was going through, she let him continue to give her a play-by-play of her heartbreak.

"We got to talking, and once you two started going out, he seemed so much happier."

That brought a ghost of a sad smile to her lips.

"He's been through a lot, you know. I did my best, but I wasn't prepared to give him what he needed. I tried, but I don't understand a lot about all of this mental health stuff. My daddy was a hard man. You had to be in those days. It was literally life and death. He loved us, in his own way. Provided, disciplined, and drug us to church. There was much more cursing than praise, and that's the way I was raised.

"I remember telling him, Dad, it's not like that anymore. We don't have to fight for everything, but you see, that's all he knew how to do. He fought for everything he had. I thought life was easier until I lost half of mine. All I had left was Troy. He's a lot like my dad in that regard. Just pushes through. That was even before the army. And then…well, he's been through a lot."

Megan nodded.

"He got me thinking though, and it turns out," he said with a smile, "I knew your parents."

Megan's world stopped spinning, and whatever it was that she thought she saw, she didn't see that coming.

"I'm sorry, what? That's amazing. I mean, I had no idea. How? I didn't realize you were the same age or class. Tommy White and Jennifer Heywood? He was in the technical program." Her hands were moving and she couldn't make them stop. The words tumbled out of her in a mad rush to get all of her questions answered. "Auto mechanic. She took typing and shorthand. Became a secretary."

Mr. Chapman smiled a wide smile, broad and true, that was identical to Troy's and nearly stopped her heart in its tracks.

"I didn't know your mom all that well, but I remember seeing her at our football games always hanging out with Tommy. They palled around together with a group of people. I could get you some of their names. They might still be around and willing to talk to you. I'm sure you have a lot of questions."

Megan struggled to speak. "Oh my God, that'd be amazing. Thank you. Thank you so much. I wanted to know so much, but my grandma… It was too painful for her."

Mr. Chapman closed his eyes and nodded slowly. "I understand."

"How did you know my father?"

Mr. Chapman smiled while looking off into the grass. "I was a senior and he was a freshman, so I didn't know him really well until we played basketball together."

"I had no idea he played."

"He was the star player. Made varsity freshman year. Blew all of the coaches away. That was the season I sprained an ankle working on the ranch. I was benched so he took my spot. Always a great defender. My dad needed help and expected it too, but he understood sports. Anyway, I wanted to apologize for not putting it together sooner.

"I was so sorry to hear about the fire. And at Christmastime. The children. It was awful. I had heard that the baby was taken by a relative and moved away. By that time I was married myself with the boys and in the thick of it all. I've thought of him often since, but didn't think much about the baby. Troy mentioned it and then your name clicked for me."

He looked at her then with tears in his eyes. "I'm sorry I didn't mention it sooner."

Megan smiled. "I'm just so glad you did."

"You favor your mom more."

"I do have a few pictures and things that were recovered, so I had seen her, but it's nice to hear someone say that out loud."

Hank looked thoughtful for a moment and then smiled at Megan. "I have something at home I think you'll want to see. Let's get out of this rain, and why don't you follow me back to the house."

CHAPTER 43

After a muddy walk back to their vehicles and a drive back to the ranch, Megan and Hank got dried off as best they could and sat down in his living room. He had pulled a book off a shelf and held it in his hands.

Megan looked down at the black leather volume in his hand. It was facedown so she couldn't see the title. "It's my old high school yearbook. It was in one of the few rooms at the house that wasn't damaged in the fire."

"Here." He passed her the book which had a few scraps from *TV Guide* sticking out. She flipped open to one and realized he had used it as a bookmark, when she saw her own reflection smiling up from the page.

Her mom's face was right there on the page— she was still a girl, and stick thin, who hadn't quite found her confidence yet. She looked up shyly, like she was mid-laugh, clearly nervous around the photographer.

Megan drank in the sight and flipped to the other page to find her dad, much thinner, his mouth almost too wide for his face in a full-blown smile completely free from worries and judgments. She flipped again to the page with the basketball team and saw him in front with one knee down, one up. His smile was still bright and bold, stretching across his face. She could see the muscles on his arms, exposed by the jersey, not quite as full as the older boys, but clearly strong.

Megan's eyes drifted across the picture, searching until she landed on Hank Chapman. He looked so much like Troy but happier.

"Troy looks just like you."

"When he smiles."

Megan heard the regret in his voice. They both knew he didn't do that anymore. What joy he had wouldn't be around now given what had happened.

"I'm sorry about what happened."

"He didn't do it, but he won't tell them that."

Megan didn't expect that. "He's not going to defend himself?"

Mr. Chapman shook his head.

"I don't understand."

"He's stubborn and prideful, and he is worried that if he tells them where he was, he'll lose his job."

Megan's mind tried to put together the pieces but was coming up short. "Did he do something worse?"

"The army hasn't always been supportive of mental health. They say they are, but he still worries that if they find out he's in therapy and trauma treatment, he could lose his job."

First, she didn't understand, but annoyance was quickly followed by rising anger.

"But it's because of the army he has trauma. He got it from his deployments. That doesn't make any sense."

"Mission first. He wants to stay deployable. If he can't be counted on with a weapon or in a high stress situation, then he can't do his job. Troy didn't want to tell me, but it all came out one night. Apparently, a lot of soldiers keep it a secret and try to handle things on their own."

"He's not doing well, then?" Megan didn't need the answer to know the truth but held her breath as he started to speak.

Mr. Chapman looked at the floor and squinted, trying to reconcile a painful memory. "He was screaming. I woke up, heard something fall, and went in to find him screaming on the floor. He was holding his head, crouched up in a ball. So much pain. I just held him. I didn't know what to do, so I grabbed him and held on. Hadn't held him since he was a boy. We talked about it that morning. He's scared he will lose his job, his benefits, his retirement. All because he might not be deployable. He defines himself by his job. Committed. Like I said. Stubborn. He tried to reach out to someone local on the day of the attack."

"But that's not right. None of that is right. What if they convict him? Why won't he tell them if he was somewhere else?"

"He did, but he isn't sharing where. Fifth amendment. Always a fan of history and the Constitution."

"God, how can he be so stubborn?"

Mr. Chapman just shook his head. "Don't worry. There's nothing we can do if he doesn't want to disclose his alibi."

"When is the arraignment?"

"Tomorrow."

"Have you spoken with him?"

"Once. He didn't sound like himself. Told me not to bond him out, and save the money instead."

"What about his lawyer? If we could let his lawyer know…" Her voice trailed off when Mr. Chapman shook his head.

"I thought about that, but if Troy doesn't want his records disclosed then there is no proof of his whereabouts on that day. He doesn't want anyone to know. I'm sure it'll work out despite that. There can't be any actual proof he was the attacker, since we know he was somewhere else."

She wasn't convinced.

Megan tried to push the thought out of her mind with a sad feeling of regret at him being wrongfully forced to go through a trial. She shouldn't feel the way she did, but everything about it was wrong from start to finish. He was too stubborn and prideful to end the whole thing. There was no shame in getting help. There shouldn't be. Especially when the alternative was sitting in a jail cell waiting for the court system to get it all straightened out. She too had seen how much pain he had. Clearly, it hadn't gotten better. To be punished more was an added insult.

Mr. Chapman distracted her from her racing thoughts by patting her hand.

"Keep going," he said, pointing at the book. "There's something else I want you to see."

There was one last slip of paper tucked in the yearbook toward the back. She peeled the page back, revealing the signatures.

A quick skim took her breath away.

Right there was a handwritten half-page letter to Mr. Chapman from her dad. The letters were in blue ink, in the clumsy writing of a high school boy. The script had an odd tilt to it as if he had written in a hurry or on something unsteady. Megan ran her hand over the ink on the page as she scoured the message again and again before going back a third time, reading through her tears.

———

Hank,

I can't believe it's the end of the year already! I'm going to miss playing with you on the court. Hopefully you can come out next year and cheer us on.

I really want to thank you for all of our talks after practice. I decided to ask Jenny out to get a milkshake because of everything you said. You were right. You can't let fear run your life. Thanks for all the good advice on and off the court. I owe you one.

Congratulations on your graduation! Go Bulldogs!
Tommy White

———

"YOU ARE the one who set my parents up?"

Mr. Chapman shook his head. "No, not really. I just told him to go for it."

He sat there, humble, so much like his son. He was more crouched down, his shoulders slumped. The weight of exhaustion was around him like a cloud. It wasn't just age or grief, but pure exhaustion. She hadn't remembered him looking that old even after getting out of the hospital, but the sadness around him was so strong. The man had lost his wife, child, his home, and now his son had been arrested.

Megan's life hadn't always been easy, but she had a lot to be grateful for. She couldn't imagine being in his shoes. The pain was too real. She could almost feel it coming off him in waves. But yet, he was talking to her about her family. Giving her a priceless gift in his own moment of pain.

"He loved her. Everyone could see it. They just needed a little push, so I tried to encourage him."

"Wow. In a way, you're responsible for me being here."

His reaction was immediate. "I didn't mean for you to think… No. No. No. I mean they would've anyway. I just sorta helped suggest. That was all."

His cheeks were turning pink, and she didn't think it was from the slight chill in the house.

"What did you tell him in those talks?"

"God, I haven't thought about that in forever." He paused and seemed to be searching his memories. "I think I remember saying, if you like her, go for it. What do you have to lose? Why wait? Why be afraid?"

"You can't live your life in fear?" she asked, pointing to the words in her dad's hand.

"I guess it made an impact on him."

"Mr. Chapman—"

"Please, call me Hank. We've been through enough."

"Mr. Hank…" He gave her a look, but hey, they could meet in the middle.

"Thank you." She held the yearbook to her chest, hugging the worn, stiff leather. "I can't thank you enough for sharing this with me."

"I owe you my life. So does Levi, and besides, it was all Troy. I was trying to encourage you two to get together. I'm sorry I pushed too hard."

Megan's heart ached for him more than she wanted to admit. "I'm surprised he mentioned me at all. We had a pretty big fight."

"He cares about you. I figured there was a disagreement about something."

"He was getting all protective, and…"

She froze.

"Megan? Is something wrong?"

"My phone."

"What about it? Do you need to call someone?"

Megan turned to him and said, "I know how to help Troy."

CHAPTER 44

Troy had been better. The past few days had gone a completely wrong direction, and things weren't shaping up to be any better. After he had been arrested, he had first called his CO and then called a lawyer. Thankfully, his CO hadn't asked about his whereabouts, and much to Troy's complete relief, the Court of Military Justice was not getting involved. Had he not been on leave, this complete shit storm would have been even more of a nightmare.

He was grateful for small miracles.

Still, the CO wasn't sold yet.

"Are you sure you don't need any help with this?"

"Yeah, I got it. They were looking for someone in a surplus coat with dark hair when they picked me up. Once everything is sorted out, I'll let you know when I'll get there."

"Alright, well, keep me posted when you can."

Troy knew his CO wasn't convinced that he shouldn't help, and why should he be? But Troy was between a rock and a hard place. He needed his job with the army. It was all he had, everything he had worked for, and if he got discharged because of a conviction, those retirement benefits he had worked so hard for were totally gone.

If he provided his whereabouts and the name of the new therapist in town, then the police could confirm the appointment which had been around the same time as the attack. He would get the charges dropped for sure, but then somewhere in some court paperwork, his therapy would be public knowledge and some tough questions would be asked. If they found he was not deployable, unable to carry out a mission… Boom. Discharged.

Troy had no education. Sure, maybe he'd be able to keep his GI bill depending on the type of discharge, but then what? Once, he had wanted to be a history teacher, but he couldn't go to school and support the ranch and his dad's medical bills. There was no way. The bed and breakfast had been a pipe dream that was a long way from bringing in any income.

That was why he told his dad to save the money and not bond him out—and why he'd stayed quiet.

As a result of this colossal shitstorm, Troy had the pleasure of spending the weekend in the county jail. Troy didn't have much of a problem with the other inmates. He understood the chain of command, the power of lying low, and had a lot of time to think. What he did mind was the nightmares.

They had gotten worse, just like always with stress. The first night had been awful. He didn't know if he had been screaming or not, but if he had, the echo woke him up quick enough not to draw attention to himself.

He didn't have access to his normal routine that helped his anxiety, so he had done his best not to sleep. Not super healthy, but what choice did he have? Screaming in the middle of the night did not suggest innocence, and he didn't need the attention.

What he had done was pace and think about Megan.

He should've told her everything. She would've understood. Maybe they could've talked it all through. He didn't like being alone but didn't like the pressure of commitment. It was all new to him, but none of those dating apps held any appeal. He would've told her that. Explained he wanted to try long distance. He had intended to. That was why he had been so insistent about her safety. He knew that was clingy. It wasn't his best moment, and she already knew he had struggled at night.

He should've come clean. Trusted her. Owned it. He wished he could go back and beg her to stay with him, to be patient as he tried long distance. Instead he had been too much—too overbearing—and pushed her away.

He hadn't even stopped to listen to what she was telling him about her power.

At two in the morning, he played it over and over in his head. Maybe it was the lack of sleep, but the puzzle pieces started to fit together, and it didn't sound crazy.

"I can't burn."

He turned that over in his head. It all lined up. She was an infant. The sole survivor of the house fire that killed her family. She had talked about her duty to be a firefighter and not feeling worthy. She shrunk back into herself when he had called her a hero. His dad had told him she had stayed to find Levi as the house was burning around her.

The longer he sat with it, the more it made sense. Well, it was actually crazy, but…

God, to think she couldn't be affected by the thing that kept him up at night. Life was kind of funny that way.

Not communicating with her was his biggest regret. By the time all of this shit got sorted out, assuming it did, he'd have to go back immediately, and there wouldn't be time to say goodbye. He wouldn't get to touch her again or see the freckles on her nose. He didn't even have a picture to remember her, and of course she would be in no mood to see him. Troy was sure he was on the news, and that meant Megan knew about his arrest.

God, what did she think of him? Did she think of him? She had mentioned she was hoping to go to that vet school. In fact, he smiled to himself at the irony. Here he was in jail alone with his thoughts, and tomorrow she would be off to her interview to get into vet school like she had always wanted. The thought of her happy and living life as she wanted was a welcome respite from the looping thoughts that plagued him, but it wasn't forever.

As much as he tried not to sleep, on the second night the body took over, leaving him open to the nightmare that followed.

His lids grew heavy and closed. All he saw was fire all around him. Dark figures reached out from beyond the flames. The first was Adam, strong and standing there while the fire licked up his old Wranglers he loved in high school. The second was his mom, looking gaunt and thin from the cancer treatments. She was standing in her old kitchen wearing an apron in front of the stove, a literal hell, with flames clawing at her skirt. His dad was running by with Levi, before he collapsed onto the floor with the flames around him. Troy tried to move to get to all of them, when the familiar screaming started. Simon looked out, his eyes wide and peeled back with complete pain and awareness of his suffering. Just like always, Troy tried. He tried so damn hard to reach him. Get there before it was too late. All of their faces mixed with the smoke until he could no longer see them. The screaming drowned out by the roar of the flames. That's when he saw Megan, crying alone in the inferno.

He jolted awake, covered in sweat.

Troy wasn't an easy crier. Never had been. But on the floor of the jail cell, he curled into himself and let the choking sobs come for all he had lost.

266

Megan sat on a worn wooden bench, clenching and unclenching her hands. Megan had tried to call the attorney's office when Hank had given her the name, but they had left for the night, so here she was outside the courtroom waiting to catch them.

She had tried to sleep last night but just couldn't, despite meditation and enough chamomile tea to choke a fish. All she could think about was Troy and everything Hank had told her.

Last night when she had gotten home, Megan had considered going to her music box and dabbing on a little of her grandma's perfume, but all of that was in the past. And none of it held answers to the future.

She already knew what she needed to do, and the choice had been clear.

Troy. He may not want her back, and between his aversion to commitment and long distance—not to mention the dating app situation—Megan wasn't getting her hopes up. Regardless, she had an overwhelming urge to come here today. Even if she never saw him again, Megan knew she needed to be here. To see him. To help him since he wouldn't help himself.

She couldn't have lived with herself any other way. She was meant to help people. That's why she was here.

Last night, when she had looked at her packed bags and new suit for her interview at the veterinary school, everything about it felt wrong.

Even though she couldn't get to his attorney until the next day, she had itched to take action. Do something.

Her cats had sat on the edge of the bed and watched as she scoured her phone again, wrote down all of the information with time stamps, and took screenshots.

Not satisfied, Megan paced while she thought through her next move. It needed to be convincing. She fired off a few ideas to Ash and smiled when she got the response in the affirmative.

The cats continued to watch from their perch on the bed. It probably was entertaining to watch her dig out the old printer from the bottom of the closet, throwing shoes in her wake and swearing as she dug somewhere in the back to shake the dust bunnies off the cords. When plugged in, it produced sounds of mashing gears and a screeching that rivaled the sounds of the damned. The cats darted away to find shelter.

To make space for the printer, she cleared off her desk, taking care to relocate her family artifacts to the windowsill before returning to the desk and propping up her laptop and connecting it to the tangle of cords.

While the computer reconnected with its old friend, Megan checked the ink, and finding it bone dry, she muttered another curse and dug around in her desk drawers looking through pens and old Post-It notes, hoping to God there was a lone ink cartridge in the back. She shouldn't have been surprised when none magically appeared. There was enough dust on the printer to grow potatoes. Clearly ink hadn't been a priority in the past.

But priorities changed.

Megan set her mouth in a line, grabbed her coat, wallet, and keys, and headed out to grab one in the pouring rain, despite her cats' obvious side-eye. Clearly, they weren't used to this new pattern of late night activity.

The drive was quick and silent except for the sprinkling of rain and the thump of the windshield wipers beating back the rain. The big store was almost deserted and as a result felt somewhere between eerie and peaceful. With no trouble at all, she marched right back to her target, snagged the ink, hit the self-checkout, and was driving back in record time. It hadn't even crossed her mind to look for cat food or anything for herself until she was pulling back into her spot.

All she could think about was Troy. Thoughts of him sitting somewhere in that jail consumed her. Was he having another nightmare? Did those other women mean something to him? Did he have them enable location services on their phone? Was that even normal or was it just creepy?

Megan turned over the thought in her head while messing with the printer back in the apartment. Given what he was clearly struggling with, probably not. Laura and Carter had location services enabled on each other. Maybe that was the new version of going steady?

He had been planning to leave, which might explain the dating apps, but now that she had some distance from it, they hadn't been messages of any substance. Did he stay late with them? Did other women console him after a nightmare?

Megan frowned at the thought, a new feeling growing stronger inside. She hadn't been able to put her finger on it before, but now identified it as protectiveness.

The idea of someone else getting him water and holding

him made her shoulders tense up toward her ears, not to mention her blood boil.

Which was precisely why, instead of using her ancient, temperamental printer to print off her resume and cover letter, she printed off the screenshots she emailed herself from her phone.

She didn't know exactly how he felt about her, but that didn't matter. He needed help, and she was compelled to go to him. Maybe this was what true love was. She might be mad, annoyed, and hurt by him, but she loved him and knew she had to go to him when he needed her. She couldn't sleep any other way.

That was how Megan ended up here on this bench instead of driving to her interview. Today was Troy's arraignment, and any minute, the lawyer would arrive to the courthouse where Megan could present the evidence that would get him off the hook and out of here.

Megan checked the time again on her phone and saw the email reply from the admissions office about rescheduling her interview.

A bubble of disappointment popped in her chest as she read what she already knew. There was no way to reschedule. She would need to wait until next year and try again.

Megan tucked her phone back in her bag and rested her hands on the folder. She was at peace with her decision. Nothing would really change, and that was okay. She would be okay.

Troy would leave and head back to the base. He had made it clear he was not interested in long-distance relationships, or anything serious for that matter. Wasn't it funny how he responded to loss with being afraid of commitment, and she took the other path? As a result, there was no future for either of them, but she would know she had helped in his time of need and that would have to be enough for her.

After that, they wouldn't talk much unless he came home. He hadn't left yet, and she was already looking forward to that first visit. He didn't like commitment, so he would probably be single, and maybe they could meet up.

That would mean her still being here, and still working at Station Three with Buzz, Jordan, and the rest of the crew. Buzz hadn't fired her after all, but had pulled out that yellow legal pad and given her the name of his counselor, a recommendation for yoga class, and a coveted week off to get some rest and sort out her feelings, which was very needed.

So it was settled.

Twenty-five years ago, Megan had been given a gift and now would continue to give back, just like how Troy had given her a gift, and now she was helping him. Everything was in balance. She was where she was meant to be, and all would be well.

Megan let out a long breath through her mouth and steadied herself for the lawyer in the blue suit coming down the hall.

Hank had given her the name, and Phil Marshall looked just like his picture on the website. Megan took great pride in her steady voice when she stepped in his way outside the door to the courtroom and said in a clear voice, "Excuse me. My name is Megan White. I have some evidence I think you need to see."

CHAPTER 46

Troy walked into the courtroom and sat where he was supposed to, grateful to be able to speak with his lawyer and hear the charges for himself. As much confidence as he had in the Constitution and rule of law, he was surprised it had gotten this far. While he sounded confident to his dad, he was really starting to get nervous. He might need to disclose his actual whereabouts on the night of the attack today.

The idea of spending another night in jail made his head pound and his stomach clench. And if this kept going, he could run the risk of obstructing justice or withholding evidence by tying up resources while the real person who attacked Keira was still at-large.

He needed to talk with his lawyer about those possibilities first before it all went any further. Either way, he was screwed, wasn't sleeping, and was so deep into overthinking he was seriously starting to question his sanity.

He had considered everything from every angle. What was he doing? Where was he going? What did he actually want?

In the long, dark hours of night, Troy had found the answers to those questions were changing.

Before, he had wanted to run away from bad memories, see something different, build up a retirement and sense of security.

Now, he was exhausted, physically and mentally. His scars were too tight and dried out from the jail soap. Nightmares plagued him. Going back to Ft. Campbell didn't feel right at all.

He wanted peace. He wanted to visit with his dad at McDonald's and argue over the answers to *Jeopardy*. He wanted to go to the barn every night and check on the horses, at least twice when it got too hot or too cold. But most of all, he wanted Megan right next to him in the middle of the night and in the kitchen the next morning. He wanted to know how her day was. How her work was. How her vet classes were going. He wanted to know everything about every moment of her day. And missing out on that for the next eight years was too much to bear.

He had to come clean. At least get out of this mess in such a way that he could recoup some of his benefits. Get what he could out of the army. He would call his therapist and see if she could transfer her notes to the new mental health clinic in town. Maybe that bed and breakfast dream could work after all. He had a little bit of savings. It would be hard, but he could start now and see where it took him. His great-grandfather had come here looking for gold, starting from nothing. He could do the same.

First, he needed to beg for Megan's forgiveness and tell her everything.

Troy had endured another nightmare last night and had hardly slept afterward. He felt like hell, probably looked worse, and...

There in the first row, he saw her hair. The beautiful red

curls were tossed up in some sort of messy bun like she'd had a late night too.

Troy digested the whole picture. She looked thinner, paler too, with dark circles under her beautiful, clear blue eyes. Her perfect lips turned upward slightly as she gave him a small, encouraging smile.

He smiled back until he realized where she should be and where she clearly was not. Today was Monday. Why hadn't she gone to her interview? She had been so excited when they had talked about it at dinner.

Guilt flooded him. After the way he had lost control, she had no reason to be here or to give up her dreams for him. He wished like hell he could talk to her, tell her to go, but he could only speak with his lawyer now.

Speak of the devil. Phil Marshall wore a blue suit today and was a man on a mission. He slapped a folder down in front of Troy.

"Why in the hell didn't you tell me about this sooner?"

Oh shit.

Troy pulled his hands over his face as the fight went out of him. He was so tired. So exhausted from the sleepless nights, the shame, the fear, the grief, the masking, the anxiety. All of it. This was how it was going to go.

"I'm sorry, I just didn't want anyone to know."

"Know that you're innocent?"

"Did Megan tell you?" Of course she did, but the question was how did she know? What did she think of him? Was that pity in her smile?

"Gave me printouts and everything. Troy, I really wish you would've just come out with this sooner. Could've saved us all a lot of trouble. Doesn't matter now. Let me go talk to the prosecutor and the judge."

"Let me take a look at these first." Better to know what kind of shit circus this would cause. The counselor said everything was confidential, but then again wasn't there some clause or something?

Troy sat down, flipped open the folder, and saw…maps.

There was no appointment reminder, no notes, no damning evidence or anything about mental health. All he saw was time-stamped maps with his location, tracking his phone on the other side of town, parked at the Brightrock Clinic right when the attack occurred.

"It may not be enough. The prosecutor will argue you could've given your phone to your girlfriend over there—"

Troy broke into a broad grin. "She's not my girlfriend." Officially…yet.

Phil just looked at him. "But she has your phone location? Okay, like I was saying, so I'll need to call and confirm you had an appointment at this time. I might need your permission for them to disclose your whereabouts and confirm your visit. Otherwise the court can subpoena the counselor and then it will be on record."

"Do we need to disclose any details of that to the courts or on my record?"

"Look, there's no shame in getting help."

"I know, I know, but I really don't want this out there."

Phil held his hand up. "I get it. I really do, but we got to keep you out of jail first. Let me go make this phone call to confirm everything."

While Phil dialed and waited, Troy glanced around him to see Megan sitting in the courtroom taking it all in. She was so beautiful, he just watched her until she caught him and blushed.

He smiled and she smiled back. That was good. He could build from there. At least he got to see her again, and hey, he probably wasn't going to have to sleep another night in jail after all. The door opened in the back of the room and his dad walked in, waving to Troy when he saw him.

Megan had turned around too and waved him down, motioning for him to join her. Troy watched as the two most important people in his life talked. The idea of leaving them felt completely wrong.

Phil walked over with a phone in his hand. "Alright, I got the receptionist on the phone. Here you go—she'll need to speak with you to give permission to send over the documentation we need."

Twenty minutes later, the judge walked in as the bailiff stood and announced his presence.

"All rise for the Honorable Judge Martin Schweider."

Judge Schweider was a broad man with gray hair and wired glasses. He sat down and without ceremony said, "You may be seated."

The arraignment began and was mostly standard proceedings with the charges of aggravated assault and felony theft. Phil did his thing and presented the evidence Megan had prepared.

While he did, Troy fought the urge to glance behind him. The courtroom was mostly empty with a few other people sitting waiting for other hearings, and one person that looked like a reporter. Great. While he tried not to dwell on that fact, he took comfort knowing Megan was just a few feet away, and she was here to help.

He wanted this to be over with so he could talk some sense into her and find out why in the hell she wasn't at her interview.

"Mr. Chapman?"

The judge's voice brought him right back to center.

Troy stood, his chair squealing back against the floor. "Yes, your honor."

The judge looked over the rim of his glasses at him, before squinting down at the maps in his hand. "I see here we have a map showing your location was nowhere near the park at the time of the attack, is that correct?"

"Yes, your honor."

"Do we have confirmation of the appointment?" he asked, now looking at the prosecutor.

"Verbal confirmation, yes. She's sending the written over now. Should arrive in the next few minutes."

The judge nodded and turned his eyes back on Troy, intent and focused. "I'm curious why you didn't share this before."

"To be honest, your honor, I didn't think it would get this far. I was embarrassed and worried about repercussions."

The judge considered him and nodded. "There's still a stigma in this country about mental health, and it's a shame. If more people got the help they needed, my job would be a lot easier. You're in the army, right?"

"Yes, your honor."

"I see. Thank you for your service." He turned to the prosecutor and the clerk. "Did my paperwork come in?"

"Yes, right here," said a woman in a blazer behind a computer.

"I miss the days when the computer announced when I got mail. All right, case dismissed. Mr. Chapman, you're free to go." He grabbed the gavel with a bang, and Troy was free.

CHAPTER 47

Troy walked out of the jail wearing his own clothes and a smile. Even through the rain, he felt lighter as he hopped into his dad's old truck.

"Ready to go?"

"More than you know. Let's roll."

They rode in silence as his dad made his way through the town he had always known, giving the two-fingered wave to every other car. "Tennessee Whiskey" played on low in the cab while they made the familiar loop into the McDonald's parking lot.

"Alright, let's go say hi to Sherry."

"Sherry?"

"Yeah, it's her shift today."

Troy followed his dad up to the counter where he placed an order for a senior coffee and the hamburger, because as he said, "The day was already a win."

He also noticed how the petite lady in the ironed polo with a perfectly cleaned visor came around to the table to wipe it down and took her break to visit with his dad.

Troy took notice over his fries as his dad smiled and

blushed, reciting the tale from the morning to Sherry who sat next to him, never taking her sparkling blue eyes off Hank. Her shiny silver hair was cut short around her ears and styled in an attractive way. She didn't wear any jewelry other than simple gold earrings. The best thing about her was her smile. Everything his dad said was met with enthusiasm and genuine interest. The woman practically bubbled joy, but not in an annoying way. Troy found himself smiling more just by being in her presence. She was the kind of person who made you feel noticed, like you were the only one in the room.

After the story and introductions, Troy learned she was a retired and widowed preschool teacher who had the job to get out and get some extra money. That's where they had met. Things had gotten more serious when he hadn't shown up after the fire. The next time they had started talking more.

He watched as they traded stories and checked in on each other. After sharing everything about his court case, his dad wanted to know about her water heater, which was apparently acting up again, and offered to stop by and take a look.

When her break was over, Troy took the trash away and was keenly aware of how much time they spent saying goodbye with plans to meet later.

He eyed his dad as he got back in the truck. His dad didn't meet his gaze and seemed oddly focused on his seatbelt for a man who had buckled himself into cars for over sixty years.

"She seems nice."

"Sherry? She's great."

"How long have you two been together?"

"Together? Oh no, no, no. We're just friends."

Troy let the silence hang in the air. "Uh-huh."

"It's called being social, son. Your generation is all about that phone or jumping into bed."

Troy let that one go right by.

"What about good old conversation?" Hank finished, despite not looking him in the eye.

"So that's all you're interested in?"

The pink on his dad's cheeks was a nice surprise.

Troy smiled and leaned back. "I think she's really nice. You should ask her to dinner."

He expected a smart remark or biting retort to throw the suggestion back in his face, but none came.

"Yeah, maybe I'll think about it."

"Can't hurt."

His dad shifted in his seat. "Nuff about me. When are you making up with Megan? You owe it to her."

"Honestly, Dad, as soon as possible."

True to his word, as soon as he got home, Troy was in the truck heading over to her apartment. Megan had ducked out of the courtroom almost before the judge hit the gavel.

There was so much he wanted to say, needed to tell her to set things right. He wouldn't have been able to catch her, anyway, since he had to process the rest of the paperwork and get his stuff, but even still, it was an act of ultimate restraint not to chase after her and make up for lost time.

Now that he had made a decision, he didn't want to waste any more time than he had already.

He turned onto her street and saw her car parked in its usual spot. Troy pulled into the parking space he had previously claimed, grabbed his bomber jacket, and ran up toward her door, hitting the buzzer twice for good measure. He paced in a circle, waiting, when he noticed the flurries starting to come down around him in a classic late season snow.

Troy looked up and down Main Street as the snow fell silent and gentle. The sun was going down, but the clouds made it look darker than normal. The warm, golden light from windows spilled out onto the pavement in a picturesque scene that felt familiar and comforting.

Home.

He was home.

Troy smiled to himself and hit the button again, happily waiting in case she was in the shower, when he heard footsteps to his right.

Megan walked up and stopped when she saw him. Their eyes met.

She was wearing her tall tan boots and her dark coat that highlighted her red hair in the dim light. To stay warm, she had on a tan knit cap and matching gloves that held a to-go cup of tea, he presumed. The tip of her nose was red like her cheeks, which reddened when she smiled.

"I didn't think I'd see you."

"You didn't stick around long enough."

Troy closed the gap between them, sliding his hands out of his coat pockets.

"I didn't know if you'd want to see me."

"How could I stay away?"

At her broadening smile, he wrapped his arms around her and planted his lips to hers. She tasted sweet and smelled like honey. Everything about her was like a summer day, and as long as he was with her, he would never be cold again.

He lingered and felt her body mold against his own. When he pulled back, there were more flurries resting on her hat and hair. He brushed a few away before bringing his arms around her again. She left her free hand on his chest. A gust of wind tried to tangle her hair around her face, but as far as Troy was concerned, a blizzard could've come that moment and he wouldn't have moved.

"When do you leave?" she asked, her eyes searching his.

"I did some thinking. This is where I belong."

"What about the army?"

Troy smiled and tilted his head to one side. "Well, that would get in the way of my bed and breakfast plans."

Megan's smile grew across her face as her eyes lit up.

"How about you? What about the interview?"

Megan looked down at his chest and wiped some snow away from the leather.

"I did some thinking too. This is where I belong."

"Are you sure you didn't skip it for me?"

She glanced up at him through her lashes, which completely undid him.

"I think I was trying to run from what I'm meant to do, but I understand now. I was given this gift for a reason. I need to learn how to honor that and find joy at the same time."

"So it's true then? You can't burn?"

Megan nodded. "You don't seem shocked."

Troy shrugged. "I admit, it's hard to believe, but I love you. I'll believe anything you say."

A laugh escaped her, and the tears spilled over her red cheeks right before she launched herself up toward him in a kiss that lit him aflame.

She pulled back and looked happier than he could remember.

"I love you too." She giggled and kissed him again. "Let's get inside before we freeze together."

"Before we do, I need to say something. I'm sorry about the dating apps and losing control. They're deleted now— they were just left over. And I should've trusted you. It's hard for me to give up control. I've lost so much, you know—"

"It's okay—"

"No, I mean that. I want you to know I regretted that. I don't want to hurt you. I've been through a lot, and I'm trying to get better. I'm not always perfect. The nightmares…"

"Troy, it's okay."

"It's important for you to know I'm going to try. I don't want to smother you. I want to love you and protect you, but I know you're your own woman. You're brave and strong and I love you."

The tears were coming down freely now. Troy wiped one away with his thumb, and feeling how cold she was, cradled her cheek in his palm.

Megan sniffed and nodded. "I love you too."

As the snow swirled around them both, Troy kissed her and let himself fall into the moment of being home and holding the woman he loved.

CHAPTER 48

Megan hung the picture and checked it with the level before climbing down from the ladder to admire her work. The framed photograph of the ranch was done by Laura who had recently taken up photography. The purple skies mixed with the golden sun created a striking water-color-like picture of the barn with the mountains in the background.

Another guest bedroom was done in the soon to open Mountain View Ranch Bed and Breakfast. Two down, three to go, and each had a theme. This one was based on the ranch, with subtle theming using artifacts Troy had found over the years. There was a belt buckle, a few buttons, and several horseshoes. The horseshoes were the basis for the equestrian theme, which she had finished yesterday. She hoped to get to the garden room tomorrow and the library room next week. Troy's room, as she had taken to calling it, was already done.

With the wall decor done and the new furniture in, all she needed to do was the linens in the en suite bathroom, make the bed, and plug in the lamps.

The past two weeks had been a blur, and she was the happiest she had been in a long time. Troy had gone back to Ft. Campbell to complete some paperwork and move out of his apartment. Megan had flown out to meet him and enjoyed sightseeing around the area. They had taken a weekend in Nashville and just enjoyed being together, taking notes on what to include in their bed and breakfast when they got back home.

Megan had come home after that weekend to keep working at Station Three, monitor progress at the house, and keep an eye on the horses. She also had enrolled in yoga per Buzz's suggestion, and Ash and Laura had joined in the classes a few times a week. The routine had been centering, and following Troy's lead, she had started checking in with a counselor every other week to work on herself. All of that meant she was in a much better place when it came to work.

Buzz, Jordan, and the rest of the guys had commented on the change. There was something they couldn't put their finger on, but she knew what it was. She went and did her best but was no longer looking for happiness from her work. Instead she was making it on her own time and own terms. She was still a work in progress, but the pressure to find joy and success in every moment of her job was gone, and a whole new world had opened up.

Once back home, she had moved into the main house and worked on the guest rooms full time. Troy's dad had elected to stay in the small house which he had made into a home. Megan still saw him almost every day, usually after she went and checked on the horses. Troy had called every night and texted as much as he could. Even though he was processing out, the army still sucked him in.

Every time he did call or text, it was very clear how badly he wanted to get home. Megan smiled to herself as she replayed some of the more romantic things he had shared while they had texted. She had never felt like this before, and now understood the constant desire to check her phone and wait for him.

But today was the day. Troy was coming home. And he'd be here any minute. They had talked off and on for most of his trip, but toward the end, she had ended the call, giving him a chance to catch up on his latest podcasts—and giving her time to work on his surprise.

Megan wiped up the dust from the drywall off the baseboard under the pictures and threw the rag in a bucket before heading to the bathroom. She folded thick, fluffy, white towels and draped them over the rod and had just laid out a wrapped soap on the new dish when she heard the door open and shut downstairs.

She tried her best to smooth out her hair to no avail. She had wanted to surprise him with some of the rooms finished when he came back and hoped he loved what she had done. Megan dropped the cleaning bucket and tools in another unfinished room and headed down the stairs.

She stopped at the top and saw him down below.

He looked up at her as he stood in the renovated foyer. He had gotten a haircut and some new clothes. His dark hair was trimmed short, and his dark eyes found her as he broke into a smile and ran up the stairs two at a time. They collided in the hallway, his hands enveloping her and crushing her to him while his mouth claimed her own as if he was starved for her.

"Welcome back. Miss me?"

"You bet," he said, pressing his forehead to her own and closing his eyes for a moment.

"Come and see what I've done." Megan took his hand and led him back to the rooms with a smile.

"Is this just your way of getting me into bed?" he asked with a sly grin. "Because if so, I'm here for it."

"Maybe." Megan laughed. "But seriously, come see what I've been up to."

She led him to the back of the hallway toward the first room, which had been his own, stopping in front of the closed door.

"Okay, close your eyes."

"Seriously?"

"Yes, just do it."

"Okay." His perfectly full lashes rested against his cheeks as his lids drew down.

"Ready? One, two…three."

Megan pushed the door open and watched his reaction as he stepped into what had been his old bedroom.

His eyes widened with shock and recognition as he took in the space and saw each of his World War II artifacts artfully displayed in the updated space. The compass, canteen, and helmet were on a newly mounted shelf, next to a collection of Life magazines she picked up from an antique market along with enamelware cups from the forties.

To match, the furniture and everything she had chosen reflected a slightly retro vibe, while still maintaining clean lines. She had his maps of London framed and mounted on the wall, and had arranged some of his books on the shelf in such a way that all of the Allied powers were together with Churchill's book at the forefront. The clocks were reproductions, with a hidden USB port in the back. All of the details were perfect, but Troy went right to her favorite one above the nightstand next to the bed.

"How did you get this photograph?" he asked, studying the framed photograph on the wall.

"Your dad, of course. He told me how much you loved it."

Troy sucked his lips into a thin line as he stood in front of his maternal grandfather's picture from World War II. He stood in his uniform looking so proud in front of an old Studebaker.

"Megan, I…"

She came up from behind him and gave him a squeeze, resting her head on the back of his shoulders.

"I love it."

"Do you? For real?"

"Yes. It's better than I could've imagined."

He pivoted and kissed her again before she pulled back.

"There's more."

"You've been busy," he said with a smile. "I can't wait to see the next one."

"Come on. Eyes closed."

Megan took him by the hand, aware that the first time she had come down this hall had been to get Levi. She was sure Troy knew every step of the way, keenly aware of where they were heading, but still she liked to think there was something to the element of surprise.

"Alright, ready?"

"Ready."

"One, two, three." Megan pushed the door open. It swung in silently on its hinges to Adam's old room.

It was almost unrecognizable with the improvements they had made and the addition, but the view out the windows was the same. The sun streamed through new windows onto the warm pine floorboards and thick braided rug, but that wasn't what caught Troy's eye.

Once again the awe of recognition and the echo of nostalgia mixed in his eyes.

The linens were mostly white with subtle lining echoing the clouds in the picture Laura had taken. Like the forties room, Megan had arranged the artifacts in here. The belt buckle and buttons were in shadow boxes, while the horseshoes were arranged all upright in a pattern flanking the bedside tables. A saddle blanket was folded over the settee on the side, but a series of photographs in black frames showed Adam as a young teenager in a series of photos from around the ranch. In the first one, he held the reins of a horses with his hand on the fence post. In another he was laughing on the back of a tractor stacking hay, and last he stood as a young man in his senior portrait, looking out over the mountains the windows framed. All of the pictures were black and white, placed there in homage to the brother Troy said had loved this ranch more than anything.

Troy blinked and blinked again, and the tears in his eyes welled up and pooled as he noticed the other little touches. The high school's pennant, a letter from his letterman jacket, and Adam's old cowboy hat all adorned the wall.

Megan had tried to honor him and the ranch but in a subtle way. Most people would have no idea, but Troy would and so did Hank. He had seen what she had done last night, and the silent smile he had given her was the most approval she could ask for. Now Troy had the same look, and she knew she had hit it out of the park.

"Well, what do you think?"

Troy shook his head and pulled his lip in tight. "I don't know what to say. I love it. You did it perfectly. He'd love it."

She stood there holding his hand for a few more moments before he met her eyes, and they walked out together toward the barn to check on the horses.

CHAPTER 49

It was so cold that night, which wasn't uncommon. Another cold snap like the last gasp of a monster before it succumbed to the sweet birdsong of spring.

Megan snuggled closer to Troy on the new couch in front of the fireplace. Her shoulders ached from all of the physical work they had done. Between getting the horses in blankets, mucking out the stalls, adding fresh bedding, and turning on the trough heaters for the first time in a couple of weeks to keep the water from freezing, plus coming back to keep painting one of the rooms, she was bone-tired.

Troy had whipped them both up a quick meal using some pasta from the pantry and a sauce he had made on the fly that tasted divine. After that they had lit the new gas fireplace and settled in to watch a rerun of *The Office* together. Megan had only picked up bits and pieces of the episode, drifting off in between the commercials which were too loud.

"Ready for bed?" Troy asked, looking down at her with a smile.

She returned the favor. "Very."

He turned down the lights while she stumbled over toward Salt and Pepper's cage, draping the towel over them. Popsicle and Lincoln both had already nestled into their new cat beds under the stairs in a little nook just for them. Megan checked their water and also saw to Leo's in his new tank near the laundry room toward the back door. With everyone ready for bed, she closed up shop and headed back to their new master bedroom.

The bedroom alone was bigger than her old apartment and newer too. Since this was part of the new addition, everything was completely fresh. Megan couldn't decide what she loved more—the master bath with the huge glassed-in shower or the huge windows which looked out toward the sunrise, framing the barn perfectly.

She washed her face, brushed teeth, and pulled on her new pajamas for this special occasion. They weren't fancy, but were new, comfy, and had a little lace around the collar while being perfectly fitted to her, making her feel pretty and feminine.

He walked in the room right on time and took a slow, sweeping look at her. Megan felt a rush of blood and goose-bumps with his passing gaze as a satisfied smile spread across his lips.

"You look perfect."

Megan tried to act coy but felt her cheeks burn. She took a breath, determined not to stutter.

"Come here."

Troy did as he was told and closed the gap between them, pressing his mouth to hers, while running his hands up and down the curves of her back over the thin, smooth fabric.

Megan did the same, feeling his T-shirt glide under her fingertips.

He broke away and ran a line of kisses down her jaw and

right to that spot she loved under her ear, making her rise up on her toes in anticipation of more.

She leaned back and took his hand, pulling him toward the new bed where she had already turned down the comforter. Megan hopped up and reached for the light when his hand stopped her.

"I want to see you."

Megan blushed again and smiled as he undressed down to his usual T-shirt and underwear before climbing over to her, kissing her into a frenzy until they were both panting for more. The heat between them made her burn with a desire for more.

Megan clawed off her pajamas to give him more access to where she needed him to be before she combusted. She threw them to the side of the room somewhere and propped up on her elbows just as Troy was all over her.

She arched her back to give him better access while raking her hands down his back. Troy was panting, leaving hot kisses down her belly when he suddenly reared up and tugged off his shirt, throwing it somewhere she didn't see because she was looking at his chest for the first time in the light.

There, all over the sculpted muscles, were the red streaks and misshapen scars marking his upper arms. The right shoulder was the worst.

Without thinking, her hand reached out to touch him, tracing the texture with the barest whisper of a touch.

"Do they hurt you?" she whispered.

He sucked in a breath and closed his eyes at her touch. "Sometimes, but not now."

Megan leaned forward and brought her lips to the physical scars of all he had been through. She took her time reaching all of them, taking care to pay attention to the sensitive areas. He had been through so much and had been strong for so long.

Megan looked him in the eye and brought her lips together, kissing him fully as she placed her hands on the muscles of his bare chest. She loved him. His strength, his kindness, his gentle side, his sense of duty. He was made for her.

To prove her point, she pressed her body against his, chest to chest, and pulled him back down with her so they got swept up again in the love of each other's bodies, pushing to new heights until they collapsed together in each other's arms.

They lay entwined together for several minutes, each trying to catch their breath as they panted in unison.

"I can see your heart beating."

Megan glanced down and smiled to herself. "A mile a minute."

He leaned over and planted a reverent kiss right on her breast where the muscle was pumping under the skin before resting his head there with his eyes closed. His breathing changed, and she could tell he was falling asleep.

"Let's get some sleep, you," she said, taking a big breath when he raised his head above her.

He smiled and kissed her again before clicking off the light. Megan got up and found her pajamas on the floor and tugged them on before looking out at the night sky again.

That's when she saw the all too familiar orange glow coming from the barn.

CHAPTER 50

The cats scattered out of his way as Troy ripped open the door. The cold dark air hit his bare legs as he sprinted in his sleep shorts and boots following Megan's shadow, two steps ahead of him, over the ground toward the barn.

This was his nightmare. The horses were trapped, just like Simon. They would either burn, suffocate, or kill themselves trying to fight against their stalls for freedom.

The orange glow from the barn flicked in the night, greedily consuming all of the dry wood and hay stored inside. It had to be the damn trough heaters. Maybe a squirrel, frayed wire…hell, it could've been lightning for all he knew. Barn fires were a rancher's worst nightmare. Fire was his own worst nightmare.

Images of Simon came back to him, his eyes looking out with terror while his mouth stretched in a scream. He tried to fight it back, struggling to stay grounded and not give in to the panic. Flashes of his mom, Adam, his dad, and the horses all swirled together in a looping, racing thought that rivaled the pounding in his head. Troy stumbled, caught himself, but dropped his phone somewhere in the dark. Troy fell to his knees to search the cold, hard-packed grass.

Megan stopped and called out, but he didn't answer her, hearing her double back to check on him. She slid down and started searching as well. He thought she asked him if he was okay, but again, he didn't answer.

Troy was searching and searching, counting the seconds while trying to stave off the memories from the past, channeling that energy to ground him. The ground was cold, hard, and damp, just like a can. He could feel the sharp blades of grass pulling him back down to the moment into the emergency at hand. Finally, his hand touched the smooth surface of glass. After a quick exhale of relief he snatched it and was running again.

Megan nodded once and did the same. It had been only a matter of seconds in a moment when every second mattered.

The smell of smoke burned the inside of his nose, and he tried to dial while running. His hand was shaking and full of sweat. Giving up, he just hit the button three times on the side, triggering the emergency call. Troy held his phone to his ear.

"911 what's your emergency?"

"My barn's on fire," he shouted while running. "Horses are inside."

"What's your location?"

Troy rattled off the address through panting breath, reaching the pool of light emanating from within the old structure. Paint was peeling off the old wooden walls, and the sound of steam was coming from somewhere. The frantic whinnies of the horses trapped inside echoed through the dark night in a scream for mercy. Sounds of banging and splintering wood mixed with pops from the flames.

Megan reached the structure first and threw open the

barn door, and a stream of smoke fled the scene, racing up to the dark sky. The rush of cold air fed the flames, which grew right in front of them. His heart pounded at the sight while the thrum of blood raced through his ears, making him dizzy and sick all at once. He stood rooted to the spot and swayed, holding his head to try and keep the nightmares and memories at bay.

Megan turned to him, dark in the night, lit from behind by the flames of hell. Gone was the shy, ethereal girl. He was looking into the eyes of a warrior who had seen hell and was willing and ready to go back. He knew those eyes and had seen them in seasoned veterans before. The wind from the fire pushed her red curls around her head in a fiery halo. She stood tall, her shoulders set, her arms tensed, poised and sprung for a fight.

He already knew what was about to happen. Just like Simon. It was just like Simon. He couldn't lose her too.

Troy reached out and grabbed her arm to pull her close to him and never let go, but the look in her eyes did more to stop him. It steadied him and soothed his panicked soul. He let go of her arm and watched her movements.

The world slowed, and it was as if someone turned down the volume of the fire and horses.

Megan somehow knew what he needed. She turned to face fully toward him, never taking her gaze off him, her shoulders shifting with the weight of her responsibility, training, and experience. She was made for this moment.

She stopped right in front of him and looked directly into his eyes. "I'm going to go in there and get them out."

Her voice was calm and steady, and all he could do was nod his head, still clutching the phone somewhere near his hip. He had no idea if the dispatcher was still listening or not.

Megan nodded once and turned on her heel, sprinting into the fire. Only then did he realize she was barefoot.

As if someone had taken their finger off the pause button, all of the noise came back at once. The roar of the flames, the screams of the horses, the pounding of their hooves against the stalls.

A searing pain shot from behind his eyes, and he pressed his shaking hand against his head to stop the pain, fighting to breathe through the smoke and memories and keep an eye on Megan's outline in the barn before it disappeared into the smoke.

CHAPTER 51

Megan threw the first two latches without a problem. The metal must've been scalding, but for all she knew it was mildly warm and gave her a tingly sensation. The real problem was trying to coax the crazed animals out of the pens that they associated with safety and urge them to run toward freedom, even if that meant running through fire first.

The smoke was quickly overtaking the barn, and the panic that the animals were in meant they were sucking in even more. She had to move fast. For their sake and for hers. The heat didn't bother her, but the smoke did. Her lungs were already getting scratchy. She tried to pull up her pajama top over her nose, but the neckline was plunging and wouldn't go. She was stuck, and time was not on her side.

The first two had stopped bucking long enough for them to realize the door was open, fleeing toward the exit where she hoped Troy would be able to catch them later.

That wasn't a today problem. Horses were herd animals and would eventually group up somewhere on the ranch. She threw another latch, and this time the animal didn't even flinch.

She ducked inside the stall, grabbed the big bay by the bridle and steered him toward the open door. Despite it being a large door, the smoke obscured everything, making it hard to see the massive exit. The door being opened had literally fueled the flames.

The fire was climbing to the roof now. The corner that housed the tack room was totally engulfed. That was where the switch was for the main trough heater. It must have been that. That was the only change. From there, the flames were greedily climbing toward the roof and spreading over other stalls.

A gust of cold wind fanned the flames even more, but caught the bay's attention who lurched forward when she threw her arm into the bridle.

Three down, three to go, and her lungs had gone from scratchy to burning now. Megan tried to swallow past it and keep going. The pounding of hooves against the stalls and frantic whinnies echoed through the roar of the flames. She headed back toward the other three, fighting her way through the thick black smoke. Sparks and bits of hay on fire were floating upward on the draft, creating a look of descending into hell despite standing right where she was.

Megan reached the next stall and threw the latch. Not waiting for an invitation, the horse was gone. The next one, a horse with a beautiful copper coat, had almost broken the stall door completely and was close to working his own way to freedom.

"Stop, stop, stop!" she cried out to the crazed animal, desperate for freedom. One big brown eye rolled over, exposing the whites before it centered on her.

"Stop!" The pounded ceased, and she threw the latch and pressed herself flat against the stall out of the way, holding it open. As the copper gelding ran by, she could see the sheen of sweat shining in the glow of the fire as the animal bolted for freedom. She knew it was warm but could clearly see it must have been scalding inside.

She was gasping now, fighting to breathe through the smoke. Her chest was burning, which was ironic.

One horse left.

Megan tugged up the thin flimsy fabric of her pajama shirt, which did nothing to stop the burning in her chest. She had to get this last one out and run for herself.

A loud crack above her was a sure warning she had to go. Her body's own fight or flight was kicking in now with memories of Buzz screaming in her ear to get out and let it go. She had pushed it too far last time and had taken heat for it. God, would he be pissed if he knew about this. He would want her to go.

But the last horse was Braxton. Troy's favorite. She had no choice. Megan pushed off the wall and tried to run to his stall.

Braxton was the biggest, strongest, and meanest horse. The pummeling of the stall was a testament to that, and the fact that the latch was still holding strong had earned it a five-star endorsement.

"Stop!" Megan tried to yell over his frantic whinnies, but it came out like a cough as she dragged in breath from the effort, only pulling in more smoke.

She tried to pull the latch, but the constant pounding wouldn't let her throw the catch.

Braxton was frenzied, and sweat was dripping down his dark coat. The whites of his eyes were clearly visible, showing his stress. They were the farthest back from the exit, and he wouldn't stop moving.

Her hands fumbled with the catch again and again, until she yanked it free and pulled it back, but nothing happened.

The other one. The one that Troy's dad had been so adamant on installing held firm.

Nearly blind, Megan fumbled over the frantic kicking, each powerful thrust throwing the door without the first catch, until her hand touched the warm metal. She tugged once, readjusted, and with a clang threw the door back, getting smacked in between it and the wall as he bolted into the smoke. His coat was the same color as the smoke in the air around him, and she couldn't track him or anything else anymore.

The smoke was pervasive. There was no exit, no steam.

With all of the horses out, she dropped to the ground in a desperate attempt to grab any oxygen she could. By now, most of it had been consumed by the fire raging around her.

Megan dragged in another breath and started crawling, pulling herself through the bits of hay, ash, and sparks of fire raining down and swirling around the inferno.

There was another crack somewhere, then a bang. One of the stalls had collapsed.

Everything felt like crawling through Jell-O, and her chest burned so bad. Megan had never known what it felt like to be on fire, but now that was the only way she could describe it.

She couldn't see where she was going. Had waited too long. This was what Buzz had warned her about. Pushed too far, gone too deep. Her breath was short now, like a gasp. She couldn't see where she was. Thought she was pointing toward the exit, but wasn't sure.

Disoriented and exhausted, all she wanted to do was rest her head and close her eyes. Just for a moment against the ground. Take a moment. She had done her best, and this was it. She was too far away. Couldn't do it.

Buzz was going to be pissed. Had her family felt like this? Was it the same when you were asleep? Would Laura's hands have healed her? What would that have felt like? What would Ash have said when she found out about this. If Buzz was a dressing-down, Ash would be a total ass-kicking. Maybe she would understand.

Troy. God, Troy.

She tried to think of him grabbing all of the horses on the other side and got a burst of energy to step up and push forward, moving another foot before collapsing again.

He had lost so many people. They had so many plans. She wanted peace for him. No pain. Just peace, and she couldn't give that to him anymore. He was right there, paralyzed with terror, and she couldn't get to him.

Megan looked up and could almost hear him now. Calling her name from somewhere outside the barn.

She tried to drag in another breath and call out "I'm here," but it was a whisper she could barely hear.

Megan would've cried, but whatever water might have come would have evaporated or turned right to steam. She closed her eyes and felt someone around her. Arms, gentle and strong, encircled her. They were warm to the touch, lifting her up. Toward where she didn't know.

She tried to open her eyes and couldn't, giving in to the sensations around her as something carried her soul away.

But then it stopped. She was going down now. There was something cold, hard, and rough under her back. Nothing like before.

Her eyes fluttered open, and there above her, she saw Troy's terrified eyes. Why was he crying? His shirt was over her nose and mouth. He pressed his mouth to her head with trembling lips and turned her on her side, covering her with something. She didn't know what. His hand stayed on her hair, combing it away from her face.

That's when she heard the sirens. Boots where everywhere, and she could hear shouting and running. Familiar voices mixed with unfamiliar ones.

Someone was running toward her, then an oxygen mask was fitted to her face with sweet cold air pushing into her more than the night air could do naturally.

Megan's eyes opened to see Laura looking down at her, pressing one ungloved hand to her throat.

Through the mask, Megan tried to smile and nod, giving permission, but drifted to sleep when a warm tingle soothed the burning like a balm.

CHAPTER 52

Four weeks later, Megan pulled out another tray of Troy's baked brie from the oven and looked out from the new kitchen at everyone in the living room enjoying the grand opening party for the brand new Mountain View Ranch Bed and Breakfast.

"Looks like we're a hit," Troy said from behind her with another case of drinks.

Megan smiled and leaned back against him. He ran his fingers down her sides of her silky green dress she'd saved for just such a special occasion. He loved the dress and how sexy she looked in it, even if he couldn't fully appreciate the green color on her.

"You doing okay?"

There was genuine concern in his eyes as he scanned over her to make sure it wasn't too much, and he didn't stop until she smiled and nodded.

So much had happened in the last month. First, she had to heal from the smoke inhalation. Mr. Chapman, Laura, Ash, Buzz, and everyone at Station Three had all been checking in and offering to help, so much so that she wondered how she ever felt alone.

Troy had stayed with her, taking her to all of the follow-up appointments, asking questions and taking notes in his phone on what the doctors said about her recovery. He had pampered her with teas, soups, and made the most delicious mashed potatoes with roast gravy when the doctors had expressed concern about her iron being low after routine bloodwork. Once she was in the hospital, it had popped the lid on the doctor's appointments and tests she had been avoiding for years. Through it all, Troy had done everything she could've asked and then some.

With Laura's healing help, and Megan's natural ability, she'd had a "miraculous" recovery from the smoke inhalation and now had full lung capacity even during a stress test her doctor insisted on before clearing her for work.

Megan had returned to Station Three a week ago, to a surprise party with a cake and everything. Troy, despite being worried, had only texted once to check in and let her know she could update him at any time, but otherwise gave her the space to do her job without interference. Buzz had called her into his office, no doubt planning a long talk, but much to his surprise, Megan had already had a few therapy sessions and reported she was doing much better. She also gave him permission to call her out if her bullshit started up again, which he gladly accepted.

She was enjoying her new confidence. Felt like she had found her voice, found her purpose, and was truly living for the first time in a long time. She still had work to do with her anxiety, grief, and pressure to be perfect from her childhood, but she had come a long way from where she was. Now her stutter only showed up when she was tired or surprised. She knew her purpose was to be a firefighter, but her joy was at home with her friends and family. And, thanks to Troy, she still got to care for animals by watching over Braxton and his five minions, as Troy had taken to calling them.

Troy had been busy hanging out with his dad and Ms. Sherry, who was an absolute doll and had accepted a position working at the bed and breakfast. Mr. Chapman had settled into the little house and turned it into a home, improving it here and there. Now it was quite nice, and almost ADA compliant with Troy's insistence. His dad had agreed and wanted to keep his independence as long as possible. They all got together a few times a week, and Troy was always down to check on him in the morning and again before *Wheel* came on.

Megan could see them now, holding court on the new couch next to the fire, talking with Laura and Carter, while Holden colored on the coffee table. Ash was talking shop with Jordan and the guys from Station Three over some drinks. The rest of them had laughed when Jordan said something, but Ash just smiled and took another sip.

Megan made a note to check in with her later. She knew she was under a lot of pressure with work. She had recently been transferred to investigation and the difference was visible. They hadn't hung out after yoga recently, since Ash hadn't made it to class two times in a row.

It wasn't until tonight that Megan noticed the change and wondered if Laura could see it too.

"Hey, want to go get some fresh air?" Troy asked as he came back into the kitchen, wiping his hands after dropping the drinks off in the cooler. "We have a big day tomorrow."

"Sure we won't be missed?"

"Nah, I put Carter in charge."

Megan glanced over to where Carter gave her a thumbs-up while Laura made a shooing motion.

"Come on. Tomorrow we'll have our first guests."

"Let's go check on the horses."

Troy smiled and led her outside with promises to be right back. She hopped up into his truck like before and leaned back into the comfortable seat as he steered them deeper into the ranch where they could see the stars.

His hand found hers in the dark and held it gently as they drove.

Megan glanced over.

Troy was relaxed and at peace. His hand was draped over the wheel, guiding them along the dark road toward one of the older barns where they had moved the horses. Since the fire, he hadn't had as many nightmares. His therapist had referenced exposure, and now he was in a new treatment. He still had hard moments, but the nightmares had subsided and routine had done him well.

"I wanted to tell you, I heard back from the insurance company today."

Megan bolted up and turned to him. "Oh good! Did they accept the appeal?"

He pulled his lips in tight and shook his head.

"What do you mean? Buzz's report showed that it was the frayed wires in the trough heaters. That was the start."

"They cited something about the wires being outside of the main structure and an add-on."

"But that's not right! They're required in our part of the state."

"They also went on to—"

"Find another loophole?"

Troy let out a bark of laughter. "You're not wrong. They said the faulty equipment hadn't been serviced, and as a result was negligent on our part."

Megan's mouth fell open. Troy shrugged. "Dad did have to sell off everything in that barn before I came home. It had been empty for a while. They're citing that as their main point, and it's something we can't dispute."

"Are they paying anything?" she asked incredulously.

"Yes, but after factoring in wear and tear, it's not even close."

"This is ridiculous. The army won't try to take the horses, will it?"

"No, not with the other barn. It's not ideal, but it's workable for now until we save up enough collateral to get a loan and rebuild."

"I'm sorry."

Troy shrugged again, but she could see the worry pulling his shoulders down. Megan shoved her own anger into a box somewhere in her mind and squeezed his hand.

"It'll all work out. Something will change soon. It has to."

Troy looked at her after he threw the truck in park. "It's just another setback in a long string of shit."

"If you can't have faith, we got to have hope."

Troy smiled and opened the door, hopping down. "One thing I hope is that maybe we can get the horses involved with TAPS or something like it eventually."

"What's that?"

"It's a Tragedy Assistance Program for Survivors. You know, like an animal-assisted therapy."

Megan's chest inflated with warmth at the possibilities. "I think that's a wonderful idea."

Troy's own smile broadened, and he glanced over at her. "Well, maybe not Braxton yet, but if you think so, I'll call the office tomorrow and get some information."

"I completely do."

"Yeah, it'll be good to give back. I have another idea I want to show you," he said as he pulled over to a place she didn't know and parked.

"Where are we?" Megan asked when he came around to open her door, after she was already climbing down herself. "This isn't the barn."

"No, it's the homestead, more of a mining shack, but still the OG. Come on, let's go take a look."

The light from the full moon smiled down over them, illuminating everything including what looked to be the remains of a partially collapsed shack. Troy led her toward it until they were under the dilapidated roof, with visible holes in it.

"Are you sure this is steady?"

"Oh yeah. The beams are all solid oak trunks. This was the original house." He patted one of the beams to demonstrate the strength. "I've always loved coming here since I was a child."

There were two windows to the outside, one with glass and one without, inviting animals to burrow within. The floor was wood and clearly uneven. While the boards were falling down outside, the walls from within seemed solid. To the left of what looked like it had once been a table for a sink or basin, there were dark stairs heading up.

"This would be a cool playhouse," she said, turning around to take it all in.

"Basic log cabin. Fireplace still looks okay, doesn't it?"

Megan took one look at the haphazard brick with crumbling, homemade mortar. "By my standards? Doubtful. But it is beautiful."

Troy laughed again and pulled her in for a hug, holding her in the cradle of his arms. "I've wanted to bring you here for a long time. I used to come out here as a child and run around and dig for treasure."

Megan smiled into his chest and let him tell the story again about the artifacts she had framed.

"There's even some sort of flower and berries growing around out back. It's all a mess now, but in time I want to clean this up. Make it a rustic cabin. Maybe even rent it out."

Troy stopped and looked down at her. "What do you think?"

"That sounds wonderful."

They lingered a few moments longer, before touring outside. Troy showed her the thicket that had once been some sort of garden. Signs of spring were apparent in the small leaves unfurling from their winter shelter, and a light, sweet scent perfumed the night air around them. On the other side, Megan could hear something and looked to Troy, who nodded with a smile before leading her down to a bubbling creek, which sparkled like diamonds in the night.

Megan leaned down and dipped her fingertips into the flowing water, feeling the water race by her with a surprisingly strong current.

"I think this is my new favorite place," she whispered.

Troy knelt down next to her. "It's always been mine, especially during a full moon like tonight. Feels like where I belong, but now with you here…it feels like home." He leaned over and kissed her, bringing her into him again. Megan let her head rest on his shoulder while he pulled her in close.

"Can we come back tomorrow?"

"Always." Troy took one last deep breath and stood up.

Megan did the same, but stepped funny and stumbled. She overcorrected and fell with a splash into the ice cold water.

"Holy shit. Are you okay!?"

Megan nodded and laughed, but her dress was soaking up more water by the second. She pushed herself up and grabbed Troy's outstretched hands, tugging her back upright and ashore.

"That's embarrassing," Megan said, looking back at where she had planted her butt moments before. Something caught her eye in the moonlight.

"Here, let me—"

Megan stopped him with a hand on his chest. "Troy?"

"What? Are you hurt? Want me to call Laura or Buzz?"

Megan didn't respond, but crouched down to where she had just fallen in the water. She plunged her hand into the icy water again, going all the way down until her elbow was submerged, and dug her hand deep into the silt.

Troy was right next to her as a brace when she turned her palm upward out of the water, revealing a palmful of mud with moonlight glinting off flecks of golden sparkles.

"Holy Mother of God," Troy said on a complete whisper.

Megan didn't answer again, but took her other hand to root around the silt until she found the thing that had caught her eye. She brushed the dirt away and angled it more into the moonlight when she heard another gasp from Troy as he laid eyes on what she had seen.

There in the palm of her hand, Megan and Troy stared at a nugget of gold.

Megan slowly turned to him and grinned. "I think we might be able to get a new barn sooner than we thought."

Troy wrapped his arms around her and kissed her until they both were laughing so hard, neither could speak. All they could feel was joy.

CHAPTER 53

Ash had stayed too late at the party and should've gone straight home. Megan and Troy's grand opening should've ended at ten, but when they had come back revealing their discovery, everyone had lost their damn minds, and it had spun out of control into a total rave, lasting until two and probably beyond.

Laura and Carter had to carry Holden fast asleep out at eleven, which everyone expected. Mr. Chapman and his new friend Sherry were right behind them, but everyone else hung out, eventually helping to set everything straight.

She had waved goodbye to the guys from Station Three, giving Megan a huge hug before rolling out herself.

But she wasn't going home.

Megan had asked her how she was doing earlier with that look of worry Ash had always hated. No one knew how much she was working. The only ones who might be able to pick up on it were Laura and Megan, and both had been busy with their own things. Not that she minded. Ash had something else on her mind too.

She keyed herself into her new office and fired up her

computer again, opening the files she had been working on for months now.

There had been a string of attacks on women throughout the area. The other guys in her department thought they had the collar with Troy, which Ash had never agreed with, but there was no stopping them. While they wasted their time with him, she had been going back to the evidence again, looking for any kind of thread to pull. There was something. She could feel it. Ash knew, like she always did. She just *knew*.

Ash clicked on Troy's file again and read the circumstantial evidence and eyewitness accounts from the scene of the attack on Keira McKinney, and then opened the one from the wreck she had responded to. She had looked at these countless times by now, so she had them memorized, but still there was something she was missing.

The only connection she could see was that the one from the wreck had security experience. The other guy looked military. That plus the connection was why they went after Troy, but there was something bigger about that—Ash could feel it.

If she could just figure this out and find the guy who did attack Keira, maybe that would free something up and lead her to the other attacks both in Goldvein and the neighboring towns.

She studied the picture again and looked even closer at the arrest from the wreck. The guy was clearly out of his mind, but toxicology came back clean. The notes from the sergeant read mental health issues, but something about that didn't sit well. It was too perfect.

She eyed him again and pulled up a different file from the courts to find where he currently was serving his sentence. Maybe she needed to pay him a visit and try to see if he remembered anything new.

Ash kept at it until the smell of coffee found its way past her door and pulled her like a siren song. The early risers on morning shift fought over who was the first to fix the pot.

She leaned back to rub her eyes, when on a whim she checked one more thing before she had to go make nice with people.

Seeing Laura had been a reminder to check that weird ping again. It hadn't moved since that one time, so as the weeks had passed, she had stopped checking.

Tonight was a different kind of night though.

Ash leaned into the screen to make sure it wasn't her eyes deceiving her. Nope. Guess who had come back.

"Well, shit."

ACKNOWLEDGMENTS

I would like to thank my best friend and writing buddy, Jenn Gosselin, who has seen me through four books. These past two years of working on this book would have been far more difficult without her. Having her cheer me on and calm me down kept me going through the last nine months and multiple rewrites.

I also need to thank my cousin and soul sister, Maria Wiggins. It is not an exaggeration to say this book would look completely different without her insight and experience, which helped shape this story and the characters. Having her in my corner cheering me on is a blessing.

I am always so thankful I get to work with my editors, Ann Suhz and Ann Riza. For a fourth time, they helped me learn more about my writing and guided me toward my vision from start to finish. I would be lost without their clear vision and thoughtful suggestions. I am deeply grateful for their patience, time, and energy.

Once again, Caroline Teagle Johnson used her endless creativity to create another stunning cover that perfectly represented the characters. I am so glad I have her to create the face of my story.

Thank you to the Virginia Romance Writers and Ines

Johnson for the craft workshops, especially when I was inspired and began drafting this series.

Of course, a huge thank you to my family, especially my husband, Kevin, who has supported and invested in me since the beginning. He always inspires me to keep going and encourages me to pursue my dreams. I can never appreciate him or my son enough.

Lastly, thank you to all readers who have read my stories. I appreciate you more than you know.

ABOUT THE AUTHOR

Kathryn K. Murphy writes action-packed, small-town romance novels bursting with emotion.

If you want to know when Kathryn's next book will come out, please visit her website at www.kathrynkmurphy.com, where you can sign up to receive email updates.